Colors of Glory

To order additional copies, please contact us.
BookSurge, LLC
www.booksurge.com
1-866-308-6235
orders@booksurge.com

Colors of Glory
A collection of short stories

Nitin Deo

Illustrations by: Nisha Deo

2006

Colors of Glory

TABLE OF CONTENTS

Dedicated to the loving memory of my father, who taught me so much about life.

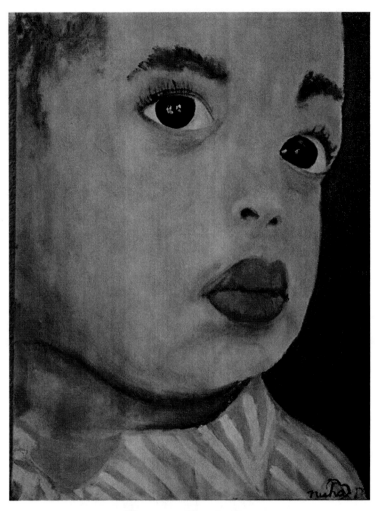

Gray Justice

GRAY JUSTICE

Ring…ring…ring….
The phone rang. Caroline jumped at it and picked it up.
"Hi honey," it was Davis on the line.
"Oh, hi. I was waiting for your call," said Caroline. Then there was a pregnant pause for a few seconds. Caroline didn't want to ask—she was hoping for the best, but in her own mind preparing for the worst.

Davis had almost finished his residency at the Durham County Hospital. It was their dream that they would move out of that tiny two bedroom apartment, have a nice house, Davis would have a nice steady job, no more long nights, no more pulling three shifts in a row. Caroline's job at the doctor's office as an administrative assistant was enough to get them and their young five-year-old son—Ryan—a good living. But their aims were much higher. Although, they were comfortable in the southern town of Durham, North Carolina, there was something about getting out of there. For the past two years, after Ryan would go to sleep, that's all they would talk about—where would they go next. They would sit down with the map of the United States and start crossing off different cities. Miami was too hot and too expensive—although there would be good chance for Davis to do something in a cardiology department. Stanford in California would have been great, but Davis could not get the right references lined up in time. Every once in a while he would blame it on racial discrimination. But, when he met Dr. Althea Freeman, the resident surgeon at Stanford, Caroline convinced him that he should really look at the merits of hospital and the town for their family, and not pay attention to any racial bias. Finally, it was between San Diego, California—because the hospital there is very good and its affiliation with University of California, San Diego would give Davis a chance to teach surgery—and Atlanta, because it would be just about an hour away from Raleigh-Durham and with a fairly large African American community there, they won't feel out of place and Ryan would have some friends at school, too.

Caroline was hoping for Atlanta's Samaritan Hospital to come through—it would be closer to her parents than going all the way to the other coast.

"Come on honey, say something", pleaded Caroline.
"Ok, ok. Mrs. Brown, here is the deal," Davis took another pause. Now, Caroline was getting excited.
"I got the job!" Davis yelled. "And you wouldn't believe the other part."
Caroline started shouting in excitement, "what, what?"

"The salary is low for the first year, but then after a year it goes to $140,000!" Davis tried to gloss over the first year salary and emphasize the following year—hoping that Caroline wouldn't catch the first part.

Caroline calmed down—"How low is low?" Caroline latched on to the earlier part that Davis was trying to downplay.

"Honey, come on. We have been making a lot less than this," Davis was setting the expectation.

"How low is low Davis?"

"Well, its $80,000 plus moving expenses."

"Davis, that's really low. And what moving expenses? We can fit all our stuff in our wagon and drive it there." Caroline's excitement was going down fast.

"You know I want to take it easy now. I have been working so hard for the past few years and with junior it is not easy. I get hardly any time between my job and the day care center. Don't get me wrong, I am willing to do whatever it takes. That's what we decided five year ago. If we had not had Junior, that would be fine," Caroline's mind was like a feather in the wind, floating in many different directions.

"Caroline, come on now. I have not regretted for a second. I love Junior. Besides, I have tried to help you as much as I could. And as I promised, once we settle down with my job, before we go for the second one, you can finish your degree. The only thing is, now we might have to wait for another year, that's all."

Caroline didn't want to discuss any further. She just asked him to see if he could convince them to get more in the first year.

"I don't want to live in another small apartment for a year. I was so looking forward to having my own house—having a swing set in the backyard for Junior, having parties without any worries that the neighbors are going to call the cops and just waking up in the morning in my own home." Caroline was slipping into the dream world until Davis stopped her.

"Ok, honey, I got to go. I am going to sign all the papers. I will see you this evening." Davis rushed and hung up.

All afternoon Caroline was making plans in her mind, going through the justification. At times she thought, maybe they should wait and see if some other opportunity comes up for Davis. Then again, she thought, what if we are stuck. Davis has to leave Durham County in a month. They have already told him that there is nothing for him there.

Finally, Caroline had made up her mind. She was going to support his decision. Her mother called to find out what had happened. But she didn't say anything definitive. She wanted to tell them when the complete decision was done. Her mother didn't want them to move. Her mother and father were getting old. Her brother didn't go to college—after a bit of rash with the law, finally became a handyman—with a small job at a large apartment complex in Raleigh. He would drive everyday from Apex for an hour and at times on Fridays wouldn't go home. Her father was so angry with her brother that he wouldn't even talk to him.

Her mother was going through all this over the phone, still trying to convince her to stay in Durham—about an hour away from her parents. But Caroline wanted to make something of their life. That was one reason she wanted to move away from that area, but not too far.

That evening when Davis came back, Ryan was having his dinner. Davis sat down at the table with a beer.

"So, Daddy, is it true that we are moving to a far away place?"

Davis didn't know how to answer the curious 5 year-old's question. He looked at Caroline with a question mark on his face.

"Well, Junior, we are going to move alright. We are going to move to a better place. Don't you want your swing set in the backyard and a treehouse?" Caroline looked at Davis—Davis sighed in relief.

'So, she IS ready to move' he thought to himself,' but what is this about backyard and stuff. Why is she setting up junior's expectation like this? What if we can't afford to buy a house in Atlanta?'

"Ok. Junior. That's enough. Now go brush your teeth. Daddy will be right there to read you a book. You have to go sleep now."

"But, Moooom, no school tomorrow."

"I know honey, but we have to go to Grandma's early in the morning. Besides, it's almost 9 O'clock. Time for bed, come on."

Then she started getting dinner ready for the both of them.

When Davis came back to the kitchen, he was a lot more relaxed after a shower. He was really surprised to see two candles on the table, a setting with two plates, the forks and knives—though kind of old and bent out of shape.

"I want to buy a new dinner set for four," said Caroline.

"Of course, THAT we can definitely afford," Davis smiled.

"Honey, come on, it will be ok."

They hugged and started floating around in the kitchen—at times kissing. All of a sudden a giggle broke the romantic silence in the room.

"Junior, what are you doing out of bed. I thought you were fast asleep."

"I want some water. But, go ahead Daddy kiss her on the lips."

"Yeah Daddy kiss Mommy on the lips," Caroline chimed in. Davis was so happy, he kissed her on the lips and then on her forehead. He was looking at her as if he had never seen her before.

"Ok, now go, tuck him in and let me get our dinner ready," said Caroline blushingly.

Davis ran to Junior and picked him up, kissed him and took him to his bedroom. For about half an hour Caroline kept on hearing giggling and hush hush sounds from the bedroom. Then Davis came back to the kitchen rolling up his sleeves and went to the fridge to get a cold beer.

"Wait, honey, don't open the beer, I bought wine for us." Caroline didn't even notice the awe on Davis' face.

Then for a long time they were having nice meal, wine and a great conversation. They made all the plans. Davis would go ahead and start looking for a place right away and then in a couple of weeks he would come back and pack the whole family into the wagon and head over there. They kept on talking about the new start and all the rough times they had over the past few years. Each tear from Caroline's eyes told a thousand stories.

As they were driving away from the parking lot, Ryan was bidding goodbye to his friends with teary eyes and Caroline was curling up her lips every second trying to look away from her parents. As they got on the highway, Davis told Ryan not to keep asking 'are we there yet', but poor Ryan was already fast asleep exhausted from crying.

"So, Davis, tell me about this house," Caroline broke the silence after a while.

"Well, it's not exactly a dream house. But the old couple I met that is selling the house is very nice. The husband doesn't keep good health and the wife is busy all day taking care of him. So, she doesn't pay much attention to the house anymore."

"I don't want to know about the sellers, I want to know about the house."

"Ok, ok. So, it's a 4 bedroom, 3 bath, 2 story house..." Caroline just gave Davis a look that made him bite his tongue.

"But you already knew that. Well, let's see, it is in a nice neighborhood. There are a couple of good schools minutes away from the house. It has a huge backyard. And there is a big tree there—perfect for a treehouse." Davis looked at Caroline from the corner of his eyes; Caroline was clearly in the world of dreams.

"Of course, if you don't want the house, we don't have to buy it right now. We could move into an apartment, wait a few more months and then see which area we like."

"Huh? No, no. If Junior likes it, we'll save a lot of trouble." Davis knew that Caroline wanted to be a homeowner!

After the walkthrough of the house, Caroline, Davis and Ryan were standing out in the front yard. The real estate agent—Ms. Curtis—was talking about all kinds of things about the warranties and termite checks and so on. But no one was paying any attention to that. All three of them were looking around—searching for something.

Right then the next door neighbor's garage door opened as a car drove into the driveway. The man looked at them and stopped the car on the driveway. The whole African American family got down from the car. Husband, wife, daughter and son. Ryan's eyes lit up. He looked at Caroline asking for her permission, Caroline understood and signed him to go.

"Hey what's up—welcome to the neighborhood. We heard from Ms. Curtis here that you had bought the place." The man introduced himself to Davis and the woman started talking to Caroline.

"Didn't I tell you Dr. Brown this is a very nice neighborhood", said Ms. Curtis.

The Browns felt relieved. Ms. Curtis mumbled something, shook hands with all of them and left.

The Brown and The Moore family kept on talking in the front yard for a while. The Moore's told them about the husband and wife that lived in that house. The Moore's had moved in their house just a few years ago. Ever since they had moved in, the husband was kind of quiet and sometimes sick. The wife was nice and every once in a while she would bring something to the Moore's—like a cake at Christmas time or cookies or something. The Moore's would reciprocate. Although there was no racial tension, somehow Mr. Moore felt that there was something between them that wasn't right. He commented that he felt the husband would avoid looking at them at times.

The kids had gotten along really well. Jeff and Ryan were just about the same age. They were already good buddies—running around the front yard and the back yard. Caroline was happy and so was Davis.

Over the next few days, The Browns had moved in. Davis' job was going fine. Caroline was looking around for a job—going for interviews and so on. Ryan was hanging out at the Moore's and Jeff would hang out at the Brown's place quite often.

One afternoon, Mrs. Moore came by and asked Caroline if she could watch Jeff for a few hours.

"Oh, sure. These guys are playing around anyway. I am busy cleaning up the attic and finally putting things where they belong. Besides, Davis will be home early today—he was on call all night."

As Mrs. Moore left, Caroline shouted at Ryan to behave and not to climb the tree beyond the half built tree house. And then she started working on her cleaning. Every once in a while Ryan would come to Caroline with Jeff right behind him, ask for something and then run away. After a while she started to ignore the both of them.

Then all of a sudden she heard Davis' voice yelling at Ryan.

"Ryan, you get back in here. And take off that thing right now. You get back in here right this minute."

Caroline stopped for a second to listen. First she thought Ryan must have done something naughty.

"Ryan, I said, get back in the house right now and take that fucking thing off." Davis yelled again. Now Caroline was worried. Davis had never used profane language before—especially in front of Ryan.

Caroline left the dishes and came out running. Ryan was wearing a long shiny white gown—which was obviously too big for him, but he had folded it up. And he also had a long white hood on. He was wearing that and running after Jeff yelling, "I am the white ghost—I'm gonna getchya" and Jeff was running around in circles. This was happening right in the front yard.

"Caroline, where did he get that thing, anyway? Have you been paying any attention?" Davis was visibly upset.

Now Ryan started crying. Caroline took him inside and took of the shiny white gown. He was clinging on to her. Jeff was scared. He didn't know what to do. Caroline hugged him too.

"Come on, Davis, they don't know what it is. They must have thought it's a Halloween costume or something."

Davis was furious. He threw his coat on the sofa and started going up and down the hallway.

He was mumbling away, 'I am the white ghost, I'm gonna getchya. White ghost! Huh!'

"Come on Davis, what does he know about what happened 40 years ago and all that?" Caroline was still trying to get her son absolved.

"I am sorry Daddy, I will never do it again." said Ryan with tears rolling down his cheeks.

Davis took one look at Ryan and melted. He ran toward Ryan and hugged him. Ryan was still shivering. Anger and hurt now started flowing from Davis' eyes. Davis stormed into the bathroom, closed the door and started washing his face.

That night the Moore's came by. They were also upset. Caroline was explaining to them what had happened earlier in the afternoon.

Ryan and their son were running around the backyard all afternoon. Then they started playing hide and seek. Ryan went to the attic to hide. He found this small door on the side. He tried to open it. After trying for a little while, it opened—just as Jeff was coming up the stairs, Ryan opened that small door and sneaked in. It was all dark in there. But there something white caught his eyes. There was a lot of dust and webs on it. He dusted it off and brought it out. He was really curious about it. He opened it. It smelled really bad. But he wore it anyway. Both Jeff and Ryan were intrigued. It was way too big for Ryan, but he folded the bottom and held it in his hands. Then they also discovered the hood—it was really cool they thought. It had these two holes, but that hood was too big for Ryan too. So, they improvised again—they tied a knot on top of the hood.

"Ryan thought it was a ghost costume for Halloween. So, they started playing ghost with it," explained Caroline.

"It's a ghost costume alright", said Davis with so much spite in his voice—as if he was ready to strangle someone.

"Davis, come on, go take a nice hot bath. You will feel better." Caroline wanted to get him out of the room.

As he left, they were all quiet. When they heard the door of the bathroom upstairs closing, Caroline started to explain.

"I hope ya'll understand. About 35—40 years ago, Davis and his parents used to live in South Carolina. Davis' father disappeared when he was only five. His mother and his uncle raised him from that point on. Nobody knows what happened to his father. But they all believe it was one of "those" kinds of kidnappings. Davis didn't know about it until he overheard his mother one day when he came back from high school. He was so upset he left the house for two days."

"Why don't you guys talk to your agent—may be...." Mrs. Moore.

"Talk to her and ask for what? There is no legal ground for them to do anything here", Mr. Moore. "The only thing to do is to search every corner of the house and get rid of anything that you find that belonged to those guys," he said it as if he knew for sure that it was the only thing to do.

"How about if we speak to that lady—she seemed nice," Mrs. Moore was still trying to find some way.

"Well, you can try. But what are you going to say? Are you going to ask them to apologize or pay you something or are you going to sue them for something someone hundreds of miles away may have done decades ago...."

"Terry," Mrs. Moore hushed her husband. Although he was making sense, the whole situation was mind numbing.

Caroline didn't say much. When Davis came back downstairs, they just bid goodbye to the Moore's. Caroline asked Davis if he was hungry. He wasn't hungry at all. She had made meatloaf—one of his favorites. They sat down at the table, not saying anything to each other. Caroline served dinner and gave Davis a cold beer. They started to eat.

All of a sudden Davis threw his fork down.

"I know those klan bastards killed Daddy. And the sheriff couldn't do anything—or he didn't want to do anything. My uncles and cousins looked everywhere. You know, we used to live near Greenville, but they went as far as Charlotte up north and Columbia on the east. But there was no sign of him. I was too little to know what was going on. "

Davis' mother had taken ill when Davis ran away hearing about all this. He remembered his mother telling him that his father had died, after he came back home after a couple of days.

"Son, it was really awful. For the next few days whenever anyone from our family went into town, people would look at us as if we had killed him. It was awful son. I had to pick up the pieces and raise all of you. I kept on hoping that he would show up one day. The Reverend—bless his soul—kept on giving me some work to do. And I kept on telling him, 'if you really want to do something for us, go talk to the governor. Ask him to question those hardware store boys and the sheriff himself.' But I think he knew what had happened. Your father was a real proud man. I am sure he must have crossed his line with those hardware store boys. But, I tell'ya boy, he didn't do nothing wrong. All his life, he didn't do nothing wrong," Davis' mother started crying.

Then she told him. "Son, do something with your life. Make something out of yourself. Get out of this hell hole. Go to school. Do something with your life son. Your Daddy gave his life for his principles, you do something that he couldn't do."

Davis' eyes had a rainbow of emotions. Caroline just looked at him. She had so much respect and love for Davis. She took his hand in her own hand and just kissed it gently.

"Davis, I am sure, just like your father, you will not do anything wrong. Just because these old folks had that KKK gown in their attic doesn't mean they might have killed someone." she gently whispered.

Ring....ring....

The phone rang.

"Davis, it's for you," yelled Caroline. "Honey, I hope you don't have to go to the hospital today. Ryan is so looking forward to this baseball game."

Davis came running down and just signed her saying wait, let me see what's going on.

"Hello, this is Dr. Brown speaking."

"Doctor, please help me doctor. You are the only one that I can go to. My husband..." there was an old lady's voice on the other line. She was crying.

"Ma'am, please calm down. Tell me what happened. What happened to your husband?" Caroline was listening to Dr. Davis Brown as she was getting the backpack ready for the game. She noticed that he was asking about what happened even before finding out who was calling. 'He is a true doctor,' she thought.

"My husband fell down as he came out of the bathroom. And he was not moving. So, I called the ambulance, we are at Samaritan hospital. We have been waiting for hours now. But no one pays any attention to us—I think it's because we are on Medicare." The lady was settling down now.

"Ma'am, that's not true. I work at the same hospital and I have treated many Medicare patients," Davis thought it was just some disgruntled patient.

"Can you come down here please? I know you are not working today. But, could you?" the lady was literally begging.

"Ma'am...." Davis hesitated.

"Oh, you didn't recognize me. I am sorry I didn't even tell you my name. I am Mrs. Noland."

'Mrs. Noland?' Davis had heard of the name, but could quite place her.

"You live in our house now," Mrs. Noland said very enthusiastically, hoping that Davis would make the connection and come help them.

Davis just froze. He didn't say anything. Mrs. Noland kept on saying, "Dr. Brown? Dr. Brown—are you there?"

Caroline was just passing by there and she saw Davis holding the phone—frozen in that state. She went near him and tried to get his attention. She then grabbed the phone from him.

"Hello, who's this?"

"Oh, Mrs. Brown? This is Laura. Laura Noland. You bought that house from us," Mrs. Noland still had hope. "Please help us. Please help my husband."

Davis just sat down at the table. He didn't know what to think.

"Mrs. Noland, let me talk to my husband and we'll see what we can do."

She hung up the phone.

"Davis. Come on, get a hold of yourself," Caroline gave him a glass of water.

Davis remembered her mother's words, "He didn't do nothing wrong all his life, son."

After a while, Caroline said, "I will leave Ryan next door at the Moore's. Let's go to the hospital together."

Davis just nodded.

When they reached the hospital, they went to the ER straight away.

Mrs. Noland was sitting right in front of the nurse's station. When she saw the Brown's coming in, she got up. Caroline went toward her and walked her back to the chairs. Davis went to the nurse and started looking at the case papers for Mr. Noland.

He immediately went in to change and told Caroline that he had to go in to examine the patient.

After a long silence for almost an hour, Caroline said to Mrs. Noland, "Mrs. Noland, would you like some coffee?" Mrs. Noland shook her head. Caroline went to get some coffee.

As she returned, she saw Mrs. Noland gazing outside the window.

"Here you go Mrs. Noland. Be careful, it's hot," she handed her hot cup of coffee.

"Mrs. Brown."

"Please Mrs. Noland, please call me Caroline."

"I sense that there is something going on here. Is the house ok? Did you feel like we cheated you or something? We did everything the realtor told us to do. But if there is something that needs fixing, please let us know. I am not sure what George can do now, but I will try to hire someone......"

"Mrs. Noland, there is nothing you can fix now," Caroline said firmly. "But, please don't worry about the house. The house is fine."

"Then what is it? Why do I sense that there is something."

"Don't worry Mrs. Noland. Davis is a good doctor. I am sure he will do whatever is necessary. He has seen many such cases." Caroline re-assured her.

Just as the ladies were talking, Davis came out in his scrubs.

"Mrs. Noland, you husband..."

"Oh my god, what happened? Is he going to...."

"No, no. He is doing ok. It's just that.... Sit down Mrs. Noland," Caroline saw Dr. Brown in Davis again.

"He suffered a mild heart attack at home. But then when he came here, he had another mild one. His condition is very sensitive right now. We are running some tests to find out....."

"Dr. Brown, we cannot afford all these expensive tests. Medicare doesn't cover it either," Mrs. Noland said matter of factly.

"Don't worry Mrs. Noland. I have told them that he is my relative," Davis said very calmly.

"But, how can that be?" Mrs. Noland asked a very simple question naively.

"Don't worry Mrs. Noland, they won't ask me how come my relative is white," Davis almost laughed.

Caroline was getting increasingly impressed with Davis and the way he was handling this whole event.

'He is born to be a doctor,' Caroline thought to herself.

Mrs. Noland was looking at Davis with such gratitude that she started crying and hugged Davis. Davis looked at Caroline, while cajoling Mrs. Noland.

The next day, they all slept in late. It was a Sunday anyway. Davis came out to get the newspaper and right on the front page there was news about a white man's criminal trial. This man was accused of setting fire to a church that was full of black people on a Sunday morning 35 years ago. Many African American people had died, including several teenage girls.

Caroline came downstairs and started making coffee. She saw that Davis was just gazing at the newspaper still standing right at the door. Caroline took the newspaper from his hands and just read the headline. She understood what was going on.

"Sit down honey, let me get you a cup of coffee," said Caroline and poured coffee for both of them. They didn't say anything much to each other for a while.

"Honey, come on. I know what you are going through, but…."

"No you don't Caroline. You haven't gone through what I have been," Davis' voice was extremely exhausted.

They kept on talking for quite a while, until Ryan came running downstairs.

"Mom, Dad, it was so much fun yesterday. Jeff and I caught a homerun ball .. we had so much fun. You want to see the ball? It will cost you. I am going to keep over there and sell tickets for my friends to come and see the ball," Ryan was going at such a high speed that Caroline's and Davis' reaction seemed like slow motion in the movies.

"And the best part was, after the game was over, McBride signed it himself—here lookit, it says, To Jeff and Ryan….. Its kind of hard to read…look… look," Ryan still had not noticed the slow motion.

"That's great, son. I am so sorry I could not take you to the game."

"That's ok, Dad. I understand." Ryan hugged Davis. Davis looked at the ball and McBride's signature. He gave one look to Caroline. She just signed him back that it's ok.

Just then, the phone rang again. Caroline and Davis just looked at each other. Davis got up and picked up the phone. Ryan started telling Caroline all about the game while she was making breakfast for all of them. She was mechanically preparing eggs and toast while nodding and saying 'Uh, huh' to Ryan, but mostly just listening to Davis' phone conversation.

"Ok, Barbara. I will be there in about 30 minutes. Just make sure Mrs.

Then Davis turned around and walked up to Mrs. Noland, "Mrs. Noland,…." he started saying something.

She stopped him, wiped her eyes and said, "I know, I know. George had signed the consent form. He had told me a long time ago," while she took out the consent form from her purse she remembered his words.

"Laura, I don't want to live like a vegetable. If anything takes me to that stage, you just pull the plug on me. Laura, I have done some things so wrong in my life. There ain't nothing that will fix it. I hope I have done good by you. But remember, Laura, don't leave me in that stage. I would rather die." Mrs. Noland remembered her husband's words.

"Dr. Brown, I love my husband too much to do that for him. Please, Dr. Brown, please do me one last favor."

"Mrs. Noland!" Davis exclaimed. Caroline was shocked too.

They sat down again. They sat there for quite a while. Davis went into the ER several times and every time he came out Mrs. Noland's hopes would rise like a candle gasping at the end.

Finally, it was late afternoon and they all walked in to the ER very slowly. Mrs. Noland was looking at George with love rolling down her cheeks. She sat by his bed. Took his hand in her hands and kissed it. She was looking at George as if she had not seen him for years….. Or was it as if she will not be seeing him for years.

After a long silence, Davis called the nurse and took out the consent papers. He told the nurse to call another doctor. Dr. Baker came into the room. Looked at the chart and papers, examined George again, talked to Davis in the corner in soft voice for quite some time. And then both of them came to Mrs. Noland and asked her to sign at the bottom of the papers. Then Davis also signed.

Davis looked out the window—the sun was just going down. He looked at Caroline. She shook her head. Mrs. Noland was still sitting by George, holding his hand. Davis put his hand on her shoulder very gently. She shook her head in consent and started crying while looking at George.

Davis went over to the equipment and turned it off. He kept on looking at the display and heard this constantly beeping sound. Then without looking at anybody he rushed out of the room. Caroline went right after him, but then looked at Mrs. Noland and decided to stay back.

The next morning, Davis woke up looking at the rising sun.

'The rising sun brings new light in your life every morning,' he mumbled.

"Huh, what was that honey?" Caroline was just waking up.

"Nothing, honey, go back to sleep," said Davis.

Noland doesn't call me at home. I will be right there." He ran upstairs to get dressed.

When Dr. Brown came downstairs, Caroline said, "Honey, eat something. At least have a toast. Here, let me bring this coffee and toast to the car. Eat while driving. At least that way you will drive slow."

Davis stopped her. "Honey, that's ok. I am fine."

"Ok, call me if there is anything..."

Davis ran out to the car while assuring her that he would call if there was something he needed.

As he arrived at the ER, Mrs. Noland got up and ran to him.

"Dr. Brown, I am so glad to see you. Please help George. Dr. Brown, we have no friends, our son lives in California—but he hasn't visited us for a long time. I will be all alone if something happens to George," she was almost at a breakdown stage.

Davis tried to calm her down, "Mrs. Noland, please calm down. Let me see what I can do."

He took the case papers from the nurse and ran inside to change.

After a while, when he came out, he didn't look exhausted. He gave the case papers back to the nurse.

"Mrs. Noland....... I am afraid I have some bad news."

She just sunk in her chair. "Oh, my lord." She started crying.

"Mrs. Noland, your husband, is in a coma. The two heart attacks damaged his brain—unfortunately, the paralysis went too far and........"

"He is in a vegetative state...." She completed his sentence.

As they were talking, Caroline walked in. She softly talked to Davis, "I just couldn't stay home. I just had a hunch...."

She went and hugged Mrs. Noland who started crying even further.

They all sat down. A lot of different thoughts were going through those three minds.

"George and I have been married for 52 years. That's a long time you know. We started dating when we were in college. We used to go to the movies—many times sneaking in—that time there were only black & white movies......" she started going through the past half century—as if she was being interviewed.

Caroline just looked at Davis. He was deep in thought.

"I know that George has made a lot of mistakes in his life. But deep down he is a gentleman. He never took advantage of anybody. After the war was over he had a job at the hardware store......"

Davis got up and walked toward the window and started gazing outside.

Mrs. Noland kept telling the whole story to Caroline—who was listening while half her attention was toward Davis.

Heaven on Earth

HEAVEN ON EARTH

A New Friend

John was standing around at the bar looking for some familiar faces. He couldn't see any. The more he searched, the more he was getting frustrated.

The atmosphere at these gatherings is very strange. Some people were there, just because they had to be there. Some of them are trying to figure some things out—how does it work, who can I meet, and so on. And then, there are people—like John. They are kind of lost. John was looking out side the window at the beautiful sunset or sunrise—whatever that was. He was so exhausted from the journey; he didn't even know what time it was.

"Beautiful, isn't it?" Ken stood right beside John with a drink in his hand. He also had one more drink in his other hand. He offered it to John. John took the glass from Ken, but didn't say a word. He just looked at Ken—as if he was searching for a friend. John was new there. He had just landed and was asked to join the group for some kind of an orientation gathering for elders over fifty years of age. John had just crossed fifty. Perhaps that's why he was attending this session hesitantly.

Ken raised his hand to shake John's hand and introduced himself.

"My name is Ken. I am from New Jersey. But please don't hold that against me!"

John smiled. He had not heard that expression in a while.

"John. I am NOT from New Jersey, don't hold THAT against me!"

They both laughed. They raised their glasses and said, "Cheers!"

"Welcome to the neighborhood," Ken added. "Don't worry, you will get used to it. Everyone does."

It was kind of informal gathering. It reminded John of some of the evening seminars he had attended in New York City—some with really highly regarded professionals from accounting, law, business consulting and so on.

Ken had been attending these gatherings quite often. He was kind of seasoned now. He was going around and shaking hands with people. Every once in a while he would run into someone he knew.

"How can anyone get used to it? I don't see anyone I used to know. I feel so out of place." John said it dejectedly.

"Don't worry about it John. I felt the same way when I attended my first session. We are all human beings. We don't like change—especially if we feel like it is being forced upon us. Do you remember when you had to do all those math problems and your Mom wouldn't let you play with your friends until you finished all the problems—with correct answers? Do you remember peeking out the window every two minutes and your friends calling you to hurry up? And then when you are finished and your Mom is checking your answers, did you feel like just bolting out of there? Isn't it the same feeling?"

John was lost in thoughts. As soon as Ken mentioned math problems, he remembered his father yelling at him. In 8th grade John had failed math and had to take a summer course to make up for it. That summer was the worst summer of his life. He remembered getting up at 5 am, doing some exercise, then a quick breakfast and off to summer school for four hours. Then he would come home and spend pretty much all-afternoon trying to revise all the things they taught that morning. By the time he was done with everything, his father would be home and John didn't dare go out to play in front of his father. His father would yell at him, "You live under my roof, you do your job. Your job right now is to get A's, you don't do your job, you don't get the benefits. Go to your room and study." John would go straight back to his room, sit in the window with the math book on his lap and watch his friends playing baseball on the street. Every once in a while someone would notice him sitting there and he would yell, "Hey, John come on down. We are in the 6th inning and those Lion Estate guys are getting clobbered. Come on!" John would just nod and say no. Then he also remembered yelling at his own daughter for the same thing. He tried to do the same thing with her, but then his wife told him that he was being too hard on her. On the one hand, John wanted to be like his father—strict, concerned about studies first and then anything else, but on the other hand, he didn't want his daughter to lose out on life. Many summers went by in this dilemma and he thought to himself, 'Why the hell did I insist on being like my father, when I am not at all like him. Why didn't I enjoy those precious days?'

"John, John…I said, its time to get back to the session. They are going start the speeches," Ken was shaking his shoulder.

"Huh, oh, yeah. Let's go." John woke up from his thoughts.

"Ladies and Gentlemen, may I have your attention please?" an older guy with southern accent called the meeting to order. He was well dressed—with a 3-piece suit, white shirt, blue tie and neatly combed hair. John thought to himself, 'why is he trying to make it look so official.'

"Well, it is an official meeting, you know," Ken whispered in John's ear.

John was totally surprised. "How did you…?"

"I know John. I know what you are thinking. Well, not exactly. But I had the same question in my first session."

The guy was talking about some processes and procedures and do's and dont's, etc. But John and Ken were not paying too much attention to that.

"So, ladies and gentlemen, let me introduce you to Ms. Regina—she will explain to you the mentor program. Ms. Regina…"

An older, but very attractive Ms. Regina stood up and went to the microphone. She smiled ever so slightly, but made everyone to go silent and start paying attention.

"Thank you Mr. Kimball. Mentor program is a wonderful program. We have had many successes over the past few years. We have Mr. Ken Cromwell to thank for it. Is Mr. Cromwell in the audience today?"

Everyone started looking around and saying, 'who is that? Have you seen him around?'

John was again shocked. 'No wonder he knew exactly what I was thinking!'

Ken stood up hesitantly and identified himself. "I am here Ms. Regina. I wasn't trying to hide from you!"

Everyone burst out laughing and started clapping. Ken was kind of embarrassed. Ms. Regina and Mr. Kimball started laughing too.

"Ok, ok, Mr. Cromwell, you can sit down now," said Ms. Regina. "So, as I was saying, many years ago, Mr. Cromwell suggested this program to us. He had been through an experience himself and he wanted to help others. So, we developed this program…

"Ken, you didn't tell me you were a celebrity around here?" John whispered.

"Well, I am not. I just don't want people to go through what I had to go through, at least not unknowingly."

"What are you talking about? What experience?"

"Do you want to get out? I will tell you all about the program. Come on, I will tell you everything."

Just as they were leaving the hall, they saw some kids playing on the sidewalk.

"Hi Grandpa," said a handsome young boy.

"Oh, hi kiddo. How are you?'

"Good and what about you?"

"Oh, by the way, Mikey, this is John—a new friend of mine."

John shook hands with Mikey.

"Ok, I will see you later kiddo. See you at basketball tonight."

"Bye Grandpa, bye John," and Mikey went back to his friends and started playing.

Ken the Mentor

Ken and John sat down on the bench. There was green, luscious lawn on the ground, some trees along the pathways. The light wind making the leaves move in a rhythm, some birds were chirping and gathering on the branches. Such a tranquil atmosphere. John and Ken sat there for a few minutes, just looking at the whole scene.

"You were going to tell me everything, Ken." John broke the silence.

"Oh, yeah. I don't know why, I feel like telling you—maybe it's you, maybe it's me," Ken started with an explanation that John didn't need.

"I led a wonderful life. I grew up in a small suburb of Chicago. There were quite a few kids of my age in the neighborhood. And also some really beautiful girls. I was not exactly an ideal kid—until one day my father passed away. I still remember that day. I was playing baseball with the kids on the street.

My mother looked down from the window and called me, "Ken, come home right now. Your father wants to talk to you."

"I'll be right there Mom," and I kept on playing. I guess, when you have an ill father and a hard working mother at home, you tend to find solace somewhere else.

When she called out again, I finally dropped the bat and ran upstairs.

I sat beside my father's bed and took his hand in my hand. His hand was so weak and cold. I started rubbing it. He was still asleep. He felt the warmth of my hand and woke up.

"Son, I wasn't really a good father to you or a good husband to your mother," my father's voice was so low that I could hardly hear him. He was gasping for air every once in while. My mother was standing by the window looking outside, but I knew she was crying.

"Son, take care of your mother. And be a good older brother to your sister. Spend some time with her. Play with her. Help her in her studies. And, son, remember one thing—god has given you hands to help others. One day he will give hands to someone else to help you." He had spoken too much in one breath. He was getting tired.

Slowly his voice went down. It was getting dark outside. I fell asleep right there by his bed. When I woke up he was gone. I cried a lot that night and for the next two days. I was getting ready for my father's funeral and all of a sudden sat down by his bed.

".....one day he will give hands to someone else to help you....." my father's words echoed in my ears.

From that day onward, I cleaned up my act. I was helping my mother around the house, spending time with my little sister, studying well and every once in a while playing baseball with the neighborhood kids. You can say that in those two days I grew up, I grew up by 20 years.

Being in good books of everyone becomes a habit. You get addicted to the compliments and all the nice things people say about you. Once you are known among your relatives, schoolteachers and your mother as a good kid, it is hard to go bad again. So, I never did. My mother used to say, 'you are an angel. Where were you hiding all these days?'

I studied very hard for my SATs. That was the first year they were going to take SAT as a measure to determine college admissions. At first, I ignored it. I thought this was a fad that would go away and colleges would go back the way it used be—based on school scores, teacher recommendations and so on. I wanted to get into University of Chicago. I wanted to complete my bachelor's degree and get into medical college right there.

Right around that same time, my sister fell sick. She was only fourteen years old. She had almost exactly the same thing my father had—kidney trouble. She was also becoming frail like my father. And that year in May, right as I was getting ready for my SATs, she passed away. That was the biggest loss to me. I felt as if I had nothing else to live for. I used to sit near the window staring at the street where all my friends were playing baseball. They used to call me to play with them. Even my mother used to say, 'Ken, you should go play with them. It will take your mind off of things.' But I never played baseball again.

After that, I took up a part time job at the local hardware store and started going to the local college for an associate degree. These colleges—what are now called community colleges—were new back then. There were very few classes and mostly all in the evening. So it was very difficult to finish all the requirements for graduation with my part time job, helping Mom at home and studying. I completed my graduation after five years.

I went to see my father and my sister—they were laid side by side. I cried a lot that day too.

Then, one day I met Susan. She walked into the store that day. She looked like an angel. She was wearing this beautiful blue dress, it was a bit short and she was aware of it. She was pulling it down every few minutes. Oh, she looked like an angel."

Ken's face was sparkling. Love for Susan was overflowing from his eyes. He sighed just thinking about her.

"We got married that summer. Everything happened so soon. I didn't even realize when we fell in love and when we got married. My mother was happy to see me happy. We had a small ceremony for our wedding and then we went on our honeymoon. Those 4-5 days were like heaven on earth. We enjoyed it so much. We had just gone to Florida and found this really nice little village nearly at land's end and stayed in a small bed and breakfast place. There was hardly anybody there."

Ken paused for a bit.

"Come on go on," John was eager to see where this story was going.

"You are not getting bored, right? Because, if you are….."

"Nonsense. Just go on."

"It was strange. I saw this couple on the beach one day. I swear she looked like Marilyn Monroe. I called Susan and asked her. Susan said I was too drunk from the rum punches I was drinking all day. And then, one day, as I was sitting at the bar on the beach—having my usual rum punch—a handsome fellow came and sat by me. He was wearing dark sunglasses. He was really handsome, tall, with well-groomed hair. He said hello to me and ordered a couple of drinks. The bartender didn't even look up—as if he had seen this fellow on that beach too many times."

"Was that John Kennedy?" John was in total awe.

"Well, I had never seen Kennedy in person, but when Susan came running to me and said she had just seen John Kennedy."

"That must have been something, huh, Ken?" John was really amazed and amused.

"Yeah, those were the days. But there were better days ahead of us. When we got back home after that incredible honeymoon, I started my own hardware store. My business just took off. I was making money hand over fist. I was spending a lot of time at the store. I started two more stores—one in Virginia and the other in Connecticut. So, I was also traveling from one store to another. Susan was a very good wife. She took the helm of my home and handled everything swiftly. She took care of my mother.

Three years after our marriage, Susan was expecting. We used to talk about how she would love to have the first one to be a boy. She wanted a son so badly, that whenever she asked me, I said, I wanted a daughter. In reality, I wanted a son also. I wanted the first son, because, when I was growing up my father was already too old to play with me and have a real father-son bond. But I pretended as if I wanted a daughter. Of course, those were the sixties and there was really no difference between a boy and girl.

Then a few months later, Liz was born—Elizabeth—but we call her Liz. Oh, she was a real bundle of joy. She was really a pleasure and I used to look forward to going home and forgetting all the things that happened during the day at the store. She was also very fond of me. Susan and Liz were getting along fine—unlike some other mother-daughter pairs I had seen. As Liz was growing up, she was looking more and more like Susan.

Then exactly four years later, Charlie was born. He was a real chubby baby right from the infancy. My mother was so fond of him that she would spend hours and hours with him. He used to call my mother Big Granny and Susan Li'l Granny. Susan used to get so mad—she used to say, 'Don't call me that. I am your Mommy and she is your Granny!' We used to laugh so hard.

I was traveling on business one time. When I got back, I noticed that my mother was losing weight and she was also complaining that she was getting tired, not feeling hungry and so on. Then later that year—in just a few months—Mom passed away. It was all so sudden that none of us really recovered from that shock for months.

Then it was just the four of us. My business, Liz and Charlie's school, tests, swimming, basketball, speech and debate competitions and Susan's constant run—as if she was on a treadmill, running exhaustively but not getting anywhere."

John was looking around. The sun was setting and the sky was looking really beautiful.

"I know, John, what you are thinking. Listening to my story, it seems like I led an ordinary life. Right? Well, let me fast forward a few more years and get to the real interesting part of my life."

Once again, John was surprised how Ken knew that's exactly what he was thinking.

"What you won't believe John is that one day when I was in Connecticut, I got a call from Susan. She sounded really happy on the phone.

'Honey, I have good news and bad news.' That was my style—I used to tease them with this good news—bad news thing all the time.

'Ok, ok, Susan, I am in the middle of something. Give me the bad news.'

'Well, the bad news is that you have to come home right away.'

'What? And what's the good news?'

'Well, you have to come home and find out,' she said it teasingly.

'Oh come on Susan. Let me guess. Charlie got into Berkley? No? Ok, ok, Liz won that scholarship for her master's degree.'

I could hear Liz and Susan giggling on the other side. So, I knew must be something about Liz.

So, finally I said, 'Ok, ok, I am coming home.'

I told my store manager that I had to rush home. He tried to warn me about the storm coming that evening.

I said, 'Ahh, come on, as if this is the first time I am driving on the highway.'

I left in a hurry. I couldn't wait to go home and find out what the good news was."

Ken paused for a while. John thought he was just catching breath.

"Go on Ken. What happened then? What was the good news?"

Ken gave out a big sigh and said, "And after that all I remember is a big white flash on my eyes—it was so bright that I couldn't even see anything for a while. I rubbed my eyes and found myself standing right by my front door. There were two cops standing right beside me.

I asked them, 'What's going on officer? Is there any trouble at home?' But they completely ignored me. As if they didn't even hear what I was saying. I was really mad. I started yelling at them. But they still ignored me.

Susan opened the door and saw the cops at the door. She was totally surprised. The cops took their hats off and one of them said, 'Evening Ma'am. Ma'am I am afraid we have some bad news for you.'

After that everything was a blur. I could not hear anything. I could just see Susan starting to cry so hard that Liz and Charlie came out in the living room.

All of a sudden I felt a tap on my shoulders. I looked back. It was Ms. Regina. I was so puzzled about the whole thing, why none of them could see me or hear me, who she was, how she got into my house and how come I could see and talk to her, but no one else could. It was too confusing to me.

So, Ms. Regina took me to the kitchen. I sat down at the table. She sat right next to me. She didn't say a word for a few minutes.

Then she started to say, "Ken, my name is Regina—Regina Williams. I am here to help you understand what is going on."

Now I was beginning to cry.

"I...I...am....."

"Yes Ken. There was a big accident on the highway. A big rig lost control and you were right beside it trying to pass it—you might have been speeding—but I guess it doesn't matter anymore."

"No, no. It can't be true. I have just started to enjoy my family, my business, my life. It can't be all over so soon." I was still in denial.

"I know, Ken. You have really lived a very sad life. Your story is so heartwarming that I decided to come and talk to you myself. Otherwise I normally don't get involved in individual cases like this."

I just looked up. I was thinking, what is this—a consulting company, where the partners take only the selected cases?

"No, Ken, its not a consulting company. But we do try to consult and help people when they come and join us."

We just sat there for a while. The cops took all the information from Susan and asked her to come to the morgue the next day. Susan, Liz and Charlie—all of them were exhausted just crying. Liz got up and called someone named, Roy. I could hear everything from the kitchen. But I couldn't say anything to comfort them.

Charlie got up and made some pasta. No one could eat anything. They took Susan to our bedroom and gave her a sleeping pill. She then lied down on the bed—looking at the wall. I sat right beside her. I wanted to touch her, I wanted to kiss her and hug her and I wanted to tell her how much I loved her. I just kept looking at her. She was crying almost all night. Her pillow was all wet with her tears. Every tear was telling me how much she loved me. But I could not tell her anything. Sometime early morning she went to sleep.

The next morning Susan, Liz, Charlie and another young handsome looking gentleman went to the morgue. Charlie and that guy asked Susan and Liz to stay out side. They went in first and came back in just a few minutes. Liz looked at Charlie and Charlie just shook his head saying no.

I was sitting right in front of them. I was staring at Susan with tears in my eyes. All of a sudden I heard a voice that had become familiar to me just recently.

"Ken, its time to go," said Ms. Regina.

"No, Ms. Regina. I refuse to go. I want to be here with them. I want to see Liz's wedding, I want to be there for Charlie's graduation, I want to be there to play with my grandkids. No, Regina, I am not done yet. I want to be here. I belong with them. I don't belong with you.'

"Take it easy Ken. No one wants to go. But we all have to."

"No. I don't agree. What have I done that I deserve such a punishment? I have always been true to myself; I have always tried my best to make sure my family gets the best I can get them. Now all I am asking is to be able to at least hang around them and see all the happiness in their lives. I want to see the happiness on Charlie's face when he graduates and pride and the tears on Susan's face. I want to see the grandmother's love for Liz's kids. I want to see my grandkids growing up and taking their first step. I want to see Susan looking at my picture with still the same love that I saw on the beach in Florida. I want to see the happiness in my family, Regina. Do something. Do anything. But just let me do this."

Regina was thinking. I got up and went toward the window. Regina came and stood beside me. The morning sun was just coming up. There was golden sunshine coming through the window. I looked on my right; Susan was standing by the next window. The golden sunshine was making her face light up. The tears were shining.

'Oh, Ken, why did you do this to me? You promised me to be with me all the way.' She murmured. I looked at her and my love for her was flowing through tears.

'Oh god,' I thought, 'what have I done.'

"Don't blame yourself Ken," said Regina. "Its not you. Let me talk to Mr. Kimball. Let me see what I can do."

The New Beginning

"Ok, Ken, you can stay."

Those were the heavenly words I was dying to hear.'

Both Ken and John laughed hard at that expression.

"But, there are some conditions," Regina continued on. "As it is, you will not be able to touch anything or do anything material. You get only one chance. If you ask us to bring you back, that's it. You cannot come back again."

I was so happy about their decision that I was saying yes to anything she was saying. But then she sat me down and looked me in the eyes and said, "Ken I hope you realize what you are just about to start. You will be able to see them, see all the happy Moments in their lives. But sometimes Ken, in a brushfire even the wet wood burns along with the dry wood. What I mean is that as you will see the all the good things, you will also see the sad Moments, but you will not able to do anything about it. And if you tried to do anything that will end your sanctions to stay on."

Again, I just kept on nodding. I was waiting to get back to my family.

After that day, I was literally in heaven. At first it was a bit difficult to get used to. I could watch Susan sitting in front of the mirror getting ready for my funeral. She sat there for over an hour, just looking at the pictures in the frames on the dressing table. She looked so pretty in that black dress. Darker colors always looked better on her. When she started crying and mumbling to herself about how bad she felt and how she blamed herself for asking me to hurry up and come home that day. This silly woman. Doesn't she know that you cannot control fate? When I hear people say, 'Oh, he came so close to dying, but his will power brought him back.' Silly. It's not his will, it's His wish. Just imagine. People say you have to be careful and not go in dark allies late at night. But then you have cases like those innocent people that die in their homes when the American Airlines plane crashed in New York. They were innocently having their morning cup of coffee, watching news on TV or getting ready for work. They were in their cozy, comfortable, safe home and all of a sudden the whole jumbo jet fell on their roof. So, you see, its all fate. Nobody knows who, when and where they will die. All you can hope for is that when death comes, it comes quickly and it comes at least after you have lived life a little. As Susan used to say, people should try to add life into the years, instead of adding years to the life.

That's exactly why I decided to take the risk and stay back—at least for a little while. As I watched Susan go through the whole day like a robot goes through the chores mechanically, I felt like telling her to just get on with her life. But I was feeling kind of good to see all those people missing me. After the funeral there were so many people in the house—we never had so many people in the house since we had that house warming party many years ago. Susan and I made a plan to celebrate our 25th anniversary in a big way. We were just a year away from our 25th. Oh well. I was beginning to get used to this arrangement. I could just waltz around the house, watch them all go through their life. Just watch them. I could just watch them for hours.

You know John, in this state you cannot touch anything, you cannot grab anything or move anything. Because, you don't have any body mass. But then how come we stay on the ground? How come gravity applies to us?"

John was totally stumped. "Huh, you are right. How come?"

"John, it's all in your willpower. We have so much willpower to stay back that it's not the gravity that pulls you down; it's the spiritual pressure that pushes you down. But I realized that willpower also has its limits.

Liz got married to Roy. What a great wedding! I was so proud of Susan. I saw them starting that day in front of my picture and ending it in front of my picture. I wanted to cry so badly that day—I don't know if it was out of happiness or sadness—but I cried without tears. It is so hard not to shed any tears, John. You have no idea.

Over the next few years, there were quite a few sunny days and some cloudy, rainy days too. Another bright and sunny day was when Roy called Susan and yelled, "Mom, it's time. We are going to the hospital. We will meet you at the maternity ward."

Susan and Charlie left in a hurry to go the hospital. By the time they went there, Liz was in her room in the maternity ward, holding a bundle in blue blanket. Roy was standing right beside her with pride and love in his eyes. Liz looked exhausted.

"Oh, look, he has his grandfather's eyes," Susan held him close to her chest and kissed him on the forehead. I was standing right there, but then I couldn't take it—I couldn't take it that I cannot hold my grandson. I stormed out. This was the first time—as I left a gust of wind came into the room and the door got slammed. All of them were startled and somewhat wondered what happened.

Then over the next few months I saw how good Roy was treating my daughter. Every time Mikey cried after midnight, Roy would get up and go to his room—without Liz even asking him to do that.

Then one morning, I think Mikey was just about a year old. Liz was working in the kitchen. I was sitting on the sofa watching Mikey playing with his blocks. All of a sudden he got up, picked up a block and walked toward the sofa and put the block on the sofa. He was walking toward me—as if he saw me and he wanted to share his toy with me. Liz came out and started to play with Mikey. And there! He did it again. Liz was so happy, she started dancing and looking at her dance, Mikey started dancing too. Then Liz went a bit farther from Mikey and started calling him toward her. I was sitting right there on the sofa between the two of them. I got down on my knees and called him as well. Mikey started walking with a wobble but he made it through me to Liz. I was very happy. But then I started to think; it would be so nice to hold him. I had such an urge to feel his touch. I thought of breaking my promise to Regina and feel that touch. But then I concluded with a very heavy heart that I am not done yet. I needed to see more of their lives. I needed to see Mikey grow up, I needed to see him ride a bike, I needed to see Liz having another baby—this time a baby girl. So, that night I slept in Mikey's room looking at him in the crib. He was sleeping so quietly and every once in a while he would smile in his sleep—as if he was dreaming about his great achievement that day.

Then it was routine for a few years. Mikey had grown up. One summer he graduated from his elementary school. He was looking forward to starting 6th grade in middle school. Liz and Roy were proud parents at the graduation. Mikey was looking so nice—with his black pants, white shirt and nice blue tie. Susan also came to attend the graduation ceremony. They didn't do that when I went to school. It seems like a new thing.

After the ceremony was over, Mikey came and sat down by Susan.

"Grandma, did you see me up there?"

"Of course Mikey. You were the most handsome kid there."

"Grandma, I am not a kid. I am a big boy now. Don't embarrass me in front of my friends."

We all laughed.

"Come here big boy," Susan hugged him and tried to kiss him on the cheeks.

"Grandma...come on," he was too shy in front of his friends. But almost all grandmothers were doing the same thing and some grandfathers too. I wished I could just pat him on his back and tell him how proud he had made me.

Suddenly Susan was overcome with grief. She started wiping her eyes with a napkin. She murmured, 'Your Grandpa would have been really proud of you.' I immediately replied, 'Yes I am. He is my boy.' A light breeze went past Susan's cheek. She started looking around as if she had seen someone or felt someone.

Then that summer Susan stayed with Liz and Roy. Liz wasn't feeling that well. She used to be sick early in the morning. And sure enough, one day they found out she was pregnant again. They were all so happy.

"Grandma, I want a little brother. I will teach him everything. I will teach him to play baseball, ride a bike, read, swim and I will even teach him how to fish," Mikey was in his own world.

"Hey, buster. That's not fair. Already you and your Daddy bother me so much. I want a girl to hang out with me at the mall and go shopping, and watch something other than baseball on TV," Liz complained.

"So, Mikey what if you get a sister?" Susan was looking at Mikey with so much love and pride that no matter what he answered, she was going to burst out laughing.

"Then, I will make sure none of the boys at school bother her. And she can make me macaroni and cheese," big brother spoke!

That afternoon Mikey asked if he could go down to his school and play basketball with some of his friends. Roy was at work, Susan wanted to take a nap in the afternoon and Liz was too tired to do anything with him, nor was she in the mood to hear loud baseball games on TV. So, she said, "Ok, but be back before sundown. Grandma is making the lamb chops that you like."

Mikey zoomed out. He went and gathered a few friends and started playing basketball. A little later a few other boys came there. At first they were just watching Mikey and his friends playing. Then they challenged them to a game. Mikey said no. So those rowdy kids started teasing them, started calling them chicken and so on. They even bet money for the game. It was just $20, but for these kids that was a lot of money. Finally, Mikey's friends decided to play the game. Very hesitantly Mikey also agreed.

The game started. I was sitting on the bench watching the game. In the first half Mikey's team clobbered them with 26 to 6. Then at half time as they were drinking water, those guys called in a few other friends. Two more people joined them. These two guys looked pretty big for their age. Mikey argued with them that they couldn't get someone else, especially someone that big. But those kids ignored him.

They started playing the 2nd half. Some of the rowdy kids were sitting on the bench smoking and talking on their cell phones. Mikey and his friends got really intimidated. They started to lose the grip on the game. And finally they lost the game. Then those rowdy kids rejoiced in their corner. Mikey and his friends were worried. They didn't know what to do.

"Yo, hey man. Good game," one of them came over to Mikey and shook his hands.

"Hey boy, where do you live?" another one joined in.

Pretty soon four or five of them surrounded Mikey. Some of his friends took off when they got the chance. Mikey tried to call them, "Hey, Ryan, wait for me." But no one even looked back. The tension started building. I sensed that something was going to go wrong. They started pushing Mikey and asking for their money. Mikey said he doesn't have the money and that he will get it to them the next day. They all laughed villainously. And then one of them noticed a gold chain under his shirt.

"Hey, what's that? Is that gold?" he yelled.

"No. No. I can't give you that. It was my Grandpa's. I will give you your money. I promise. Just meet me here tomorrow."

"Yeah, right. Who do you think we are? Morons? Give me the money now or give me the chain."

"We will come back here tomorrow and give you your chain back—you give us 100 bucks and take your chain."

"100 bucks? The bet was for only 20."

"Yeah, that was before we knew you have no money."

"Hey kid, why don't you just give us the chain? Your grandpa won't even know."

They all laughed while closing in on him.

"No, No. I won't give that chain. My grandpa died several years ago. That's the only thing I have to remember him."

"Ahh, kid. He is dead anyway. Why do you want to remember him now?"

I went and started pacing up and down the court. I wanted to do something. But I couldn't. The only thing I could do was to go around them so fast that it would create a breeze. But those guys were too busy bullying and poking at Mikey. They didn't even notice.

Mikey was getting angry and also scared. He started pushing them back. At one point he saw an opening between two guys and ran—he ran with all his might. But they started following him. One of them got real mad and he took a big knife out. I saw that. I wanted to shout and tell Mikey to run to the nearest house. That guy took one of the bicycles and went after Mikey. The whole mob followed them.

I ran after them too. Mikey was running as fast as he could. He was looking back with such a scare in his eyes that I had a split second to decide what I had to do next. And just as that guy was approaching Mikey from behind, he was getting ready to swing his knife as he was coming closer to Mikey. I went from behind and I ran from behind and pushed that guy on the bike and yelled, "No, Mikey, run".

That guy fell from his bike on the right side and Mikey fell on the left side. I was relieved. The words I yelled echoed around all of them. They all stopped. They knew something strange was going on. And then they all turned around and ran away. I went closer to Mikey. He was not moving. All of a sudden I saw something shiny oozing out from under him.

I started crying, "No, Mikey, no."

"I am here Grandpa," someone spoke from behind me. I couldn't believe my eyes. I looked at Mikey lying there on the ground—now the blood from his neck was all around him. I looked back—there was Mikey.

I got up and hugged him. "No, Mikey no. You are so young. You cannot die. You have so much to look forward to."

Regina was standing behind me. She walked up to us and patted me on the back.

"I am really sorry Ken," she said.

"No. No. I am sorry. I couldn't do anything. What good is my being here if I cannot do anything to prevent these kinds of things."

"Well, Ken. Don't be too hard on yourself. It's not just you, I am not sure if anyone could have done anything."

"No, Regina you don't understand. Sitting on the sidelines and watching all the good things is one thing, but the frustration of not being able to do anything when they need me the most is too much to handle. That's it. I want to come back. I don't even want to go through anything any more."

"I understand Ken. Come on let's go."

We started walking back. We could hear the police cars approaching with loud sirens."

The Decision

Ken was visibly exhausted. He was looking down—trying to avoid looking at John. John just asked him, "But look at the bright side. You are spending a lot more time with Mikey here."

Ken looked up. Wiping his tears, he laughed meekly.

"But you know what Ken. I have made a decision. You see, you have to take the bad with the good. When there is sunshine, there is always going to be darkness. Where there is day, there is night too. Besides, if you want to see heaven, you have to die yourself—you can't see it through someone else's eyes—right?"

Both Ken and John laughed. "No pun intended, right?" Ken said. "Right," John chimed in.

They both sat there for a few minutes. Someone calling Ken broke the silence.

"Grandpa," Mikey was walking toward them. Ken got up and hugged Mikey.

"Now this is real heaven John, this is real heaven," Ken looked at John as if he was asking him to reconsider. But when he knew that John wasn't going to budge, he said, "Ok, come on. Let's go talk to Regina. After all, if you want to see heaven, you have to die yourself right?"

They all laughed and started walking toward the main office.

Mirage

MIRAGE

"Natasha, come on, it's getting late. And where are Nathan and Maya? Why aren't they still here?" Kevin yelled from downstairs looking up the staircase.

It was graduation day at Lowell. Natasha had just graduated with honors in Law. Everyone was very proud of her. Her mother—Tina, her father—Kevin, her grandfather, and even her big brat brother—Nathan, were all proud of her. All that week Tina was talking about how much of a pain Natasha was initially; how they were both worried about her future as a parent and now that she is ready to step into her real life, how Natasha has changed.

"Ok, ok, Mom, now can I enjoy my Moment?" Natasha grumbled.

Kevin and Tina had raised their children with a lot of love and care. Kevin used to have a lot of high expectations of his children, but then Tina always used to tell him to be realistic.

Kevin used to say, "Look guys, my father was just a small town guy. But he went to Boston and made a name for himself as an honest lawyer. He always taught me to expect more. Shoot for the moon, he used to say, even if you miss, you will be among the stars."

"There you go Kevin, you and your clichés," Tina used to try to bring him down to earth.

When Natasha was in the 10th grade, there were a lot of arguments in the house—especially around the time when grade cards were expected.

"What the hell do you mean—be realistic? Is it not realistic to expect that she gets at least a couple of A's? Its ok, I understand that she gets a C every once in a while, but her GPA below 3.0 is just not acceptable to me. And its not about me—it's about her, it's about her own life. Doesn't she get that?" Kevin used to be extremely frustrated.

"Stop talking about me like a third person when I am right in front of you Dad. And, it's my life—right? I know which schools I can get in and I know what I can do. Why don't you just trust me?"

"Yes, Natasha, I trusted you. I trusted you that you will get a GPA of at least 3.4. When you go to your room and say you are studying, I trust that you are studying. Trust is a two-way street, Natasha. If you close a lane even once, that's the end of the road."

"Oh, Dad, come on. You and your metaphors! What the heck does it mean—if you close a lane, that's the end of the road?"

"You know what I mean. Come on Natasha."

Before they would continue, Tina would butt in and break it up. Or some times Nathan would do something crazy—just to change the subject. At the dinner table that evening, there would be pin drop silence. Then Kevin would start with something silly, like talking about Natasha's friends or commenting on how badly he did when he was in the 10th grade.

Kevin sat back on the sofa waiting for Natasha and Tina to come down. Last few years passed by in front of his eyes like a movie. He sighed. His father was sitting right beside him.

"Don't worry son, she will do just fine. I used to be worried about you just like this. But you did fine in your life."

Now it was Kevin's turn to get mad, "What do you mean? I used to drive you crazy. I don't believe it Pop. I had to do everything around the house, take care of little Mikey, study and on top of that you were never satisfied—until I got my first job at IBM. Then all of a sudden you became my friend."

"Well, son, isn't that the same thing you went through with Natasha? As soon as she got into Lowell, didn't you guys become best friends? Remember all those sudden visits to her dorm, then buying her a laptop, going shopping with her for her roommate's wedding, waiting for her at home restlessly when she came home for summer vacation! Remember all those days? You were her best friend—and I must say, that made Tina so jealous!"

"Noooo, you really think so? Tina and Natasha used to sit in Natasha's room for hours. God knows what they talked about! I am sure they were talking about boys as if they were fast friends of the same age. And of course, every once in a while, I used to hear my name—in vein, I might add."

"Well, son, that's the bond I am talking about. There is a different kind of bond between a mother and a daughter. When the daughter tells her mother all about her life—everything about that cute boy in her class and even that hand-some young professor, that's when you know that this bond will stand the test of time."

"Yeah, I know Pop. They became really best friends of each other. Didn't they?"

Kevin and his father just sat there reminiscing for quite a while.

"Thanks, Pop," Kevin took his father's wrinkled, but soft hand in his own.

"What for son? I was just doing my best to be a father."

"That's what I was thanking you for. I tried to teach my kids whatever you taught me."

"Oh, come on Kevin. Get out of that sentimental slush. That's one thing I could never teach you. Everything doesn't have to finally end up in tears. You always loved that emotional enchilada! That comes from your mother's side."

"Now, don't drag Mom through this Pop. She was a good lady—so kind-hearted and...."

"And so full of sentimental slush!" he laughed.

After working for IBM for over a decade, when Kevin has an idea to start a new company based on some technology he tried to convince IBM to develop, he went to talk to his parents. His mother tried to convince him not to do it.

"Why do you want to this? You have a nice job. Nice family. Why do you want to disturb all of that?" she said.

"What do you mean why? Go ahead, son, do what your heart is telling you. But make sure your head tells you the same thing. Don't make a silly mistake. You are allowed to make a smart mistake, but not silly mistake. And...."

"...and not the same mistake twice. Yeah, yeah, Pop, I know. You have told me that a thousand times."

So, Kevin set out to start his own company. Nathan was not even a teenager and Natasha was just turning 7. Tina and Kevin thought long and hard about the decision. But then they decided to go for it.

The next few years were very hard for all of them. Long hours for Kevin, stressful times, working on weekends and holidays; but most of all missing kids' birthdays really got to Tina.

"Come on, Kevin, I know we took this decision together. But I didn't think it would be this hard. I didn't think you will get addicted to work that much."

"I am not doing this just for me you know. I am doing it for all of us."

"Please, Kevin. Don't give me that. You are doing it for yourself. And if you are doing it for us, I will tell you right now, go ahead quit. Go back to IBM and go back to that 9-to-5 routine. Can you do that Kevin?"

"Be realistic Tina. You are always telling me to be realistic about things. Now, you be realistic. I can't go back to IBM. I have moved on, that company has changed so much and besides they have closed down the Boston design center. If I go back to IBM, we would have to move to Vermont. Anyway, give me just two more years. We are doing so well with our product. I am sure the board will do something."

Years passed after that. Kids grew up. Nathan went to college in Connecticut and then got a job on Wall Street. He started coming home for Thanksgiving and Christmas. Natasha was going through high school—with frequent fireworks at home about her grades, followed by door slamming contest and loud CD player.

Then one day Kevin called home and asked Tina to meet him at Viccaro's in downtown.

"Why Viccaro's Mom? Didn't you say it was really expensive?" Natasha asked while driving over there.

"Knowing your Dad, I am sure he has something big to announce. I kept on asking him the reason, but he wouldn't tell me. So, let's just go there and find out."

When Natasha and Tina arrived at the restaurant and asked for their table, the maitre de said, "The rest of your party is already here Ma'am."

"The rest of the party?" Natasha asked. But before the maitre de could answer she saw Nathan coming her way.

"Nathan? What are you doing here?"

"Come on at least give me hug first!" He hugged her sister and then his mother.

They walked to the table. Kevin was sitting there with a gorgeous young brunet. They were both laughing about something. As soon as they saw the three walking toward the table, they got up.

"Nathan?" Tina guessed.

"Mom, meet Maya. Maya this is my Mom and this is my nasty little sister—Natasha."

They all sat down. Tina couldn't take her eyes off Maya. Maya had very sharp features.

"Ummm, my father is Caucasian and my mother is Japanese. They met in Japan when my father went there as an exchange student. Then my mother came to New York and stayed with my grandparents."

They talked for a long time. Mostly Maya was telling them about herself and her family.

"Well, folks, I propose a toast. A toast to a very smart young man—for catching such a beautiful fish—and to a very dumb young girl—for falling for this young man's charm!"

"Kevin, what are you saying? You just called her dumb. You don't do that when you meet someone for the first time!" Tina yelled at Kevin.

"Yup, you are right dear. You can't do that when you meet someone for the first time. But who said this is the first time I am meeting Maya?" Kevin laughed.

"What? Nathan you kept this secret from your poor mother? How could you?"

"Well.…." Nathan couldn't say anything.

"Oh, come on Tina. Remember last fall when I went to New York for analyst conference? I met Nathan for dinner there and I met Maya. But we decided that we are not going to tell you until it is 'official'!" he gestured quotes with his fingers.

"Ok, ok, can we do the toast already? My hand is getting tired holding up this glass of water!" Natasha yelled.

"Hold on a second dear. I have another announcement to make. Just this morning my company got a term sheet from Informatica. They want me to head to California for final negotiations the day after tomorrow."

"Oh, honey, that's great news. Congratulations!"

Everyone raised their glasses and hailed cheers. The clinking sound of the glasses spread around the almost-empty restaurant.

The clinking sound of keys that Natasha was dangling in front of Tina, woke her up from her deep thoughts. Tina was standing in front of the mirror thinking about those days.

"Come on Mom, let's go now."

"But, what about Nathan and Maya?" she tried to buy some more time.

"No, I already called them. They are on their way. They should be here any minute."

"Ok, give me a minute. I will be right there."

"Alright, Mom, I am going downstairs. Hurry up now."

Natasha started hopping down the stairs. Kevin was looking at looking at her from the bottom of the stairs. He had tears in his eyes. "Oh, my big girl," he thought.

Pop came from behind and put his hand on Kevin's shoulder. "She sure is, my son, she sure is." Pop also had tears in his eyes.

All of a sudden, Tina came out of the bedroom and yelled, "Hold on Natasha. Aren't you forgetting something? Come on up here."

"Oh, yeah. I am sorry Mom," Natasha took a u-turn and went back upstairs in to Tina's bedroom.

They both stood by the small nook in her bedroom, right by the computer desk. They stood in front of a large size portrait of Kevin. They stood there with utter silence.

"Kevin, look at your daughter now. You would have been so proud of her. She really has lived up to your expectations." Tina started crying.

"Come on Mom." Natasha said very softly.

"Thanks Dad. Thanks for everything you taught me. I don't know where I would be today if it were not for you. I wished you were here to see me today."

Kevin was watching from the door.

"But, I am right here dear. I am so proud of you."

They stood there for a few minutes—with tears in their eyes—tears of joy, sadness, reminiscence and full of hope for the future.

"HELLO, anybody home?" Nathan came in from the front door yelling. "Ladies, come on let's go."

Tina and Natasha wiped their tears and started hurrying down.

"Your Honor, I move to make a move," Nathan tried to act.

"What? What was that? Do you know anything about the law?" Natasha remarked.

"Where's Maya?" Tina asked coming down the stairs.

"She is in the car. It takes her hours to get in and out of the car Mom."

"Well, young man, you should be 6-month pregnant and then only you'll know," Tina slapped back at him.

Kevin was watching all of them from behind as they left the house—with tears in his eyes.

"Come on son; don't tell me you still like that sentimental slush! You will never learn!" Pop slapped him on his back.

Checkers

CHECKERS

The Beginning

"Hello Mom, how are you?" Jeremy sounded very happy when he called home from Chicago.

"How are you Jeremy? We have been waiting for your call. Did you get the contract?" an old motherly voice from the other side.

"Yeah, Mom, we got the contract—I got the contract. It was really hard, but we did it."

"Congratulations. I knew you could do it."

"Thanks Mom. Is Dad there?"

"Yeah, here he is."

His father took the phone from his mother.

"Good job, son. Have you called Jennifer? She called here a couple of times."

"Hi Dad. No, I first called you guys. I will call her right after this. This was really invigorating. At times we thought we lost it, but then again, we brought it back to life. It was tense, but a lot of fun."

"I know Jeremy. It's a lot of fun negotiating these contracts, I am sure you will do it many times."

"Oh, I know Dad, I am sure you have done this many times. Anyway, how's the weather in San Francisco?"

"Well," his father moved the curtain and looked out the window, "it's cloudy and cold, what else can you expect?"

"Ahh, too bad, its nice and sunny here in Chicago. But all I have seen is the conference room and my hotel room."

"Yeah, yeah…ah huh…ok Dad. Well, Dad, I've got to go now. We are all getting together for a little celebration. Yeah Dad, thanks."

He hung up as he pulled up right by the restaurant. He was going to go in right away, but then he thought he better call Jennifer also.

"Hi, Jenny, this is Jeremy," he started to wear his coat as he was talking.

"Yeah, we got it. We did it Jenny, we did it," his voice was so manly now.

"Yeah, well, I still have to stay for a couple of days to work out all the details with these guys," he could hear the disappointment in her silence.

"Say, Jenny, why don't you fly here on Friday? We'll spend the weekend here in the windy city and then go back together on Sunday night," he thought he was on a roll with his ideas.

"I am staying at the Marriott by the water. I will arrange a small meeting on Sunday morning, so we can stay in the hotel."

"Oh come on, honey. I am so excited. I wished you were here right now."

"Ok, ok. Go look into it. I am sure Ted wouldn't mind if you left a little early one Friday. Book your ticket on the web—just go to Orbitz.com, they have great fairs. . And make sure you get on American. I will upgrade us on the way back."

"Ok. Ok. But it'll be fun. See what you can do. Gotta go now. Love you too honey. Oh, I am so excited."

Jeremy Chapman had started his own software company couple of years ago. He left his nice, cushy job at Oracle Corporation. First year was really rough. Now things seemed to be turning around. And that day was the greatest. It was a large multi-year, multi-million dollar project for Citi Bank. They all knew that once they land that deal, there would be no looking back. Jeremy had spent over 3 weeks in the Chicago office. Although it was a small office with only 4-5 people, for those three weeks the office was packed with workstations, laptops, whiteboards and sleeping bags!

When Jeremy went into the restaurant, they guided him to this small room in the back. As soon as he entered, everybody turned around and yelled, "Hey, Jeremy, congratulations!" "You did it Jeremy", "Great job Jeremy". Someone gave him a glass of wine.

He raised the glass and yelled, "Folks, we all did it. Congratulations to everybody. Now get back to work!"

Everyone laughed. And started to mingle. Some people came up to Jeremy and started raising issues about daily or weekly meetings, software development and support, expanding Chicago office, and all kinds of things.

The party went on for quite a while. There were rounds of toasts and cheers. After a while, some of the local people started to leave. And some of the others decided to take the party to the bar.

Jeremy went and sat down at the bar. His cell phone rang.

"Oh, hi Jenny. What ? I can't hear you. I am in a bar. No, I am not drunk. So, what did you find out? Really, that's great. Ok, we'll talk in detail tomorrow. Love ya."

He asked the bartender for another scotch. Just then he saw a man sitting at the end of the bar. He looked very sad, almost as if, he had lost something. That man gave Jeremy a bleak look. Jeremy raised the glass to him and said cheers. The man just laughed awkwardly and raised his glass just slightly.

Jeremy felt something strange. He got up, went and sat down beside the man.

"Hi, I am Jeremy", he took his hand forward to shake hands.

The man looked up with a little surprise. "I am Mick." He shook hands with Jeremy. As he shook hands, Jeremy felt as if he had met this man before somewhere. But then he thought to himself, 'Ah, everybody has that de ja vu feeling once in a while', and he ignored it.

The man looked about the same age as Jeremy. Jeremy had triumphantly loosened his tie, so had Mick—but with a more tired look. They started talking to each other. Jeremy ordered another round of drinks. Mick kept on refusing, but with a tone of want.

Mick was from New York City. He had come to Chicago on business. He was a sales executive of a company that sets up and supports internet support centers and call centers. One of his big clients was in Chicago. Another large company had just acquired this client. The news came as a total surprise to Mick and his company. His boss—the self-made millionaire—was upset at Mick and wanted him to do whatever it takes to keep the account. Mick had been in Chicago for a couple of days, meeting with various people. At times, getting humiliated by having to sit in the lobby because some managers just didn't want to talk to him—may be because they themselves didn't know much about how things are going to pan out going forward. And then in the afternoon, the vice president of customer support told him that at the end of the month they would start the termination process and end the contract with his company in 90 days. Mick did everything humanly possible to save the account—offered to lower the payments, prolong the payments, no payments until the customer's acquisition was complete, etc. etc., but to no avail. He called his boss and told him the whole story. And for the first time in his life, he laid down his sword.

"Wow, Mick, I feel for you man. I really do." Jeremy sympathized with Mick.

"Well, Jeremy," Mick said with a sad smile, "it's really hard to forgive yourself. When others make a mistake, and you decide to forgive their mistakes, that's one thing. But, when you know, that you have made a mistake and you cannot forgive yourself, that's really hard."

There was a long silence. They kept on sipping their drinks.

"I am sorry Jeremy, I didn't ask you about yourself. What was that celebration for?"

Jeremy told him everything about his new company, the contract and the celebration. Mick congratulated him. Jeremy saw a slight shine in Mick's eyes, he wasn't sure if it was envy or joy.

Jeremy asked the bartender for another round. The bartender said, "Alright guys, are you driving? Should I call you a cab or give you guys some coffee?"

They both got the hint and started packing up. They exchanged their business cards and promised to keep in touch.

The Bond

"Jeremy, there is somebody named Mick on the line for you", Barbara—Jeremy's assistant—peeped in Jeremy's office.

"Who? Tell him I will call him back. I am busy. I have to get this design done today," Jeremy didn't even look up. He didn't even listen.

Barbara wrote down Mick's number on a note pad, but before she could give it to Jeremy, he called and asked to get the design team together in his office right away.

The whole day Jeremy was really busy. But finally the design was done and he was ready to call it a day—at 11 O'Clock at night. By then he had called Jenny three times and postponed dinner half an hour every time. She was getting angrier every time. But Jeremy couldn't help it. The design was overdue by a week or so and the Chicago client was getting increasingly anxious.

On the way out, he saw the note pad with Mick's name and number on it. And then he remembered who Mick was. He looked at the time and thought it's too late to call New York right now. But then he saw the number was a 415 area code—it was the number for San Francisco Hilton. That means Mick is in town he thought to himself. He went back to his office and called the Hilton for Mick. Mick answered the phone with a very groggy voice.

"Hi Mick, this is Jeremy. How are you buddy?"

"Oh, hi Jeremy."

"I am sorry, were you asleep," Jeremy said apologetically, "oh, that's right, its past 2 am your time, you must be sleepy. I am sorry, I will call you tomorrow."

"Yeah, that'll be great Jeremy. I'll be here for the rest of the week. Let's get together sometime later this week."

"Ok, I will call you tomorrow. Go back to sleep. Good night." Jeremy hung up. He started to leave the office while turning off all the lights.

While he was driving home, Mick's words kept on chiming in his ears, "Its hard to forgive yourself, Jeremy."

How true, Jeremy thought.

The next day was also another busy day. Jeremy had sent the design to the client. There were several tele-conferences to discuss the feedback and by the time he got back to his desk with a Diet Dr. Pepper in his hand it was 5:30 pm. He sat in his chair, sipping the soda, looking out the window and saw the dusk light mixed with sporadic street lights. All of a sudden he saw this note on his desk with Mick's phone number on it. Right then the phone rang.

"Hello, this is Jeremy" he answered with a tired voice.

"Hello Jeremy," the lady said.

"Oh, hi Mom,...no, no, I am fine. Just a little tired that's all. How are you doing?"

"Oh, same old, same old, you know."

"And how's Dad? Did he go to the doctor for that knee?"

"Yeah he went to the doctor. The doctor gave him some pills. And I had to keep his schedule for him. Here, talk to your Dad."

"Oh, Hi Dad. How's your knee?"

"Its fine. Beth just worries for no reason. The doc said I may have just twisted it somewhere."

"Oh, ok. I am glad it was nothing. But be careful, don't go jogging around now. You always have this trouble when the weather changes."

"Ok, ok. You sound like your mother. Anyway, we don't see you these days. Looks like you are really busy at work."

"Yeah, I am really busy at work. Its been one heck of a ride for the past few months. I didn't realize this contract would be so much work."

"Well, son, like I always say, anything worth doing........."

"I know, I know Dad.. anything worth doing is worth doing well. That's why I am here till 11 O'Clock at night and spending weekends here."

"So, what are you doing tonight? Why don't you and Jenny come over for dinner?"

"No, Dad. I can't. I have a friend of mine in town. You remember Mick—that guy I met at the bar in Chicago I was telling you about."

"When did you tell me about him?"

"Oh come on Dad. I told you, but you don't remember. Anyway, he is in town. So, I have to take him out to dinner. But I will see you tomorrow maybe. Bye now Dad."

He cut the call rather abruptly. Because he knew that his mother would force him to bring Mick also to the house and then he would have had to make up another reason and so on and so forth. He was too tired to deal with it.

"Cheers, I am glad you called me," Jeremy raised the glass of wine to Mick.

"Cheers, yeah me too!" Mick was truly happy to see Jeremy.

They shared stories of what happened over the past few months. Mick got back on track with that big company that had acquired his client. They had decided to give him a chance to pitch his company's services to the management.

"And then Kate called me back one day," Mick had a sparkle in his eyes.

"Kate?"

"Oh, yeah, I didn't tell you about Kate. Kate is my girlfriend."

"You never told me about Kate. You dog! I told you everything about Jenny," Jeremy was kind of mad but very interested to know more.

"I am sorry. But when we met in Chicago, it was a rough time between Kate and me. I wasn't doing good at work and I was under a lot of pressure. Mom had just started falling sick. So, I couldn't spend much time with Kate. But, lately things seem to be turning around. Now Mom is living with Kate and me. So, I don't have to worry when I am late at work or if I am travelling. Kate takes good care of Mom."

'Mom? Mick never told me about his mother either. And what about his father?'

"Oh, I didn't tell you about my Mom much either. My father left New York when I was little and ever since, she has raised me all alone. I not only love my Mom, but I admire her. Raising a kid in a city like New York in the tough times of the eighties and that too when she hardly knew anybody—heck for that matter she didn't even know how to speak English very well."

'Wow, there is so much more to Mick than meets the eye,' Jeremy thought. 'My life has been so boring. Good parents, good house in a nice city like San Francisco. All the fun during school and college years and then my own company, a beautiful girlfriend that my parents approve of. What more does a guy want?' he just realized how lucky he had been. And all the pain over the past few months started to fade away.

"So, when things started to turn around with that company in Chicago, once again I knew where I was going. And then, another hitch came in just a few days ago. My boss brought in his own cousin into the company and gave that account to him. I was really disappointed and felt betrayed, but the economy was getting tougher by the day and I didn't want to walk out at such a time. But then a few days ago I found out that the manager at that small company had moved to San Francisco and that manager called me to come and talk to his new company. That's why I am in town."

It was getting late. The restaurant was getting almost empty. The waiter came by a couple of times and then finally told them that the restaurant closes at midnight. So, they had to wrap it up and leave.

Over the next few months, Jeremy was really busy. He had some rough months with the new contract and making sure he had account control at the same time, he didn't want his colleagues to feel that he was hogging up everything. And then troubles started a few weeks ago. That's when his personal life was totally shattered. Jenny was getting mad at him for working long hours and weekends. His parents were not happy, because they hardly ever saw him. Only once in a while on Sunday mornings, Jenny and Jeremy would make it a point to go to church with his parents. Jeremy didn't know whether it was for his parents or because he himself needed some tranquility at least for a couple of hours every week.

As Jeremy was giving a synopsis of the past few months, something just struck him. It was kind of odd. It seemed like whenever Jeremy was going through trouble, Mick was doing great. And the exact opposite was also true. But then he thought to himself, 'that's absurd. That can't be.'

They kept on talking for quite a while. Both of them felt as if they had been friends for a long time.

Finally, when the waiter came back just before midnight, they both decided to get up before he even said anything.

They promised each other to keep in touch. And then they went their own ways.

"Hello Mr. Chapman's office," Barbara answered the call.

"Hi, is Jeremy there please?"

"No, I am sorry he is not here today. He is out on personal account. Is this urgent?"

"No, it's not urgent. But….. Well…this is Mick Boskava."

"Oh, hello Mick. You had called the other day right? Jeremy told me about your dinner with him couple days ago. Is there any message for Jeremy?"

"No, just tell him that I have to go back to New York today. I will call him sometime later this week."

"Ok, ok, I'll tell him."

"By the way, is everything ok? I thought he was really busy with this contract, so how come he has taken some time off?" Mick suspected something was wrong.

"Well,…errr..I don't mind telling you, Mick. Jeremy's mother is very ill. She was hospitalized late last night. That's all I know."

"Oh that's really too bad. I am really sorry to hear that…...Well, tell him I called."

Jeremy, Jenny and Jeremy's father were in the hospital waiting room trying to read some magazines just to keep their minds busy. Jenny was going from Jeremy to his father, comforting them. Jeremy was giving a sad smile and his father just wouldn't say anything.

The doctor came in and asked Jeremy to speak to him alone. They were whispering in the hallway for a few minutes. Then Jeremy came back to the waiting room after thanking the doctor for doing everything he can.

Both Jenny and his father came to him and started looking at him with the looks of a small boy asking his mother for permission to have a cookie before dinner.

"Well, Dad," Jeremy sat down, "Mom had a blood clot in her brain it seems. She is stable now. But the doctor doesn't know which way it is going to go. She may get better, but….."

"Jeremy," his father almost started crying, "Not my Beth, Jeremy. I am the one who should be going. Not her, Jeremy. I am the one who has made uncountable mistakes, not her. She kept on forgiving me all my life. I should be the one going. Jeremy, do something, Jeremy, I don't want my Beth to leave me."

His father was really restless, he was holding Jeremy's hand in both his palms. This was the first time Jeremy was noticing his father's sweaty palms.

"Dad, Dad. Take it easy Dad. Nobody is leaving anybody." Jeremy looked at Jenny with teary eyes seeking some consolation.

After a while, Jenny said to Jeremy, "Jeremy, why don't you and Dad go home. Take some rest. Take a nice hot bath and come back. I will stay here."

That sounded like great idea. Jeremy took his father home.

Jeremy didn't even realize how long they had been sleeping. He was woken up by phone ring. It was just getting dark outside, or was it getting bright. For a second, Jeremy couldn't figure out, was it dusk or dawn? He looked at the watch, it was 6 O'Clock—was it 6 PM or 6 AM?

"Hello Jeremy, this is Jenny." Jenny sounded really upbeat.

"You wont't believe this Jeremy. The doctor is saying it is a miracle."

"What, what?"

"Mom is awake. She is responding very well to the medicine. She is responding to the questions. The doctor said, she is still not completely out of danger, but he was very hopeful."

"Dad," Jeremy started yelling. "Dad, wake up Dad. Let's get ready. Mom is waking up," he was like a boy with a cookie in his hand.

"Thank you very much doctor," Jeremy shook the doctor's hands as he was walking out of Beth's room. Tired Jenny and ecstatic Dad were looking at Beth and the doctor with teary eyes.

"Don't thank me, Jeremy. Thank Him," the doctor pointed upward. "We doctors cannot give life, we can only try to improve quality of life."

Jeremy shook his hand with both hands and came back to talk to his mother.

For the next few days, Jeremy was going to the office only for a few hours. He had made arrangements for a nurse to be at home for 24 hours a day, but even then, he was spending a lot of time at home. For some reason he felt that staying home with Mom, Dad and Jenny was more important. He would get up late, finish his emails, phone calls etc. while still in his pajamas. Then he would sit down with his Mom, feed her breakfast, help her get cleaned up a little and then sit down with his father talking about various things like economy, business environment, and so on.

His Mom could hear them talking sometime. His Dad giving him some advice with his typical clichés and pro-verbs and before he could complete those, Jeremy would join in.

"...........son, you can't leave things hanging like that. You know what happens to things that are hanging for too long, don't you?"

"Yeah, Dad, they become bats and are afraid of coming to light!"

His MMom would chuckle at these things.

Check

Jeremy went to the office on Monday morning. It was as if he had never taken a single day off. He started the day with his usual staff meeting and informed everyone that the Chicago client would be in town later that week and handed out all the objectives that needed to be met by the middle of the week.

"Remember, guys, I really don't know why all of these guys are coming here. So, this Friday night we will either be drinking to celebrate or to forget about the week! Now, I don't know about you guys, but I sure want to get drunk while raising our glasses, and not looking down," Jeremy was trying very hard to sound enthusiastic and hide all the lethargy. As he was trying to pump the team up, he was thinking to himself, 'oh, well, here we go again. Do I really have to do this?'

That whole day he was really busy. His father had called twice, but he was really busy and had to hang up in just a short conversation.

"Hello this is Jeremy," when the phone rang again, he answered it on the speaker phone in a tired voice thinking it was his father again.

"Oh, hi, Mick, how are you? Are you in town again?" all of a sudden he perked up.

"No, I am calling from New York. I was going to be there this week, but I couldn't," answered Mick.

"Oh, I see. You sound kind of tired, are you ok?"

There was a long silence on the line. It seemed kind of awkward to Jeremy.

"Hello, Mick," Jeremy picked up the receiver and sat down. "Are you ok?"

"Yeah, I am ok Jeremy. But......." Another awkward pause.

"But, what?"

"My mother passed away a few days ago."

"What?" Jeremy almost yelled. "My god, Mick, I am so sorry to hear that. When did this happen?"

"Well, next week it will be a month. On the 14th of last month."

Jeremy sank in his seat. He just could not believe it. It was the same day his mother had recovered miraculously.

"Yeah, I was in San Francisco that week. I got a call from our neighbor that she fell down at the stairs and they called ambulance to admit her in the hospital. So, I took off. I tried calling you that day, but you were out of the office. When I reached New York it was early in the morning. I went straight to the hospital. The doctor said that she had stabilized. So, I went home, got cleaned up and went back to the hospital later that afternoon. As I was leaving that evening to get some dinner, the doctor again said that he was hopeful that she would be out of danger by the next day. When I got back from dinner it was late at night. I think it was almost II o'clock at night. I sat down by her bed and held her hand. As I was thinking about my whole life and how she had helped me become what I am, I fell asleep. Sometime after mid-night I felt her had kind of clinching my hand and then all of a sudden the clinch was gone. I knew it deep down that I had lost her then. So, I ran out and started yelling out for the nurse and the doctor. They all came running in, but there was no use."

Mick's description was so vivid that Jeremy almost felt as if he was right behind the camera as all the actors were moving around performing their parts. But he had still not recovered from the shock of knowing the date of Mick's mother's death.

He finished that conversation somehow making sure the Mick understood his sentiment. Then he hung up and hurriedly picked his jacket and ran out.

"Jeremy, where are you going," Barbara yelled out, "If you are going out to dinner, don't bother. We are all working late tonight, so I just called for some Chinese."

"No, no. You guys go ahead. I have to go home."

"Jeremy, what's wrong? Is your mother ok?"

"Yeah, she is fine. I just have to go home. I will see you in the morning."

"And what about the presentation? Did you finish at least the draft?"

"Yeah, almost. I will get it to you tomorrow."

Jeremy felt as if he had a sticky gum on his hand and he couldn't get rid of it. The more he shook his hand, the more it got stuck.

"Dad, Dad,.... Are you home? Mom, is Dad home?" Jeremy started yelling out for his father as he entered home.

His father was sitting on his favorite chair watching TV. He shut the TV off and said, "I am here Jeremy. What's wrong?"

"Dad, I have to tell you something," Jeremy was almost panting.

"You remember Mick? I was telling you about my friend Mick?"

His father had a big question mark on his face.

"Dad, come on. I told you I met him in Chicago and then he was visiting here last month, I went out to dinner with him one night?"

"Oh, yeah, Mick. I remember. What about him?"

"Dad, ever since I met him, I knew there was something really weird. He was a great guy. I hit it off with him right away. But then I noticed something very unusual."

"What?"

"Well, I am not sure. But it just seemed like whenever I had something good happening in my life, he had something exactly reverse. And when I had something bad happening, he had something good happening in his life."

"What are you talking about Jeremy? I have no idea what you just said," his father was confused. "Are you ok? Maybe you are tired. Let's have a drink. You relax and then we will talk tomorrow."

"No, Dad. I am fine. Just hear me out. Remember? I was in that bar in Chicago celebrating that big contract we had just won."

"Yeah, what about it?"

"Well, Mick was there too. He had just lost a client. Then, remember? He was in San Francisco to meet a potential huge customer? I was going through a tough time right then."

Jeremy sat down and gave a few more accounts of how he came to that conclusion.

"And then, the biggest shock was what I found out today."

"What? What did you find out?"

"Mick called after a while. I had even forgotten about him. But he called today and explained why he had not called for a few weeks. His mother passed away last month on the 14th."

"Oh, that's too bad. I feel sorry for him," his father's immediate reaction.

"No no Dad, you didn't hear me. His mother passed away on the 14th. That was the same day Mom recovered all of sudden when even the doctor was surprised."

His father was surprised. He realized that Jeremy's observation was something to think about.

He got up and went over the bar and started pouring a glass of scotch for himself and Jeremy.

"What is this fellow's name you said?"

"Mick...Mick Boskava. What an unusual last name. His parents are from Slovakia."

Jeremy's Dad was pouring his scotch and when he heard the name, his hand shivered. He suddenly came back to his chair and sat down, rather nervous and restless.

Jeremy looked at him. He looked pale. Jeremy yelled, "Dad, are you ok? What happened?"

Jeremy got up and sat on the arm of his chair. "Do you need a drink?" His Dad just nodded.

Jeremy went up to the bar. The two glasses were filled with scotch with a puddle of scotch around it. Jeremy was totally surprised. He didn't know what to make if it. He gave the drink to his father and sat down thinking.

The phone rang just then. Jeremy picked it up. It was Barbara.

"Yes, Barbara, I will be there. I am sorry. I just had to come home for a minute. No, no. Everything is fine. I will see you guys in a few minutes."

He told his parents that he would be back just as soon as he could finish the presentation and then after dinner they would have their regular game of gin rummy. And he ran out.

For the next couple of days, all three of them were doing things rather mechanically. All the laughter in the house was gone. They were just smiling at each other—awkwardly.

Friday morning Jeremy got up early and got dressed in a very casual elegant way. He wanted to come across professional and that he cared about his east coast client—who tended to be a lot more formal than Californians—but yet he didn't want to look too patronizing. He wore his silk white stand-up collar shirt with a blue blazer. He was looking good. He was feeling good too. He was ready for them to come and see the progress on the project. He has orchestrated the whole meeting very well.

All morning and early afternoon he was busy. He had told his team and he wanted to make sure they knew he had it all under control, so he had already apologized to all his staff before the meeting started.

When the visitors came, he was kind of relieved, because they were all wearing casual clothes. Barbara had shown them to the conference room. Jeremy got his laptop, his packet of presentations and went in to the room. He shook hands and as he was saying, "Welcome to California. You remember my staff—Paul, Tony, Hamid,..." he closed the door of the conference room.

Late in the afternoon when he was walking back to his office, he looked exhausted. The visitors were all gone. Apparently, they had a sales conference in Hawaii and they thought they would stop by on the way. So, they had to leave around 4 O'clock anyway. In his exhaustion was also a slight smile of relief. As he was walking by Barbara's desk, he whispered, "Your Dad is waiting for you in your office."

"What? My Dad is here?" he rushed into his office.

"Dad, is everything ok? How's Mom? Is she ok?"

"Yes, Jeremy, she is fine. Everything is ok. I just wanted to talk to you."

"But Dad, I wasn't going to work late today. As it turns out our client had to leave early anyway," Jeremy dropped everything on his desk and sat down in his chair.

Then there was this awkward pause. Jeremy felt some familiarity with that pause. He felt uncomfortable. His Dad was just sitting there, looking down.

"Their last name is actually Boskoytlava. But they changed it to make it easy for their immigration," his Dad spoke softly.

"Whose last name? What are you talking about?"

"Mick's. Mick's last name."

"How do you know that? You haven't even met Mick. Do you know him?"

"Yes and no."

"What? Dad? Are you ok? What the hell are you talking about?" Jeremy was getting restless.

"The other day Mick called home and I talked to him. He was also surprised, but I didn't tell him how I knew his real last name."

"Ok, Dad. Now you are freaking me out. What's going on?"

"Can we go somewhere and talk?" his Dad got up looking out the window. It was still sunny. That beautiful orange sun, just before the dusk.

"Yeah sure."

They both walked out. Jeremy told Barbara that he would be back soon. But if he cannot, ask everyone to go home early and they would talk on Monday.

"Is everything ok, Jeremy?"

"Yeah, its fine, Barbara. Thanks."

They both sat down on the bench in the park looking at different kinds of people around. Rollerbladers, bicyclists, a family with a couple of cute kids and at a distance this homeless looking at them.

"I know Mick's mother, Jeremy."

Now, this was getting even more weird for Jeremy.

"Look Jeremy. I wanted to talk to you for a couple of days now. I just couldn't gather up courage." His father looked up at the tall skyscrapers. "I feel very small today. But I know that if I don't tell you this, I will never be able to forgive myself."

"Dad, come on. What's wrong? How bad can it be?"

His father just looked at him.

"It was 1975. You were just 2 years old. I used to travel a lot those days. Your mother was not happy about it, but I had to do it. I was trying to prove something, I guess. I used to go to New York quite a bit. My company was doing well here and we were expanding to the East Coast. I met Maria at a bar. She was bartending. She was not very good at it. I went to the bar quite often, it was right next to the Holiday Inn—where I used to stay. We just started talking. And then I found out that she had fled from communist Russia. She had left everything behind, including her identity.

After a few visits to the bar, we met for coffee and things like that. I found out that she was a trained nurse. I knew this doctor at the New York City Hospital, I introduced them to each other. And then in the next trip I found out that she had gotten a job at the hospital. She was so happy about it. She invited me to her apartment for dinner one night."

Anticipating what's coming next, Jeremy looked at his father in shear disbelief.

"No, no Jeremy. I had told her all about your Mom and you. Showed her pictures and so on."

Jeremy was kind of relieved, he just signaled him to continue.

"So, that evening I was also happy. I had gotten the whole New York office started. I had hired a sales manager and now my job was kind of done there. She looked very sad to know that I might not be coming to New York frequently. She was very lonely. She could never go out openly and mingle with people. She was afraid that every man that looked at her was a KGB agent to bring her back to the USSR.

Then that night, we kept on talking for a long time. When I woke up, she was sleeping in my arms. The morning sun was shining through the window and she looked so beautiful, so peaceful. I don't know what came over me, I just kissed her." Jeremy's father went into a trance, as if he was floating in memories. Jeremy had never seen this emotional side of his father.

"Then a year later I got a letter in the office with her picture holding a baby. She had written that those days were the best days of her life and she wouldn't trade those days for anything. She was not sending the picture to get anything from me, but she just wanted me to have it." His father took out a folded picture from his wallet. The fold had worn out a line exactly in the middle between the baby and the mother.

Jeremy looked at that picture. He could barely see it, as it was getting dark. He asked very softly and very hesitantly, "So, is that Mick?"

His father just nodded. Jeremy's heart sank. His eyes were flooded. He just looked elsewhere. He couldn't look at the picture or his father. His father was now looking at him with a thousand apologies in his eyes. He took Jeremy's hand in his and just then a tear fell on Jeremy's hand. His father wiped it off and held his hand with both of his.

'So, Mick is my little brother.' He thought.

"Does Mom know?"

"Huh, uh. She doesn't know. Maria never called or sent any letters home. She used to send a letter to my office every once in while. But that's it. Not every story has an ending Jeremy. Maria's story ended with her. I am so sorry for her, I feel for Mick, but I don't want to give up what I have with your mother. Maybe I am too selfish. Maybe that's why god is punishing me. Contrary to common belief, you pay for your sins in this life itself Jeremy. And I haven't paid my dues for all the things I have done."

His Dad was crying. People started looking at them. Jeremy hugged him and wiped his tears.

"Let's walk Dad."

They walked around for a while without saying anything much.

"But, Dad, do you think this has something to do with what I noticed?"

"Huh? What have you noticed? What do you mean?"

"Dad, this is weird. But, ever since I came in contact with Mick, it seems like his luck and my luck are exactly opposite. When I am doing well, he is not and vice versa."

"I don't know son. Maybe it is just a coincidence."

"No, no Dad. It is too much of a coincidence. It happens every time."

They had walked back to Jeremy's car. The conversation ended there. They both went home. When they reached home, Jenny was already there. She and Jeremy's Mom were sitting and chatting. Jenny was wearing an apron. So, it was clear that she had made some dinner.

When she saw both of them coming in, she got up and took off her apron and said, "Ok, guys we are all going out to Scott's Grill today!"

"But, I thought, you must have made some dinner," Jeremy was surprised.

"Yeah, dream on buddy. I don't cook on Fridays. You are buying us all dinner because you guys are late. And for committing that sin you have to pay."

Jeremy and his Dad just looked at each other and smiled.

Check Mate

Ring, ring. The phone in Jeremy's office rang.

"Hello this is Jeremy."

"Hey, Mick, how are you?"

"Oh, you are coming here tomorrow? What? Oh, just an interview. Here in San Francisco? That's great."

"Oh, I am sure you will work out all the details. You are a star sales guy after all. I am sure you will convince them…..yeah, ok. Let's meet on Friday, at my place. I will fax directions to the Hyatt. Ok? Nice to hear from you Mick."

For some reason Jeremy felt really good. He felt like a big brother. Encouraging someone, showing affection. He smiled.

When he went home that night, he told his father about Mick while having dinner. They both looked at each other.

"It seems like things are going well with Mick." Jeremy commented.

"And how about you son?" his Mom asked.

"Oh, I am doing fine Mom. Things seem to be in order at the office. Dad, can you pass me the potatoes?"

His Dad was thinking about something.

"Dad,"

"Huh?"

"Pass me the potatoes please!"

"It's ok, Dad. Everything is ok."

"There's only one thing. Mick said they haven't actually given him the offer yet. Being a sales guy, he wants to make sure his commission schedule is done right. And they are hesitating to do that. But I am sure he will work it out."

On Friday night when Jeremy got home, it was kind of late. He had to stop over at the wine shop to pick a couple of bottles of good red wine. He knew Mick enjoys a good wine. When he came in, Jenny, Mick, and Jeremy's parents were all sitting and talking. Mick looked a little exhausted.

"Hey, Mick how are you bud? Sorry I am late."

"Oh, no problem. I just got here myself."

"You look exhausted man. Is everything ok?"

"Oh, yeah, everything is fine. I am still on the East Coast time. Its about 11 at night there. I am just a little beat. That's all."

"Oh, ok. Well, let me just take a quick wash. I will be right back. In the mean while, Jenny daaarling, would you please do us favor…." He handed her the two bottles of wine.

She made a face at him and said, "would you do us a favor?...go—you late comer, make it quick."

Everyone laughed.

At the dinner table, Mick was kind of quiet. He was just answering the questions and going with the flow. They were talking about all kinds of things. It was kind of ironic though. Every time they would talk about something, Mick always made a small comment that got everyone kind of silent for a second. Then after dinner, Mick took his plate and went to the sink to rinse it. As Jenny brought a couple other plates, he took them and started rinsing those too. All of a sudden, he was at the sink rinsing all the dishes while talking to Jenny about her job. When Jenny asked him about his future plans, he just shrugged it off and said he was thinking about it.

In the mean while, Jeremy took his mother to her bedroom and helped her get ready for bed. He sat down by her bed after tucking her in.

"Oh, I forgot to say good night to Mick."

"That's ok Mom, I will tell him. He will understand."

As Jeremy started to leave, his mother held his hand.

"Are you ok Jeremy?"

"Yeah, Mom I am fine."

"Well, I know you. I know that there is something bothering you from the inside. You were always good at not showing it on the outside."

Jeremy sat down and just smiled like a boy that just got busted by his mother eating a cookie.

"Its ok, Jeremy. Everything will be alright. I am sure Mick will be fine. He looks like a fine gentleman and smart too. And your Dad...."

"Dad? What about Dad? What has he got to do with anything?"

"Come on Jeremy. You think I don't know? When a cat is slurping her milk, she shuts her eyes, and she thinks that the world cannot see her. I know about Mick."

"What? What are you talking about?"

"Ok, now. You don't have to pretend as if you don't know. I have seen the letters from his mother years ago. I never thought he would be a part of this family. I ignored all those letters. I did not confront your father at all. After being married for 37 years, it is kind of hard to keep anything from each other. I am sure he knows that I know."

Jeremy thought to himself, 'what a lady!' To keep her family together, she ignored such a significant thing in her own marriage. And here he was making everything that bothers him a big deal and taking everyone down with him when he was going through hard times.

"When you are married for decades you will know that proving yourself right is one way of satisfying your own ego. But, sometimes, forget and forgive is the best way to have a peaceful life. And after seeing the bright white light in last month's experience, I am not about to make a big deal out of something that happened so many years ago. I just hope that your father realizes what he has done and at least now does the right thing."

"What is the right thing, Mom?"

"I don't know, Jeremy. He has to figure that out himself."

"Jeremy, hey, Jeremy. . ." Jenny was calling Jeremy from the drawing room.

"Its ok, Jeremy. I will be fine. Go ahead. Join them. I will ring the bell if I need anything."

Jeremy just held her cold and frail hand in both his strong and warm hands and thanked her, said good night and left.

"What was going on there? Talking about me?" Jenny.

"No, we have better things to talk about!"

"Oooh, you are in big trouble mister!"

All of a sudden, Jeremy went to Jenny and hugged her. Looking straight into her eyes he said, "You know I am only kidding right? You know that I love you right?"

Jenny was totally surprised. And just as Jeremy was about to kiss her, Mick and Jeremy's father coughed and started laughing.

They all sat down with a glass of sherry. His father took his usual warm water and brandy, sat down in his favorite chair with a warm blanket on his feet. To get everyone in a light mood Jenny told a joke. Everyone laughed and then there was silence.

"So, Mick, how did it go with your interview today?" Jeremy broke the silence.

Mick was kind of sad. He smiled and said, "Well, I tried to negotiate as much as I could. But it looks like these guys are not ready to budge. The executive vice president—Steve Kelley—will call me tomorrow and see where we go."

"So, that's good right? It doesn't sound so bad. Right?"

"Yeah, maybe. But I doubt if this guy is going to call tomorrow."

"Oh come on now. I am sure he will call. They wouldn't have brought you all the way out here if they were not serious. Granted that these guys are just starting off, but I am sure they have their strategy well thought out."

"Yeah, we'll see." Mick sounded as if he was ready to give up.

Jeremy just looked at his father—who was staring at Mick continuously.

They kept on talking for a while after that. His father didn't say much. He kept on pressing his left arm. When Jeremy asked him if he was ok, he just said, "Yeah, I am fine. I must have sprained a muscle or something when I was helping Jenny prepare that wonderful meal."

Everyone laughed. Then Jeremy helped his father get up to go to bed. While taking him to the bedroom, Jeremy said to Mick, "Mick, it's late. Why don't you sleep here tonight in the guest bedroom?"

By the time Jeremy got back from his parent's room, Jenny had convinced Mick to stay for the night.

The next morning Jeremy, Jenny and Mick woke up early. They were having their coffee at the dining table and all of a sudden they heard Jeremy's mother's bell ringing and her shouting, "Jeremy, come here. Jeremy, oh my god!"

They all rushed to the bedroom.

"Mom, are you ok?" Jeremy yelled—looking at his mother standing by the bed.

His mother was crying. She was trying to stand up straight—still leaning on the bed.

None of them really looked at his father until she pointed to him and started crying.

"Dad, are you ok?"

There was no answer. Jeremy felt as if the whole room was revolving around him. He rushed to his father and held his hand—it was cold. He frantically tried to shake him to wake him up. But soon realized it was too late.

"What happened, Mom? Why didn't you wake us up?"

"I don't know. I was sleeping. I just heard him mumble something. I thought he was just telling me about something you guys talked about."

"Come on Mom, I am sure he must have been in pain or something. I am sure he must have cried out for help."

"Come on Jeremy, go easy on her. Its not her fault. What did he say? Do you remember?" Jenny tried to calm Jeremy down.

"Oh, he said,…." She was still crying. "He said something like, I am sorry. But I hope at least now, both of them will be ok. Forgive me. But take care of both of them…and then he mumbled something I couldn't understand."

"Let's call his doctor." Jenny started looking for the phone.

Just then, a cell phone rang. With a natural reflex action Jeremy reached out to his pockets. Then realized it was Mick's cell phone. But Mick was just standing there looking at Jeremy's Dad.

"Mick..it's your cell phone."

"Huh…" Mick woke up.

"Hello this is Mick……Oh hi Steve…………." Mick started to walk out of the room. He spoke very softly.

"Can I call you back later?…Oh, no,….this is just a bad time…..Ok, I will call you in your office this afternoon."

There was a slight smile on Mick's face when he came back to the room.

Jeremy was standing by the bed over his father, his mother was still crying sitting on the other side of the bed and Jenny was calling the doctor.

Mick walked up to Jeremy. Put his hand on Jeremy's shoulder and just patted him gently. Jeremy thanked him with his eyes. Jeremy realized what his father meant when he said, 'Now both of them will be ok.' He looked out the window. The fog was just clearing and the sun was peeking out.

Colors of Glory

COLORS OF GLORY

CHAPTER 1

Reminiscing at dawn

It was a clean, crisp and somewhat cold Sunday morning. The rustling leaves of the mango and banyan trees were dancing swiftly to the soft whistling tune of the wind. Katherine was really tired that morning. Little Margaret kept her awake almost all night. It was only a few hours before sunrise that Margaret went to sleep. Her fever was down and she had fallen asleep in Katherine's arms. Katherine also had gone to sleep sitting in the rocking chair. The barking dogs in the neighborhood at the crack of dawn awakened her. She gently put Margaret down on her bed, pulled a light blanket over her and collected all the books spread on the bed—some of her own favorite books—Jim Corbett's Maneaters of Kumaon and Kipling's famous Jungle Boy. Katherine used to read these books to Margaret and Seeta used to sit right beside them listening to all the stories. That used to be their favorite thing to do on Saturday nights before going to sleep. Seeta used to sleep over on most Saturday nights, because she could sleep in on Sunday morning—only if she was staying at the haweli with Katherine. Otherwise Seeta's mother used to wake her up at 6 am every day.

Katherine pulled a light shawl over her shoulders and tip toed across the room. On her way to the door she saw Seeta curled up on the floor. Ten-year-old Seeta looked so innocent that Katherine kept on gazing at her for a few minutes. Katherine grabbed a comfortable, warm quilt and pulled it over Seeta. As the cold sheet made Seeta even colder, she shivered. Katherine put her hand gently on Seeta's shoulder and patted her a little. Seeta took a deep breath and went back to sleep with a light smile on her face. Katherine sat there for a minute just looking at her with a lot of affection in her eyes.

These were testing times. It was 1945. The war in Europe was just over. But Katherine had been away from Europe for a couple of years before it ended. As soon as the war ended, the tensions in India had started mounting. David—her husband—used to be away a lot on duty. Most of the time he was in Delhi—in charge of security of top British officers. Katherine and 1 year-old Margaret were living in this large house—haweli - right outside of Durgapur—a small town on the train line that went from Delhi to Madras. They had purposely selected this town—it was away from all the unrest against British raj and it was right near the station—so that David could stop by anytime he was going from or to Delhi. At first, Katherine did not like the arrangement, but she had no choice.

When she arrived in town and they found out that they had to rent the house from the local sahookar—the wealthy moneylender. Katherine did not want that at all. She insisted that she would live in a smaller house, but it was below dignity for David. David couldn't understand why she was paying attention to such a small issue. They had a big argument about it.

"David, you don't understand. These sahookars are not good people. They are known for their extortion of poor people. I don't want to encourage them."

"Katherine, you are the one who doesn't understand. If we rent this haweli from the sahookar, he will take care of you. I have already talked to him and he has assured me that he will look after you. Besides, what will people say, if the Security General's wife lives in a small house?"

'Nonsense. David, you would never understand,' Katherine thought to herself and decided to give up.

Besides, the other problem was that the haweli was so big, she thought that without David being around she would not feel comfortable. So, they closed off some parts of the haweli and started living only in one part of it—the part that had a large balcony overlooking a large meadow.

Katherine stretched her body and went to the kitchen to make some tea. She pumped the kerosene stove and fired it up. She rubbed her palms vigorously and got some warmth from the stove. She put some water to boil and added tealeaves, sugar, a small piece of ginger as well as some milk. She was moving so mechanically—as if she was programmed to make tea that way. Even though it was quite cold, she sat on the ground and folded her legs to sit in padmasana pose. Despite the clearly visible wrinkles due to exhaustion, there was a little glow on her face. She took a few deep breaths and then got up to wash. The water was also very cold. She shivered a little while splashing some water on her face with a tumbler in her left hand. But it felt good as it woke her up. She went into the verandah and sat down on a long cane chair and started sipping hot cup of masala tea. The long wooden armrest of the chair was slightly damp and cold, but she ignored that and started watching the sunrise. This was the part that Katherine liked the most about living in Durgapur. She wanted to stay away from the hustle-bustle of the big cities like Delhi and Bombay.

The last time she was in Delhi announcing to her friends at the club that she was going to leave Delhi and live in a village, her friends thought she was crazy. After all, why would anyone leave the comforts of nice quarters, servants, the club and all the hob-nobbing with the British dignitaries? But, Katherine knew what she wanted from her time in India and she knew that she would not get that living in Delhi.

Katherine's eyes were reflecting the orange rays as if she saw the sunrise for the first time. The birds had started chirping and fluttering as if they were in a hurry to go somewhere. Katherine looked at the birds and smiled a little. She finished her tea and sat back looking at orange, white and blue skies. A few birds started to fly around from one tree another. So, did Katherine's mind. She didn't realize when her mind had drifted about a couple of decades back in time.

"Katherine! Katherine, wake up! Look who is here!" Katherine's grandmother woke her up.

Little Katherine got up and while rubbing her eyes she wore an old army hat, which was too big for her little head. She tucked her hair in the back of the hat, wiped her face and ran downstairs. It was early morning and the sun was shining from the back. Little Katherine could only see a dark figure of a large man right in front of a slightly ajar door—holding a small stick in his hand and his hat pressed to the side of chest with his left elbow. Even in that darkness she could see the well-ironed creases on the side of his brown army jacket. Then she began to notice his long mustache and well-groomed short hair.

"Come, my little princess, I have been waiting for a kiss from you for months now," said Lieutenant Arthur Whisman.

Katherine jumped up and hugged her father. Her hat fell off, but she didn't care. Her father was home. Arthur's hat also fell down while holding Katherine with both hands. He didn't care either. Katherine's grandmother looked at both of them with tears full of affection flowing freely.

"Well, princess, you are not little anymore. You have grown so tall. How old are you now? Eight? Nine?"

"Daddy, I am eleven. I was eight when you left for India. You know, Daddy, I thought I was dreaming when granny woke me up. I thought you would never come back from India to get me," grumbled Katherine.

"Not even the queen can stop me from seeing my little princess. As soon as some of the riots in India were under control, I caught the next boat here. Oh, I almost forgot..." he gently put her down and started looking for something around him.

"Ram Singh," he yelled out a name. Katherine was totally surprised. What kind of a name is that—she thought. Arthur opened the door again. There was a young man standing outside with his hands folded and head down. He was shivering in the cold wet weather outside. He was wearing white clothes—with long shirt that was below his knees. He was wearing—what looked like Arthur's old army jacket and a funny thick skullcap. He was still shivering.

"Come inside, you silly boy. You will freeze to death. And bring my suitcases inside. What were you doing standing outside anyway?" yelled Arthur.

"But,...sahib...", Ram Singh could not say much.

He brought the luggage inside. He was avoiding looking at Katherine as she was staring at him trying to catch his sight. The luggage consisted of a large wooden bag—with a big lock on it—as if it was a treasure chest of some sort. It looked kind of beaten up by weather, but still in a sturdy condition. Then there were other small bags—they looked exactly the same, except one of them was packed to the rim. Then there was the good old army gray colored hold-all—it is like a rolled up giant sleeping bag, except more rugged looking and with leather belts around it. The hold-all looked like it really held all kinds of things in it. It also had a large umbrella stuck between the belts. And finally there was a briefcase—very typical brown leather with shiny aged look to it. Obviously, this was all Arthur's luggage, lying right there by the door—slightly inside. Slightly outside the door was a small beaten up metal trunk.

He introduced Katherine and Ram Singh. Katherine greeted him with a lot of curiosity in her eyes and Ram Singh was still trying to avoid looking at her.

Arthur walked up to his mother.

"Hello Mum, how are you?"

"I am fine Arthur. Now, I am fine." She had tears in her eyes.

"Come on Mum, I told you I will be back. So, here I am."

Ram Singh was looking at this re-union of a mother and a son. He felt kind of odd that they hugged each other and Arthur—seeing his mother after so many years—did not touch her feet. Arthur sensed it.

"Well, young man, you are in Queen's Land now. This is how we greet our loved ones here. Bring all those bags to my room upstairs, Ram Singh," said Arthur while walking up the stairs.

"Come upstairs princess, let's open up all the bags and see what kind of magic I brought for you from India," said Arthur while extending his hand toward Katherine.

Arthur was looking around the house and noticing that nothing had really changed in the house. It was almost the same as he had left a few years ago.

"Isn't this magic enough for one day?" whispered Arthur's mother.

"Mother!" said Arthur, "Mother I am so hungry, I could eat a horse. I am dying to have some baked beans on toast and some sausage."

"Yes, dear. Why don't you take a bath and come down for a nice English breakfast," said granny.

"Oh, and mother, in my small black bag, there is some chili powder wrapped in a newspaper bundle. Go ahead and use a spoonful of that and mix it up with the baked beans. Come princess, let's go."

Granny was totally dumb founded, she once again whispered, "Chili powder? In baked beans? What kind of a recipe is that?"

Ram Singh took his shoes off, kept it neatly in a corner and grabbed two bags like a porter—one on his head and the other one in his hand—and started to go upstairs.

Granny was watching all this with awe on her face.

"RAM SINGH, TAKE ONE BAG AT A TIME. DO YOU SPEAK ENGLISH?" said granny in a high tone voice and her thick British accent.

"Mother, he is not deaf. He speaks good English and if he didn't understand English, what's the point in shouting at him? Is he going to know what you are saying?" said Arthur from the top of the stairs. "Ram Singh, bring one bag at a time, alright?"

Granny realized her mistake, but she was not happy that Arthur made her look like a fool in front of everyone—especially a stranger—that too an Indian! Katherine chuckled and ran inside the room. Granny loved her son, Arthur, but sometimes she would get really upset at him. After his wife passed away, he had started drinking a lot. Granny didn't like that. After all, Granny had also lost her husband right around the same time. Her husband, Arthur's father, was a dare devil pilot in World War I. He was sent on many missions that would start late at night. One night when he had already completed his mission, he was flying his plane back to London and the Germans spotted the plane. They shot it down and Arthur's father was never found. For a few years Granny believed that her husband was still alive, but as days became months and months turned into years, she gave up hope. Right around the same time, Arthur's wife fell sick. They couldn't diagnose what was wrong with her. The local doctors and physicians were too busy to look at a civilian patient. That's why Arthur was so angry with the Germans. After her death, one day when an opportunity came to be posted in India for a few years, without even blinking, he accepted it. He left little Katherine with Granny and promised that he will be back in a year and bring both of them to India. Granny didn't like the idea of him going to India.

'It is awful there. So I have heard. There are no educated people there. They are all peasants. They couldn't even develop their own railroad and postal service. The British gave it to them.' She tried to dissuade Arthur in many ways, but couldn't succeed.

So, finally she agreed to be Katherine's mother only for a year. And Arthur left for India. He used to write a letter once in a while. Granny and Katherine would read it together. All the letters started out with 'My Little Princess'—except the one around Christmas. That would start out with 'My Dear Mother'. Arthur knew that Granny would feel very lonely and sad especially around Christmas. Except for those special letters to Granny, Arthur had not expressed how he felt about his own mother. Deep down, Granny knew that he loved her.

'When you love someone, you don't have to express it in words,' she would mumble to Katherine.

Ram Singh put down two of the bags and carried one bag to the room upstairs. When he saw Arthur was unbuttoning his shirt, getting ready for a bath, he hesitated to enter the room. Katherine was sitting on the bed with her eyes full of admiration for her father.

"Come in, come in, Ram Singh. Now you are part of the family. Just put those bags on the bed," said Arthur.

Arthur went to the bathroom with its door open and started shaving, while talking to Katherine about his trip. Katherine's eyes were full of imagination and intrigue. She was listening to every word he was telling her very intently. Every time Ram Singh came to the room with a bag, she looked at him and he, in turn, avoided to look back at her.

"Go ahead Princess, open that big bag over there. See what I brought for you. I hope you like it"—Arthur.

Katherine opened the bag and she had to gasp at the glow from the bag. There was a shiny beautiful gold and peacock colored dress. She picked it up, unfolded it and ran toward the mirror. She held it at her shoulders and started to admire the dress.

"Ram Singh, look, doesn't she look like a beautiful peacock?" exclaimed Arthur.

Ram Singh looked at her hesitantly while putting things out of the bags and started to giggle a bit.

Katherine looked at him with some anger and asked,"Now what are you laughing at?"

Ram Singh realized his mistake and wiped the grin off his face immediately.

Arthur stopped shaving and said, "Go on young man. Speak up."

Now Ram Singh was in trouble. He didn't know how to get out of this.

So, hesitantly he proceeded to say, "But Sahib I just meant that .. umm.. I mean male peacocks are the pretty ones, the female peacocks are not so pretty....." and he hurriedly started to unpack the bags.

Arthur and Katherine were dumbfounded. It is true that the male peacocks are really pretty and have multi-colored feathers—feathers with a golden eye and rich shiny colors fanning out from a white stem. The dress had exactly that kind of a design right in the middle of it.

Arthur remembered the good times in India. He remembered the time he had visited a ranch that belonged to his friend—a wealthy diamond dealer. The ranch house was almost in the jungle. One late afternoon it was getting cloudy and the clouds were thundering. It got dark a little bit. All of a sudden Arthur noticed a peacock in the woods dancing gracefully with all its feathers spread around like a rainbow. Everyone came to the varanda and started watching this magic of Mother Nature. That's when he got the idea of getting a dress for his little princess with colors of that peacock's feathers. But he did not know—he had no way of knowing—that it was the male peacock that was dancing. He naturally assumed that it was a female peacock—with such spectacular spread of colors and rhythmic dance.

Katherine thought Ram Singh was pouring cold water on her happiness. She threw the dress on the bed and yelled, "Fine! You wear it then!!"

All of a sudden there was silence in the room; everyone was looking at each other. Then Arthur burst out laughing and then Katherine slowly started laughing. Ram Singh was still puzzled, he did not know whether to laugh or not. He just stood there awkwardly—but with a slight smile on his face. He looked at Katherine with apologetic eyes and Katherine responded back with 'its ok' look in her eyes. Then Ram Singh started to laugh as well. Ram Singh looked out the window and he saw bright sunlight sneaking in from behind the trees. It was going to be a beautiful sunny day.

Downstairs, granny was rocking in her favorite chair knitting something and still mumbling. When she heard all the laughter, all of a sudden her face changed. She stopped rocking. She was really happy.

'I heard laughter in this house after such a long time. It sounds wonderful,' she mumbled. She took the cross in her necklace in her right hand, looked at the portrait of her husband on the wall right above the fireplace and closed her eyes to mumble prayers. Deep down inside she wanted to hear that laughter. But it was clear that she was still not ready to be a part of that laughter.

"All right now, Little Princess, let us all get ready for some nice breakfast. Ram Singh, why don't you unpack my entire luggage here. Just leave that leather bag alone and then go downstairs and go in the outhouse—there is a nice room there and a washroom too. I am sure you must be cold, so have a nice bath with hot water. Get ready quickly and help Mother in the kitchen," Arthur said it all in one breath.

Katherine was kind of surprised. She did not expect her father to get that personal with Ram Singh. She thought here is my father, a rich Englishman, an army lieutenant—why is he being so friendly with an Indian fellow.

"Yes Sahib," said Ram Singh and started to unpack the bags.

Arthur looked at Katherine and winked with a smile. He went into the bathroom and closed the door.

Katherine still stayed there and started talking to Ram Singh asking him all kinds of questions.

"So, Ram Singh, where are you from?"

"My parents are from a small village called Ram Gadh."

"I didn't ask you about your parents, I asked about you."

"Princess," said Arthur popping out from the bathroom, "In India, that's how you identify yourself—by the place where your parents come from and by your parents' names."

It occurred to Katherine that Arthur was listening to their conversation. She did not want that. She was extremely curious about Ram Singh, but she did not want to show that to Arthur. So, she just nodded her head and started to leave the room.

"Dear, can you crank up the good old phonogram, please? Just put any one of my old records on. Thanks."

Now Ram Singh was puzzled.

'Why is this 'bada sahib' (big boss) being so polite saying please and thanks to his own daughter?' he thought. 'If it were my bapu, he would have just ordered me around. Its that English etiquette!' he thought.

"Sure, Daddy", said Katherine and ran toward the phonogram on the desk. She cranked it up and started the music. She ran downstairs to her room to get ready. Arthur started to whistle to that tune—although it had a lot of static noise, he was still enjoying it. Ram Singh stopped for a second and then started to unpack the bags rather quickly.

"But, why did you have to bring that peasant all the way to England?" asked granny sitting at the breakfast table. Katherine was still in her room getting ready and Ram Singh was also in the outhouse. Sipping a hot cup of English Breakfast tea, Arthur told her the whole story about Ram Singh.

CHAPTER 2

Where fate might take you

"Mother, he is a poor fellow. He comes from a village called Ram Gadh. His parents were ordinary farmers with a small piece of land. They used to grow wheat and some vegetables in that field. Their two sons—Bahadoor Singh and Ram Singh, and the boys' uncle—Ajit Singh—used to work in the field Ram Singh used to study mathematics and English at night. In the famine of 1898 almost all of North India got totally wiped out. This poor family had nowhere to go. Lots of families were leaving the villages and going to big cities—like Delhi and Amritsar. Delhi is in the heart of India in the northern part."

"But, I thought you were stationed in the southern part of India—what is called Madras state or something," said granny curiously.

"Yes, Mother. But in the past 6 months or so I was stationed in a small town called Nagpur—which is kind of half way between Madras and Delhi. And now there is a train that goes all the way from Madras to Delhi via Nagpur. I met Ram Singh in Nagpur itself. I think his maternal uncle used to live in Nagpur."

"So, how did Ram Singh go from Delhi to Nagpur?" asked granny. Now she was really curious.

"Ajit Singh had disappeared a few months after that famine started to hit farmers. Everyone thought he had fled the harshness of life and gone to the city to work. But, Ram Singh's mother used to tell him how she missed her brother and that she knew that he had left the house to do something good for India."

"After the famine, Ram Singh's parents decided to leave Ram Gadh. But by that time they had lost everything. On top of that they had borrowed money from the local money lender—who is famous for lending money to people in trouble and then extorting them. There is at least one of those in every village in India. They are called the 'sahookars'. Sometimes these sahookars themselves have their own thugs that go around and harass people. Sometimes the only way poor families can repay their loans is to marry their young daughters to these old bastards that are older than their grandfathers......bastards..." Granny could sense the deep detest in Arthur's voice.

Arthur paused for a second, staring blankly at the cup in front of him. Then he realized that Granny was looking at him in awe. He kept quiet, but his eyes apologized for using this kind of language. But Granny also understood. She coaxed him silently.

Katherine had been listening in from the dining room door. She came in and sat beside Arthur. Arthur held her hand and kissed it gently.

"Go on, Daddy", said Katherine.

"Unfortunately for Ram Singh's father, he did not have a daughter to give away in marriage to pay off the loan and Ram Singh's cousin, Chunni, was only 8 years old—too young to be married. Obviously they could not repay his loan and one day the sahookar gave them an ultimatum that if he did not get all his money, he would simply burn their house—which was a small hut anyway—and make sure they did not get any money from anybody else."

Ram Singh was listening to all this from the kitchen. He sat down hugging his knees with tears in his eyes. He was shivering. Was it really cold for him or was it too emotional? He was gazing helplessly at the floor. It was as if he heard the kicking and screaming of the helpless mothers and young daughters mixed with wicked laughs of the sahookar and his men.

Arthur poured another cup of tea. Granny offered him a piece of lemon, Arthur refused it and without saying a word added some milk and sugar to his tea and started stirring it. Granny was again in awe. But she let it go and just signed him to go on with the story.

"Hearing this news, Ram Singh's uncle came to visit them. He came late at night—I think he was a freedom fighter. So, he did not want anyone to know he was in town. Otherwise, some of these sahookars and their people would turn him into the authorities."

"That night, there was a meeting at Ram Singh's house. They were all arguing about what to do next.

Ajit Singh said, "I am involved in something so big and so sacred, that I don't think I will be alive for too long." Ram Singh's mother started crying and pleading to him to quit all that nonsense of freedom and get back to his family.

"I am serving my mother—Mother India—that's the noblest thing anyone can do," said Ajit Singh with a strange power in every word he said.

Granny interrupted again, "How do you know all these things and exactly what happened that night?"

"I have seen it with my own eyes, Mum—not this family, but some other families. I have seen all the sahookar types in all parts of India, trying to please me with all kinds of things—just because I am English. And I have also seen some of the young people mesmerized by the freedom fight movements—looking at me as if I had barged in to their house without asking them. I have seen the spite in their looks, but I also had to learn to ignore it."

"Ok, so, what happened then?" Katherine could not wait to get to Ram Singh's story.

"Well, to make a long story short, they all came to the conclusion that the sahookar will kill Ram Singh and his father for sure. So, they decided to make up a story that police from Delhi came and took away Ram Singh to find more information about Ajit Singh and they decided that his parents would surrender to the sahookar and work at his house for food and shelter. Very reluctantly, Ajit Singh and Ram Singh left early in the morning before the village woke up. On the way, Ajit Singh met up with some of his cohorts and they started marching southward. Some times taking a bus—crowded with people feeling the villages going to the city, some times taking trains—not sitting on a nice cushioned coupes, but riding on top of the train in cold wind blowing in their faces."

"Wow, that must be exciting, riding on top of the train!" Katherine was intrigued.

"No, princess, it's the most treacherous travel—just imagine—all the coal dust from the engine flying straight into your eyes—I have seen these people—they look like black beard ghosts when they get down. But there is no other way for some of them to travel. They are not allowed to travel in coupes, even if they can afford to pay for it. Only some of the richest and most distinguished people can travel in coupes."

During those times in India, only rich people, politically connected people and British people were allowed to travel in coupes. Everyone else was allowed to travel in Third Class compartments or on top of the trains—although traveling on top of the trains was considered illegal. There were many deaths of people falling off from the top.

"And what about you, how did you travel in India?" Granny was curious.

"Well, for British officers and dignitaries there are reserved coupes", as Arthur explained he saw that Granny was relieved. But Katherine was again hurrying Arthur up to continue with his story.

"So, finally one early morning Ajit Singh and Ram Singh arrived in Nagpur. They stayed with a friend of Ajit Singh. In a few days after good rest, one late night, Ram Singh heard some whispering in the other room. He peeked in and saw 3-4 people he had never seen before, they were talking about 'Project Mother India"—he didn't really understand much, but just understood that something was going to be blown up the following week on Tuesday—a holy day in the name of a goddess."

"What goddess?" Katherine was curious.

"Well, you see princess, Hindu religion has thousands of gods and goddesses. Nagpur is dominated by Hindus and there are all kinds of religious festivals all year long."

"And what about Muslims—our teacher was telling us the other day that there are Hindus and Muslims in India—and very few Christians." Katherine was proud of her knowledge.

"Yes, that's right. But I have seen that the Hindus and Muslims Delhi working together—unlike Catholics and Jews inn London."

Granny just shook her head and started taking the teapot away. Arthur signaled Ram Singh to help her, Ram Singh jumped up and took the tray from Granny into the kitchen.

"So, anyway, the next morning, Ram Singh found himself alone in the house. The police were banging on the door shouting that they would burn the house down. So, Ram Singh came out and started saying, he was alone in the house.

The police grabbed him and started dragging him down the road—beating him up and asking where the others were and who their leader was. Poor Ram Singh had no idea what was happening. Crowd was gathering along the road and no one was doing anything. I happened to go by in my car—on the way to the base—when I saw this whole show, I knew there was something wrong.

I interrupted this procession. The policemen saluted me and stopped. When I asked them what was going on, they explained that this boy was part of a cult that is creating the some trouble and plotting to kill some people for money.

I went up to the boy and asked him in my broken Hindi, "Kya yeh sach hai? (Is that true?)"

I was completely surprised to hear this boy speak in English,"No sir, I do not know what they are talking about. I came to Nagpur looking for work from a village. Please sir, do something. They are beating me for no reason."

I asked the policemen to release him and said that I would take him in my own custody. I asked him to sit in the back of my GeePee."

"What's a GeePee?" curious Katherine.

Arthur—the proud father started to explain—"Well, there are these military type vehicles we call G.P.—that stands for General Purpose Vehicle."

"Oh, I know, there was this American chap living across from my friend Rita. He calls it a GeePee too—J E E P I E", Katherine the scholar again.

"Anyway, so I took Ram Singh home and fed him—that poor lad, he had not eaten a proper meal in days. He took a bath and wore some of my old clothes—the ones that don't fit me anymore', Arthur put both his hands on his belly—as if he was proud of it!

Granny and Katherine both looked at each other and smiled.

"So, from that day onward, Ram Singh started living with me. Every once in a while when he would go out for shopping, the local goondas—the local thugs—used to tease him that he is my pet and insult him with all kinds of foul language. But Ram Singh had more class than them. He would ignore them and keep walking."

Ram Singh was standing right by the kitchen door very silently, still looking down. Katherine and Granny looked at him—with admiration, pity and affection.

"Sir, thank you very much sir. But, you know, I don't want anyone to pity me. So, please, sir, ask them not to repeat this to anyone, sir. Mai kahin ka nahi rahoonga sir—I will have no dignity, sir."

"Of course, Ram Singh. I have always treated you with respect and so will they. I…."

"Dad, I always wanted to have a little brother, but I will settle for a big brother," chimed in Katherine.

Granny didn't say anything, but just nodded.

"Ok, so, let's get some lunch ready. And then if it is still sunny, we will go to the market and show Ram Singh around," Granny broke the silence.

They all started laughing.

The house that looked empty for months was now all of a sudden full. Granny took out the old china from the cupboard and started making the table for lunch. Katherine went into the kitchen, signaled Ram Singh to follow her and started to take out eggs, meat, bread etc. Arthur went into the living room and started looking at a pile of mail, books and things that he had not seen for years. There were some old newspapers with headlines about the great depression in the world.

He looked out the window and he could hear a train whistling and taking off from the station.

CHAPTER 3

Dark Clouds, Silver Lining

It was 1940. Katherine was looking like a real lady now. Just as the war broke out, she had finished her high school. As the war became increasingly intense, many parents stopped sending their children to school. Walking to the school, open playgrounds and all children coming home in the late afternoon was too risky for those times. Any time of the day the sirens would go off and everyone would scramble around to find a secure shelter. There was kind of a gloom over whole of London. The London streets—once very lively, bright and full of music in the air—were now lonely and dark with lots of debris fallen everywhere. The only music one could hear was that of the sirens followed by bombardment.

So, Katherine had started her own little school at home. She was teaching about 10-12 children of various ages—history was her favorite subject to teach. She would sit down all the children and talk about some of the glorious stories from history. In that her most favorite ones were the stories from India—Indian mythology, history of all the great kings like Ashoka the great, Akbar Badshah and the stories that followed those two great emperors.

"You know, there are only two kings in the whole history of mankind that are given the title of 'the great'", she would tell them.

"Alexander the Great and Ashoka the Great. But the sad part is that both these great kings caused so much destruction and killed so many people that their titles didn't really mean anything after a few years of their death."

"And then there was Akbar—a muslim king who was so kind hearted that people from all walks of life admired him—muslims and hindus alike. He has assembled a very talented group of seven in his court. A singer—who could sing and bring tears to gods and bring wild animals to knees, a mathematician—that brought forth various theories that later German and Greek scholars claimed they invented, a musician who could keep thousands of people listening to his music for hours, an architect that created monuments that are now national treasures in India, a politician who gave him advice that was written and referred to by several generations, a warrior who fought and won many wars for Akbar and most of all, a very clever fellow named Birbal—a witty, smart and tactful person who won many kingdoms for Akbar without fighting any wars," Katherine would get so immersed in these stories sometimes, only to be woken up by sound of sirens or bomb blasts.

The boys and girls would stay glued to their seats listening to the fascinating stories. And then ask Katherine if she was just making them up or they were real stories. Even Ram Singh would sit down listening to those stories. And then Granny would get mad him for not paying attention to the chores at home. Every once in while, Arthur would sit in his easy chair and listen to her stories too. He would get a smile out of pride for Katherine and a chuckle out of granny's reaction to the stories.

It was also stressful times for Arthur. He had taken ill and was given desk duty. He had lost a lot of weight. He was coughing all the time. When asked if he was alright, he would get mad at them. One day he came come home looking rather disgruntled mumbling to himself, 'I am an army officer. Not a clerk. If they wanted a clerk they should have looked in the bank. I can still hold the gun in my hand. I am ready to battle the enemy—not a pile of papers.........' and so on.

Katherine would always try to calm him down.

As he came home, she called Ram Singh, "Ram Singh, saab ke liye pani garam karo."

"(Heat up some water for your master)."

She was very proud that she had learned some Hindi. Arthur also looked at her with pride and joy. And then he got sad again, "Oh, its my fault. I know how badly you wanted to go to India. But I am sorry princess, I can't do that now."

"Its ok, Dad. You get better and we will all go to India. After all, we have to make sure Ram Singh goes back there safe and sound, right?" Katherine would explain to Arthur as if he was a five year old kid.

Ram Singh was kind of smiling when he brought a pail of warm water at the sink for Arthur.

"Now, what are you chuckling at? Go get my newspaper and put on the gramophone." Arthur started splashing water on his face.

Granny was also watching all this. She also chuckled and said to Ram Singh, "Ram Singh come on help me start this oven so I can start this pot roast." Ram Singh just stood there for a second. "Come on now, I know you don't eat beef. But Katherine stood in that line for four hours yesterday to get this much beef. I am not going to let it go waste because of you." Granny was not happy that he didn't follow her orders right away. She always thought that Ram Singh immediately did whatever Katherine told him to do.

The next day, Arthur did not wake up at 'o six hundred hours' as he always used to. Katherine went up to his room to wake him up. He was tossing and turning in his sleep—obviously feeling extremely uncomfortable. Katherine was really scared. She went running near him and realized that he was running high temperature. She called Ram Singh and asked him to bring some cold water and a towel to clean him up and then she started putting the cold wet towel on Arthur's forehead. Granny made some hot tea and brought it to him. After the sun was up, Katherine hurriedly went out and brought a doctor with her. The doctor gave Arthur an injection of antibiotic and hoped that the fever would be under control within a day or so.

Katherine and Ram Singh stayed in Arthur's room all day. Katherine and Ram Singh were taking turns to wipe Arthur's face with cold water, put some cold water strips on his forehead and massage his forehead or his feet to make him feel better. Both of them looked exhausted by the end of the day. Finally in the evening, Katherine asked Ram Singh to go downstairs and help Granny with dinner. When Ram Singh went down stairs, he found Granny just sitting at the table staring emptily.

"Granny-ji"—he used to call her by that name. 'ji' in Hindi is added to the name to call someone respectfully.

"Granny-ji, do you want to make pot roast today?"

Granny just looked at him, gave him a slight smile and just nodded. Ram Singh went to the kitchen to start the oven.

"And Ram Singh, start cutting that cabbage also. We have some of that spice left over from last week. You can have that with some bread and rice."

Ram Singh smiled and started cutting the cabbage.

Ram Singh was part of the family now. He was Katherine's big brother. Even granny had accepted him in the family. She had realized that he was a gentleman and he helped her at home, helped Katherine in anything she needed and also helped Arthur get some things done that Katherine couldn't do. In addition, he respected granny in spite of the fact that initially she didn't like him at all and didn't want to make him part of the family.

By dinnertime, Arthur was feeling much better. All four of them actually brought the whole dinner in his room and had dinner with him. He ate only some rice and some soup. Again, there was some laughter in the house.

Ram Singh insisted that he stay in Arthur's room for the night in case he needed something at night. Granny supported that request and asked Katherine to get some sleep. Arthur was fine with it too.

"Arrey Ram Singh kyo mere liye yeh sab kar rahe ho?"

"(Why are you doing all this for me?)"

Arthur was happy he had not forgotten his Hindi. Ram Singh also felt quite touched.

"Saab, aapne mere liye itna kuchch kiya hai, muze aapki itni to sewa karane di jiye"

"(Sir, you have done so much for me, let me at least do this much for you)" he replied.

Arthur sat up in his bed and asked Ram Singh to sit down. Ram Singh sat down on the floor by his bed. Arthur signed him to sit on his bed, not on the floor. As the night rolled down, they had to close all the curtains and have only very small candles for light. The war time in London had brought the strict rules of curfew and blackouts. Every house on the main streets was required to put black curtains and make sure there was no light coming through at night. If the German planes spotted any light, they would start bombarding all the area around that light.

Arthur was telling Ram Singh stories about the war and how he fought in World War I.

"Some times I get really sick and tired of these wars. All my life I have either fought a big war or small battles. Even in India, the environment was always tense. It was only after Gandhi took over the freedom fights that things calmed down a bit."

Ram Singh's mind also started floating. He had tears in his eyes thinking about homeland and his parents.

"Don't worry Ram Singh, I am sure you will go back one of these days and meet up with your parents. Don't worry Ram Singh. You are not a traitor to your Mother Land. You did not run away. I brought you here. There are a lot of traitors here too in England. Just like that Hansaraj—the famous traitor that helped General Michael O'Dwyer and Brigadier Edward Harry Dyre on Jalianwalah Bagh in Amrtisar, Punjab. Just last week I was at my favorite Indian Restaurant—Pujab India in Soho. There were a few people from India—Surat Ali, Shivsingh Johan and this bright young fellow named Udham Singh. They were all telling me about this O'Dwyer and what he did to all those 2000 innocent people. Now, that's a traitor. You are not a traitor."

Ram Singh just gave him a weak smile and started rubbing his feet. Arthur started telling him a story of a traitor that gave the German bombers a very small clue and that destroyed the Middlesex County near London to a point of total destruction. A German descendant who had lived near London almost all his life was contacted by the German secret service. He was given two choices, either to help the Germans locate some strategic areas around London at night for a lot of money and a small villa for his family right outside Nurnberg or all of his family back in Nurnberg will be sent to the 'special' camps. So, they decided the time and place. The place was right outside the entrance of the public library of Middlesex County. This library had secret passageways down to the underground offices of the Royal Secret Service.

One clear night, after dark, this traitor went outside and started smoking cigarettes—one after the other. When one cigarette was finished, he would light up another one with a match. And before he went on to smoke the fifth cigarette, German bombers had spotted him and they bombarded that whole area so badly that even the roads were completely turned upside down.

Katherine was also listening to the story from the door. She came in and sat on the other side of the bed. She took Arthur's hand in her hand, kissed it and said, "Everything will be fine Dad. Everything will be fine."

They all sat there for quite a while. Arthur had fallen asleep and so had Ram Singh. Katherine got up and tip towed across the room to go to her bedroom.

The following morning as Katherine was getting ready to go to the basement to start her school, there was a knock on the door. Katherine opened the door. There was a tall, handsome military officer standing at the door. They both stared at each other for a few seconds.

"Hello, my name is David. David Sutherland. I work with Lieutenant Whisman."

Arthur was just walking down the stairs—still in his pajamas and robe. "Oh, David, come on in lad. Why are you so hesitant? Katherine, this is David Sutherland. He is one of the most dynamic young lieutenants I know. Well, come in, come in David."

"Well, I haven't made it to Lieutenant yet, sir."

"Oh, don't be too modest young man, it's not a question of if, just when," Arthur had always been impressed with David's modesty.

Granny came out of the kitchen listening to all the conversation in the hallway. Arthur introduced David to her. David was very a gentleman. He took off his hat and shook hands with Granny.

"Very pleased to make your acquaintance Ma'am," he said.

Ram Singh was watching all of this from the kitchen door. He didn't want to come out until someone asked him to. This would happen once in a while. Whenever a visitor came to their house, all the members of the Whisman family would be engrossed in conversation. But before they would forget, they would introduce Ram Singh to the visitor. It was not unusual for Ram Singh.

"Would you like to have some breakfast? We were just about to have ours." Katherine was hoping David would stay for a while.

"No, Ma'am. I usually have my breakfast early—half passed six."

Arthur and Katherine looked at each other and laughed.

"You military men are all alike."

"Well, David. Come here in the study. I will give you the papers you came here for."

They both went into the study. Katherine was getting breakfast ready, but half her attention was toward the study. She heard some laughter and then some whispering. Arthur gave David a brown envelope and again whispered something more. When she saw them shaking hands and David thanking Arthur, she went into the study.

"At least have some tea with us, Lt. Sutherland," she asked politely.

"Sure. I will have some tea. And call me David, please. I know Lt. Whisman for long enough to be friends with his daughter."

Katherine liked his polite yet forceful way.

"Ok, David. Do you like tea the Indian way, like my father?"

"Oh no Ma'am. I like it the good old English style. I have heard about this Indian way of adding some spices, some sugar and milk to the tea. These Indian fellows have to make up their mind. Either they need to drink tea or milk. Either it needs to be spicy or sweet. They need to be either free or rich!" There was a lot of arrogance on his voice.

Katherine was about to say, 'Well, why not both? Does it have to be one or the other?'

Arthur knew what she was going to say. He just shushed her with his eyes.

"Ok, ok, Lt. Sutherland. We will have tea the English way. Alright?" Arthur said laughing.

They all went into the kitchen, sat around the table and started having some tea, Arthur's favorite baked beans on toast and eggs. Along with that they were having good conversation. David had moved into Arthur's division just a few months ago. He was considered to be one of the most promising candidates to rise through ranks. His attention to detail, his discipline, and his drive to make something out of his career was noticed by a lot of senior officials. With the war looming over their heads, the seniors had not gotten around to write recommendations to the Commander to promote David. And when the war actually started, they were all very busy working long hours and implementing changing strategies. David was also getting frustrated, but he didn't say anything to anyone. Arthur knew all of this and any chance he would get he would talk to his senior officers and recommend they do something about it.

Ram Singh was in the kitchen, just getting everything ready. Katherine would come in the kitchen with a smile on her face and take something back to the dining table. She had completely forgotten to introduce Ram Singh. Ram Singh was feeling bad, but he didn't say anything.

Finally, when David started to leave, all three of them went to the door. Once again, as a gentleman David bid good bye to all three of them. He suddenly realized that he had left the papers on the table. Arthur called Ram Singh and asked him to bring the papers.

When Ram Singh brought the envelope, Arthur proudly introduced him to David.

"David, this is the lad I was telling you about—Ram Singh. He has almost become a part of the family now."

Ram Singh heard that 'almost' part loud and clear. But again, he didn't say anything.

"How do you do sir?" Ram Singh said with almost a perfect English accent and that stunned David.

"Fine. Fine." He said. He couldn't say anything more. He took the envelope from Ram Singh and said thanks.

There was an awkward silence for a few seconds. Then David said he had to rush to the office and hurriedly took off.

Ram Singh closed the door behind him.

"Fine lad isn't he Ram Singh?" Arthur purposely asked him.

"Yes, sir. He seems like a gentleman."

"What do you think, princess?" Arthur purposely asked Katherine with tongue in cheek and smile on his face.

"Well...he seems like a gentleman, Dad." Katherine was almost blushing. She ran into the kitchen and hugged Granny with her back to Arthur. Granny looked at Arthur with awe.

"Why don't we ask him to come over for dinner tonight?" Granny asked.

"Yes, Mum, that is a fantastic idea. It has been a long time since you had a fantastic idea!" Arthur started teasing her. "But we have to make sure its ok with Katherine."

"Of course, it is up to you Daddy." Katherine was blushing, but she didn't want to show. She hurriedly got ready to head down to the basement. The children had started gathering and making some noise.

Katherine's school was unique. They had made a different door to enter the basement from the side door. So, every morning the children wouldn't have to enter through the house. Generally, everyday Katherine would go downstairs and get a few projects ready for the children. So, when everyone got together, she would start the school right away. Today was different.

Katherine went downstairs and hushed everyone. But, then one smart kid asked her, "Ms. Whisman, who was that?"

"Who was who?" Katherine tried to plead ignorance.

"I saw that handsome Army man leaving from the front door with a smile on his face. Who was that?"

"Yes Ms. Whisman, who was that?" a few other kids joined the chorus line.

"Nobody. now, sit down and let's start working on our projects." Katherine wanted to move on.

"Yes, Ms. Katherine," kids chimed again. And then there was some laughter and giggles.

Katherine gave them their projects and started to get herself busy.

By the time it got dark and the children had started to leave one by one, Katherine was very tired. She had not slept very well for the past couple of nights and then all day she was running between her school and making sure Arthur was taken care of.

Finally, she went upstairs after the last child had gone home. She had almost forgotten about the conversation about David coming over that evening. She went and sat at the dining table and asked Ram Singh for a hot cup of tea.

"He is coming over for dinner on Sunday," Ram Singh whispered while giving her the tea.

"Huh?" Katherine was still lost in her thoughts.

"That gentleman that came this morning, he cannot come for dinner tonight, but he is coming over on Sunday."

"Oh, ok. Thank you Ram." Katherine remembered about David.

Katherine used to call Ram Singh, Ram. She liked that better. She thought it was more affectionate than Ram Singh. Her pronunciation was also very good. After Ram Singh had been with the family for a few months, Katherine asked him if she could call him Ram.

"Whatever you please Ma'am." Ram Singh had replied.

"Now, you have to promise me, if I call you Ram, you must call me Katherine."

"I cannot call you by your name Ma'am. That will be an insult to you."

"Oh, come on. Why do you have to make everything so emotional?"

"Its not that Katherine-ji, my mother always told me that you must show respect to people in everything that you do. Just by saying 'I respect you', you don't show respect. How would you feel, if the children in your school said, 'We respect you' in a rude voice while putting their feet up on the table? My mother used to say, just like love is shown through your actions and not words, respect is also shown, not spoken."

"Ok, ok Ram. I know almost everything your mother used to say." Katherine pleaded.

"Oh and one other thing. . ."

"Now what?" Katherine was a bit annoyed.

"You may call me Ram. But I don't ever want to hear you say, Hey Ram."

Katherine just smiled. She knew exactly what Ram Singh was talking about. For any Hindu, Ram is god's name and it is believed that when you die, you go to Ram. That's why the last words out of a true Hindu's mouth are 'Hey Ram'. Or when someone dies, that person's relatives and friends place the dead body on a stretcher and then four people carry the stretcher to the crematorium. While they carry the stretcher a procession of friends and family members followed them chanting, "Ram naam satya hai" (The only truth is the name of Ram).

This is similar to what they say when they bury a Christian, 'Soil to soil…..'. Many people also convert that phrase into a verb—"Usaka Ram naam satya ho gaya" (He became one with Lord Ram).

"But, Ram Singh, aren't you Sikh? You are not Hindu, are you?"

"No. My mother is a Punjabi-Hindu, but my father is Sikh. So, we follow many Hindu and many Sikh customs. But, sometimes, you know, I cannot tell the difference, which one is which."

"That means they are both fundamentally the same."

"In that case, shouldn't all religions fundamentally the same?" Ram Singh asked innocently.

'That's what god, religion and faith is all about. Even this uneducated man knows that. He is so much better than all those so-called scholars that keep arguing about which religion is better,' Katherine thought to herself.

CHAPTER 4

Delicate Bonds

On the following Sunday, David came for an early dinner. Surprisingly it was a great day. It was sunny and nice. It was also relatively quiet. There were no sirens going off and no bombarding. Even the war had taken a day off, it seemed. So, they all decided to sit in the backyard to have dinner. It was still a bit cold for Granny, she was all bundled up in wool. Ram Singh was also cold. He was wearing his nice Indian clothes—kurta & pajama. But he had to wear a thick wool sweater over it and a wool cap covering his ears. In short, they looked like a couple of polar bears.

Katherine was busy right from the crack of dawn to get ready for the dinner. She had done all the preparation—marinated chicken—tandoori style, marinated beef and cut all the vegetables for salad, started baking fresh bread for dinner as well as many kinds of condiments. She was ordering everyone all around, telling them to get this and that, and every once in a while she would get mad at Arthur for just sitting there reading his newspaper and all the propaganda leaflets and making comments about the Nazis and how the Royal Army should just take over Germany, etc.

Granny was sitting in her favorite chair and watching this whole drama unfold for the whole day. She would ask Katherine if she needed help and then get back to her knitting. When Arthur made any comments or didn't listen to Katherine, Granny would yell at Arthur and ask him to behave himself. Finally, at around 'Seventeen Hundred Hours' they all decided to set up dinner in the backyard, since the day had turned out to be a good one. Then, again, there was scrambling around on Katherine's part. She asked Ram Singh clean the backyard, clean the wooden deck table and the chairs and spread a beautiful Indian thick blanket with lots of pretty colors on the table. She brought out the salad bowl and the dishes, the beer glasses and the napkins etc. Then she stood there for a minute planning the whole evening in her mind and then decided to take the salad bowl and the plates inside.

Arthur was now getting a bit frustrated with all this running around.

"Princess, slow down. Don't run so much, I am getting tired!" he laughed.

"YOU are getting tired, Dad? I am the one doing all the running around. If you could just help a little bit...."

"Ok, ok, Lieutenant Whisman at your service, Your Majesty!" Arthur stood up straight and saluted her.

Now, Granny and Ram Singh both started laughing.

"Alright, Katherine, take it easy now. Relax. After all, he is just Arthur's colleague, not Winston Churchill." Granny tried to get it under control.

"Oh, no. If this is the condition when David is coming over for dinner, I can't even imagine if Churchill himself came to our house for dinner!" Arthur exclaimed.

Katherine just gave him a look and didn't add anything to that.

Ram Singh whispered in Arthur's ears, 'Lekin saab, Churchill to shadi shu-da adami hain na? Wo kyu ayenge hamare ghar khana khane ke liye?' (But, sir, Churchill is a married man, why would he come to our house for dinner?)

"Well, young man, you have a point there!" Arthur.

They both laughed.

Katherine laughed at them rather sarcastically and said, "I know what you said Ram Singh. My Hindi is not good, but I know what shadi-shuda means."

They both shut up and Granny also asked them to shut up.

When David came that evening, he was looking really handsome. He had a polo turtleneck and a light jacket over it. The Navy blue color reflected in his eyes and they looked even more radiant. He brought a bunch of flowers for Katherine and a bottle of Scotch whisky for Arthur. As he entered, he first gave the flowers to Katherine in a very English gentleman way.

"You look beautiful in that colorful dress, Katherine." David said.

"Thank you, so do you......errr I mean….."

"I hope I don't look beautiful Ma'am and I am certainly not wearing a dress!" he laughed lightly.

She was embarrassed. Her heart was running at a thousand miles an hour. As David came close to her to give her the flowers, she smelled his cologne and knew it there and then that he was also just as excited to be there as she was. David liked the way Katherine has dressed up—simple, but elegant. There was a unique elegance in her simplicity. In his military days, going out to drink with his army friends, he had met a lot of women at these bars with loud make up and gaudy colored dresses with slits on the side of their skirts going too high above their knees. Katherine was wearing a make-up, but with such subtlety that David could almost feel it. It's just like the difference between the orange red sun at dusk—accompanies by the wind that blows away someone's hat or someone's scarf—and the same reddish orange sun at dawn with gentle breeze that invigorates and fills you up with new breath of life.

They were still looking at each other. As this exchange was going on, David and Katherine both were oblivious to the world, while Arthur, Granny and

Ram Singh were just frozen in their positions watching the two. Ram Singh had always felt gratitude and a strange kind of affection—maybe brotherly love—toward Katherine. He was looking at her with a lot of pride and joy in his eyes. Arthur was looking at her with a lot of pride in his eyes too. But it was hard to know if that pride was for his daughter or for himself—for introducing them to each other. Nevertheless, he was happy that Katherine was meeting someone that put a smile on her face in these stressful times. Granny's face was so bright with joy—one could have lit up a room with it. She was happy for Katherine for meeting someone nice—of course with a possibility of getting set for life together, she was happy for Arthur since this was the first time in days she had seen a smile on his face. And she was also happy for Ram Singh—for being so affectionate and for being a part of the family. Three different colors of pride, three different happy faces. Each one of them cheerful in its own way!

"Hummm, aag dono taraf-se baraabar lagi huwi hai….kyon Ram Singh hain na?" ("The fire is lit from both sides, isn't it Ram Singh?) Arthur said with a smile coming out from under his big mustache.

Ram Singh started laughing. Katherine looked at him and hushed him. Granny and David didn't understand what was said. But he knew it was some lighthearted humor about him and Katherine.

The whole scene was ruffled by Granny when she brought everyone down to earth, "Come on everybody, before the Germans realize we are having a good time and start bombarding my back yard, we should have some good food!" Everyone was visibly annoyed by this comment that was disheartening yet true. Those were very stressful days. One the one hand, people knew the reality that there is war going on and every day there was news of someone known to you had died. On the other hand, life had to go on. Whatever little time everyone had together, they had to enjoy it. That feeling was indescribable.

They all hustled to get the dinner started. Katherine was ordering everyone around and asking them to do things the way she wanted. She was even dictating who sits where for dinner. But all of them were just listening to her like obedient children. Ram Singh was in the kitchen when the rest of them started with dinner.

Katherine paused before starting to eat, "Should we wait for Ram Singh? He is just getting things ready for the dessert."

"Well, he is a servant, is he not?" David remarked quite matter-of-factly. Granny and Arthur just looked at each other. They couldn't believe he just it and that too in such a dry tone of voice.

Ram Singh had heard what was going on. He peeped out of the kitchen and said, "Please do not wait for me Mem-sahib. Today is Sunday. I was fasting all day and I can only eat after the moon rises."

Katherine knew he was lying. But she didn't want to say anything. She was a bit embarrassed.

After a couple of minutes of awkward silence, Arthur said, "Ok then. Bon Appetite everyone." Katherine had made a combination of English and some mixed Indian—not-so-spicy—kind of food. As usual, Arthur asked for some more chili powder in his vegetable curry. He was enjoying the curry with bread. The bread also seemed fresh. Granny told them about how Ram Singh and Katherine had ventured out in the morning and got a lot of things like bread and meat. Katherine looked at David and smiled.

"Thank you Katherine. It's delicious." David commented.

"Well, dear, everything is great. But you must add some spice to your life.... err...I mean to your curries!" Arthur started teasing Katherine.

"Come now, Arthur, leave her alone. That poor girl has been sweating over the oven all day."

"Come on Mum. If she needs spice in her life, she will tell someone. Won't you dear?"

Again, Katherine started blushing. She was avoiding looking at David, but wanted to see if David was looking at her. Ram Singh was looking from the kitchen. On the one hand he was sad that they didn't invite him again to join and on the other hand he was happy for Katherine that she was finding some relief from her hectic schedule. She was the man of the house for all practical purposes. She was also managing the school very well and lately with Arthur's illness she was stressed out even more.

Just as the dusk started to turn into night, they all moved in the house. Closed all the doors and windows. The rules of blackout had become a routine in everyone's life. Ram Singh lit up some lanterns and dimmed them enough for everyone to see each other, but not bright enough for the light to show from outside. The black paper they had stuck on the windowpanes was beginning to peel off. That faded and tired paper was reflecting people's emotions. This was not just in Arthur's house, every house had the same thing. Arthur's house was especially melancholy because of the large French window in his living room that had to be covered with that black non-transparent paper. Being an officer Arthur had to be even more careful. Sometimes he had some classified papers in the house; sometimes he would meet some key people and have discussions. So they all had to be extremely careful.

As they all sat down in the living room, Arthur offered a cigar to David. They both lit up their cigars. Arthur poured two small glasses of scotch and gave one to David. Just as he was doing that Granny and Katherine walked into the room.

"Arthur dear, where are your manners?" Granny yelled at him.

"Oh, I am sorry Ma'am." He replied politely. "May I pour you a nice glass of sherry or would you prefer brandy tonight?"

"I will have brandy," Granny said firmly and sat down in her favorite chair.

"And how about you miss?"

"No thanks, Dad, I am alright."

"Are you sure?" Arthur tried again.

"Yes I am sure."

"Please don't be shy dear. Feel at home, ok? If you want something else….." he paused. Katherine knew what was coming next. "…..go get it yourself!" Arthur started laughing.

Katherine made a face at him and went in the kitchen.

Arthur, David and Granny were sipping their drinks, talking quietly about the war and other happenings.

Katherine came back in a few minutes with Ram Singh. Ram Singh was holding a nice tray with four small bowls with small silver spoons sticking out.

They both went toward David. Katherine gave one bowl to David. The bowl had something that looked a pudding, but it was different. It was white in color—made with crème or milk, there were lots of almond pieces and raisins sprinkled on it. It looked interesting, but David was puzzled.

"What is this?"

Arthur was so excited. He kept his drink and cigar down and looked at the tray.

"Ahh,…let me see, which one is most full?"

"Dad, come on. If you want more, we have plenty in the kitchen."

"What is this?" David had still not eaten it.

"Young man, this is my favorite dessert. This is called Shahi Tukda."

"Shahi what?"

"Well, literally it means, Royal Treat. Try it. And if you don't like it, I will take your bowl too!" he laughed.

"Dad…" Katherine yelled at Arthur's childish remark.

David tried some. He liked it. He had some more.

"I can taste some vanilla. Where did you get vanilla essence?"

"Dad had brought from that Indian restaurant—Punjab India Restaurant in Soho. He goes there quite often. Sometimes, he goes there and forgets that he is in England now and he has his family waiting for dinner at home."

"Yeah, I go there. Even Ram Singh likes to go there with me sometimes. Right Ram Singh?"

Ram Singh was going back to the kitchen. He just nodded.

"Well Dad, you feel more at home in that restaurant than Ram Singh! You love telling them your jokes in Hindi and brag about how much you know about India."

"That's true. But sometimes I meet very interesting people there. I met this fellow—Jawahar Nehru there. He is a big shot in India now. A simple, but bright man. He told me all kinds of stories about how he is going to free India."

"Yeah, right. Free India. Who is this nut case?" David laughed. But soon he realized he was the only one laughing.

"Look, David, with all the plans the queen had for India, many officers— my fellow officers—twisted her commands in many ways. It was never her intention to kill all those people mercilessly and ruin the freedom of that country."

"Well, sire, with all due respect. It was never a country. In fact, we—the British—made it a country. Look at the prosperity ahead of them—they are now exporting cotton, silk and spices to all of Europe," David spoke like a true Royal Army Officer.

"Is that all that country is for you? A piece of land? All those people are nothing but farmers to you? They are supposed to make silk and spices for you all their lives and what do they get in return? Your abuse and getting innocent people—even women and children—killed?"

"Sir, we are protecting them from the evil German and Japanese empire. We need all the soldiers here in Europe, but still there is a full battalion of army in India."

"Yes, of course, there is a battalion of army in India, but it's not there to protect the Indians, it is to protect the British officers and businessmen."

Granny was just observing this dual going on for some time.

"Well, David, we also have some bread pudding with raisins and rum. Would you like some of that?" Granny wanted to change the subject.

"Would you like some more brandy David?" Arthur asked.

Arthur and David had worked together for quite some time. David knew how passionate Arthur was about India. He also couldn't agree with him all the time. Because of Arthur's views on India, he was kind of an outcast at the office. Except for David and one or two other fellows, no one would go out to even a pub with Arthur once in a while. Then Arthur would go to Punjab India Restaurant and hang out there. There was also some talk about the fact that he was called back to England because of his views on the British Raj in India and he was identified as a troublemaker.

Arthur and David kept on sipping on the brandy while Katherine and Ram Singh cleaned up in the kitchen. Granny was just sitting there on her favorite chair, knitting the sweater she had started last winter! All of a sudden they heard some loud blasts of bombarding nearby, immediately followed by loud sirens. The whole house shook. Katherine and Ram Singh ran into the library, shut all lights off and made sure that all the dark curtains of windows were properly closed. They were so used to this routine during the blackout hours at night that they were mechanically doing everything to make sure they comply with the blackout rules.

Arthur became quiet. He was visibly upset. He was mumbling something. Katherine came and sat down right by his chair holding his hand. David was watching this bond between father and daughter. They all just sat there for what seemed like hours.

"Well, looks like it has stopped. Before it starts again, I'd better get going" David started to get up.

"Nonsense, I am not letting you go home at this hour. Why don't you spend the night here?" Katherine said it and then realized she sounded awfully presumptuous. David was also surprised. But before he could say anything, Arthur re-emphasized, "Well, young man, the judge has spoken. The verdict is guilty! You are sentenced to one night at the Whismans. Do you have anything to say?"

"Well......"

David just looked at Katherine and couldn't even complete his sentence. The small lantern looked dimmer than the light of hope in Katherine's eyes.

"I will get you a pillow and a blanket, you can sleep right here in the library. Ram Singh..." Katherine got up.

"Ji, Mem-saab, I will get it." Ram Singh promptly got up to get all the necessary things.

Both Granny and Arthur got up and said good night to go to bed. Arthur shook David's hand with both his hands and without any words said a lot of things.

Ram Singh came and gave pillow and a blanket and left to go to bed as well.

"Sometimes I get really scared," Katherine sat down to talk. "I feel like there is so much going through Dad's mind, but there is nothing I can do about it. He won't talk to me. But I know something is bothering him. Do you know anything? Does he say anything at the office?"

"Huh uh. He used to talk a lot about his experiences in India. Sometimes with a lot of sadness in his voice and sometimes a lot of spite. I think he is very sympathetic to Indians and what he has seen over there and he is angry at the officers that are twisting their orders for flexing their power and for personal gains. He is angry and sad at the war. After all, he lost his wife due to the war." David analyzed Arthur so swiftly in just a few seconds that Katherine was also surprised.

"Katherine, from what I see, he has loved three things in his life more than his life—his wife, India and you. And he has lost two out of three. That's why he is angry. He does not want to lose the third one. That's why is sad."

David came by and sat beside Katherine. He took her hand in his hands and started to say something. Katherine put her finger on he lips and asked him not to say a word. She just looked at him. The lantern was coming to its end and the light was flickering. In that flickering light, David looked so bright. She kissed him. He didn't kiss her back. He just looked at her as if he was asking, 'are you sure?' Katherine understood and just shook her head. Then David kissed her gently.

Arthur was right at the door and he saw their shadows getting closer together.

'I hope I don't lose anything, I hope I gain something,' he thought to himself and tip toed upstairs to his bedroom.

Katherine and David kept on talking for hours and finally fell asleep right there in the library.

CHAPTER 5

Ram Hey Ram

David started visiting the Whismans' quite often. Sometimes he would come straight from the office and stay for dinner; sometimes he would come early in the morning to accompany Arthur to office. He was becoming part of the family.

He was warming up to the idea of having Ram Singh as part of the family. Every once in while he would ask Ram Singh about India and the life in India. But Ram Singh still wasn't comfortable with David around. As soon as David would enter the room, Ram Singh would get up and leave the room.

One afternoon, Granny was sitting in her favorite lazy chair and knitting something. Ram Singh sitting right beside her cleaning spinach leaves to get ready for dinner. The weather was kind of cold, cloudy and gloomy.

"Ram Singh, what do you think of David?" Granny broke the silence.

"How do you mean Granny-ji?" Ram Singh knew exactly what Granny was asking, but he pretended as if he had no clue.

"Come now, Ram Singh, you know exactly what I am asking. How is David for my little Katherine?" Granny out the knitting down and went straight to the point.

"Granny-ji, who am I to say anything in that matter?"

"Do you not approve of David?"

"Oh, no ma'am. He is a fine gentleman. Of course, Kathy-ji will be very happy with him. I just hope...."

"What? You hope what?"

"Well, I don't want to say something, I am just a....."

Granny just looked at him.

"Well, I just hope David would show some compassion toward the Indians."

Granny was kind of surprised with the heavy English words Ram Singh was using. But then she really didn't like that. Who knows whether she didn't like Ram Singh's comments about David or that he had made accurate observation about David.

"Well, keep you opinion to yourself. I think David is perfect for Katherine. If Arthur asks you about David, don't say anything like that to him. He listens to you too much."

"But, Ma'am, have you asked Kathy-ji?"

"Asked Katherine about what?" Granny was getting visibly annoyed now. "Of course, Katherine likes David."

"Then it really doesn't matter what I think about David, right?"

Granny got even more annoyed. Ram Singh was right again.

Just then the clock struck five.

"Well, Ram Singh, hurry up. Arthur should be home soon. Go get ready for dinner."

Ram Singh left that room and went to the kitchen to get ready for dinner. As he began to stir fry the vegetables, he started thinking about something. His hand stopped and he started to stare in vacuum.

He remembered the days in India. He heard the girls giggling and running around in the verandah. The whole house was alive with a lot of laughter, people talking, music playing and girls singing. He was visiting his uncle in Delhi. That afternoon his aunt told him to get ready for some visitors.

She said, "Chalo chalo Kaake, achchi tarah se naha dho lo, woh log abhi aate he honge."

"(Come on hurry up little brother, those people should be coming soon)."

"Woh log? Kaun aa raha hai Mami?"

("Those people? Who is coming Auntie?)

"Arrey buddhu, Chunni ko dekhane ke liye ladake wale aa rahe hai."

("You silly, the groom and his folks are coming to see Chunni.")

He went into the room. Chunni's friends were getting her ready. She seemed kind of little to get married so soon, he thought.

Chunni looked up at him.

It wasn't Chunni looking at him; it was Katherine in a beautiful peacock-colored Indian dress with gold border—looking at him. He was startled.

But his hand touching the hot pan and the vegetables getting burnt startled him. He shook his hand and yelled meekly, 'Oh Maa'. ('Oh mother').

His eyes were full of tears. Was it because he got burnt or with the thought of getting his little sister married or was he nostalgic?

He started stirring the vegetables in the pan.

Granny was watching this from the hallway. She knew what was going on. When she saw him burning his fingers, she almost got up from her chair to help him. Then she sat down again and resumed her knitting.

'I know Maa means mother. I know that much Hindi now.' She muttered to herself.

At the dinner table that evening, everybody was very quiet. The usual routine was that the three of them would eat first while Ram Singh served them and then Ram Singh would eat in the kitchen. But something happened and Katherine stopped all of sudden while eating. Both Granny and Arthur looked at her without saying a word.

"Ram Singh, chalo tum bhi aaj hamare saath hi khana khao," she said.

("Ram Singh come eat with us today").

"Yeah, sure, why not?" Granny joined her. "We have everything here. Come lad, sit with us today."

David was a bit taken aback. But he didn't say anything.

They all sat down to eat. The whole table came back alive. They started talking and teasing each other. Arthur and Ram Singh would say something fast in Hindi and laugh at Katherine and Granny.

All of sudden they heard a few bombs and the emergency sirens going off. Ram Singh immediately ran into the kitchen and turned off the light in the kitchen and brought a small candle with him.

The whole house was in the dark for a minute or two. They just sat there— completely still. Then Arthur lit up the large candle in the middle of the table with a match.

They were still quiet. Looking at each other. The bombarding went on for a while.

"These bloody Germans," Arthur started swearing.

Ram Singh got up and started cleaning up. Arthur got up and went into the library and poured himself a brandy and gulped it down. Granny followed him and patted him on the back, 'Calm down Arthur. Calm down.'

That night bombarding started again. It would calm down for a while and then again it would start. Arthur was tossing and turning in his bed as this went on. Almost everyone was awake all night.

The next day, of course, no children came for school. They all got up a bit late and started looking through the windows to see the damage. It was pretty bad. The whole neighborhood was hit very badly. Rubble everywhere, people running around, some children crying and their mothers screaming.

That whole day, no one went out. There were all walking around the house, not knowing what to say and how to pass time. At dusk, Katherine started wearing her shoes.

"And where do you think you are going young lady?" Arthur asked.

"Dad, before it gets dark, let me go and get some milk and bread. Otherwise we won't have milk for the tea in the morning."

"That's ok, you don't need to go out there. I can drink tea without milk for one day."

"That's what you say right now Dad. But tomorrow you won't even finish a whole cup of tea without milk. I know. Now, come on. It's not that bad out there. I will be back in a jiffy."

Before Granny and Ram Singh could say anything, Katerine slipped out the door.

"I will be back in less than 10 minutes. Don't worry."

It was as if she just wanted to get out of the house. She was walking as fast as she could. Almost all the streets were empty. Only some shops were open with their door half ajar and only a dim light inside. She went to a couple of shops asking for milk and bread, but to no avail.

She had to walk much farther than she thought. Now it was getting dark and she was also getting frightened. So she started walking briskly—almost running.

Finally, she found one shop open and they had milk and bread to her surprise. She paid the shopkeeper and just halted right there. She could see a swarm of planes coming. The shopkeeper immediately shut the light off and closed the shop. Katherine didn't know whether to turn around or run forward. She knocked on the shop and yelled, "Come on open. Let me in." But no one opened the door.

So she decided to start running. She was hoping that those planes were from the Royal Air Force. But to her dismay, they started bombarding and flying almost exactly over her head. She was scared. She started running. The bombs were exploding right around her. She tripped on the rubble and fell down. The bread fell off from her basket and the milk spilt all over the street. She still had one more loaf and one bottle of milk. She held that to her chest, got up and started running again.

As the bombarding started Arthur, Granny and Ram Singh all got startled. Arthur stopped to drink and went near the window to look outside. Granny missed one knot and the whole bundle of wool fell off from her hand and rolled away from her. Ram Singh was washing something in the sink. He stopped. The water was running. He shut the tap off, wiped his hands and came running to the living room.

"Granny-ji,....." he yelled.

Granny just nodded her head saying Katherine wasn't back yet. Ram Singh threw the napkin away and ran to get his shoes. When he came back with his shoes on, Arthur was standing at the door with Arthur's own overcoat and torch-light in his hands. No one said a word, but they all said a lot of things to each other. Granny came near the door and just put her warm hand on Ram Singh's hand. It was as if she was begging him to find Katherine and bring her back. Ram Singh just nodded and assured her that he will do whatever it takes to bring Katherine back.

Katherine had gone into a dark alley. She sat there for a few minutes. And as the bombing seemed to have stopped or paused, she got up and started running towards home.

There was the big city hall building on the way. It was on the main street, just a few blocks away from home. The city hall used to be pride of everyone there. They used to have many town meetings, celebrations and other gatherings there. It was in that same hall that they all heard about the war starting and all the rules of blackout and curfew etc. The building had grandeur with its big entrance and two tall and broad pillars right in the front Katherine used to think while walking past the hall many times and think of those two pillars and the big strong pillars in her life—Arthur and Ram Singh.

As Katherine was running toward the city hall, she saw Ram Singh. She recognized him right away with his turban. Ram Singh waved at her and sighed in relief. As they both approached each other right in front of the hall, a plane swooped down and bombarded the city hall. That huge building started collapsing like a house made from playing cards would crumble down with the slightest wind.

Katherine ran toward Ram Singh and everything all of sudden went into slow motion. She felt as if she was running for minutes—not seconds. She vaguely remembered seeing on the pillars collapsing right on top of her. But then something pushed her away. She let go of the bread and the bottle of milk she had held to her chest. The bottle fell down and broke. The milk spilt all around her.

God only knows whether it was seconds, minutes or hours when she woke up slowly. She saw the milk spilt around her and on the edge of the milk she saw blood flowing in.

"RAM SINGH….NO…..NO RAM SINGH," she yelled and frantically started looking around. She saw Ram Singh buried under the large pillar. She could see only the upper part of his body.

She ran to Ram Singh and sat down right beside him. She took his head and rested it on her lap. She could hear him breathe. She called him out very softly, "Ram Singh". She was trying not to cry. "Ram Singh say something Ram Singh."

She heard the Red Cross car coming from the corner of the street. She started waving to the car, meekly yelling, "Help, please someone help here."

Ram Singh could barely breathe. With a lot of effort he said, "Kathy-ji, suniye…" ("Kathy, please listen to me").

"Yes Ram Singh," Katherine said hurriedly, "I am here. They should be here in a minute. Help…here….please help," she kept on waving.

"Kathy-ji…mere paas ab jyada waqt nahi hai…."

("Kathy, I don't have much time").

Katherine took her scarf off, folded it to make a small pillow and put it under Ram Singh's head. She took her jacket off and laid it on him to keep him warm. She wiped blood off his head and face.

"Aap logon ne mere liye itna sab kiya hai. Mai appke kuchch to kaam aay-aa"

("All of you have done so much for me, I am glad I could be of some service to you").

"No, no. Ram Singh. Don't do this to me. Don't do this to Dad," she started crying.

Ram Singh brought his hands together with great difficulty and joined his palms to do namaskara.

"Granny-ji.... Arthur-ji..." and he laid his head on the ground, his hands still joined.

"Noooooo" she shouted. Her cry was muffled in the noise from those planes swooshing down and in the bombardment right behind her. Those did not deter her anymore. She just sat there for many hours.

Finally when dawn broke out, she got up. She had gone to sleep right beside Ram Singh. Her tears were frozen on her cheeks. She was now shivering from the cold. She got up and started running toward the house.

Arthur and Granny had both fallen asleep right near the door. Granny was sitting on the chair and Arthur was sitting at the bottom of the stairs. When the heard the door opening, they both got up with oozing hope. Katherine slowly opened the door. She was visibly exhausted. Her clothes were muddy and torn; her hair was dry and spread all over. But most of all her eyes had lost the youthful look. She had Ram Singh's turban in her hand. When Arthur saw that he knew. He knew that a true sikh like Ram Singh would never take off his turban, unless....

"Kathy, what happened? Where is Ram Singh?"

"He ran to save me Dad, he ran to save me. He pushed me aside and the whole pillar dropped on him. He saved me Dad, he saved my life."

Tears were flowing from her eyes limitlessly. She handed the turban to Arthur and went upstairs. There was a dead silence in the house. Arthur took the turban in both his hands and hugged it tight to his chest as if he was giving a warm hug to Ram Singh himself. Granny had nothing to say either.

Arthur went into the study and poured himself a drink. Just as he was about gulp it down, Ram Singh's words echoed,

"Sir-ji, subah subah daru peena aap ki sehat ke liye achcha nahi"

("Sir, drinking alcohol early in the morning is not good for your health".)

"Yeah, yeah, I know. Don't treat me like a child......" Arthur threw his glass on the floor. As it broke, both Katherine and Granny got startled. They both ran into the library.

Arthur was sitting down and crying.

Although his voice was muffled, Granny could hear him say, "Why Ram Singh, why did you have to be a hero?"

Granny went forward and hugged Arthur.

"Why, Mom, why does this happen to me? First they took my Elizabeth and now Ram Singh. Why do these Germans hate everyone I love?"

Granny just coaxed him. He sat down beside her and rested his head on her lap.

Katherine went upstairs and straight away leaped in to her bed crying.

They were all so exhausted that all of them fell asleep right there. In the middle of the afternoon they all woke up because of big knocks on the door.

David was yelling out loud, "Arthur, are you in there? Katherine, open the door. Are you all alright?"

Arthur got up and opened the door.

"Arthur, what took you so long? Is everyone alright? Where is Katherine?"

"Katherine is sleeping upstairs."

David was surprised. Katherine sleeping? At this time of the day?

"We are ok. But…."

"But what?"

"Ram Singh was trying to save me," Katherine spoke up as she was coming down the stairs.

"He WAS?" now David was getting the whole picture.

"Where's he now?"

"Under the rubble at the town hall."

"Town hall? Oh boy. That whole area is completely leveled. I saw the rescue workers and Red Cross trucks on my way here. They said hundreds of people around there got buried in that rubble."

"Yeah, and Ram Singh, too." Katherine was so cold saying that. Even Arthur was surprised.

"Well, do you want to go there before it gets dark and the curfew starts again?"

"Yes, Katherine. We need to give Ram Singh a proper cremation."

"Cremation?" everyone thought all at once, but only David said it out loud.

"There is no way anyone will let us light a small fire, let alone a fire that creates a lot of smoke."

"And what about all those fires started by the bombs?"

"Well, the fire trucks are out there trying to put out all those fires before it gets dark."

They all looked at each other and started to rush out to the site.

When they reached there, they found it to be a total disaster. There was chaos with lots of people running around. It reminded Arthur of the war zone when he was trying to help his friends and fellow officers out of the rubble. There was smoke everywhere and the whole area was kind of dark because of the black smoke. At first, Katherine could not orient herself. She couldn't find the place where she had left Ram Singh just a few hours ago. Arthur and Katherine were desperately looking for Ram Singh. David was helping Granny. He actually didn't want to look for Ram Singh anyway, helping Granny was a great excuse.

Finally, they arrived at the place where they saw a big pillar lying on the ground along with a lot of brinks and other rubble. They frantically started to remove the rubble. As Arthur was removing it as fast as he could, all of a sudden he stopped. He saw a pair of hands right by his feet. It was as if someone was touching his feet. He removed more rubble and yelled for Katherine. He could now clearly see Ram Singh's bloodied face. He stopped and cleaned Ram Singh's face. The blood was literally frozen on his face. Arthur was crying when Katherine got there.

She sat down beside him and could not control herself but started crying. A few minutes later David and Granny arrived there.

"Oh, poor Ram Singh." Granny also had tears in her eyes.

Noone said anything for a few minutes.

"Uhh, Katherine, I hate to say anything, but we really need to get moving. Before it gets dark or before the rescue team comes here and takes the body away."

They wiped their tears off and started to remove the rubble again. Finally, they cleared all sides around the body and pulled it to one side.

"I will go get a stretcher." David ran toward the Red Cross truck.

By the time he got back with a stretcher, they had cleaned up the body as much as they could. They put the body on the stretcher and lifted it up with Katherine and Arthur in the front and Granny and David on the back. Granny was so weak, but still she did her best.

They took it toward the back of the building. Many trees in the back yard of the city hall had fallen down and a few things were still on fire. Wherever a bomb exploded there was fire there. They laid him between two such places, gathered a few logs of wood and branches of those trees lying around and arranged it around his body. Arthur was directing them all along. Just as they were getting ready to light the fire, Arthur yelled, "No, wait."

He went near Ram Singh, kissed him on his forehead and then took one of the twigs and poked his own right hand thumb with it. Everyone was watching this intently. Arthur started bleeding. Then with his bloody thumb, he drew a line on Ram Singh's forehead from his eyebrows to his turban. This is a sign of decorating a hero. Usually the ladies of the house or the elderly people would put this mark on the forehead of someone returning as a hero from war or something like that. They also follow that custom when someone is leaving for war. It is a mark for good luck or a decoration for a job well done.

Then Arthur took the torch from David's hand and lit the fir around Ram

Singh. Katherine started crying and hugged Granny. Granny was also crying, but she was trying to console Katherine. As the fire started to catch on, Arthur stood back and saluted Ram Singh's body. As he stood there saluting Ram Singh, he saw the past 15 years in that smoke. He didn't even realize when he had started crying. A streak of tears was flowing from his eyes on his cheek and all he could think of was all the good times they had together.

After a few minutes, David walked toward Arthur and patted him on the back. He softly suggested, "Arthur, we should get going before......"

"Yes, David. I know," Arthur nodded and turned around and started walking. On his way, he came toward Katherine and Granny. He put his hand on Katherine's shoulder and said, "I never thought I would be doing that. These Germans have now taken away another part of my heart."

Katherine burst out crying and hugged Arthur. "He came to save me Dad. He came to save me. How am I going to live with myself now? I killed him. I killed the only brother I had."

Arthur put his hand around her and started walking—as if he wasn't going to let go of her.

For several days after that, Katherine didn't teach at school. Everyone was walking around as if there was no reason to live any more. Katherine used to go the outhouse and sit there for hours, thinking of Ram Singh. Granny would stand in the window to the backyard and look at Katherine weeping. David used to come by every once in a while, and try to cheer everyone up. David and Katherine used to sit in the living room for hours without saying much to each other. David used to just take her hand and try to comfort her. Then he used to start talking about all the things that he used hear at the office. Katherine would just nod and give a weak smile every so often.

David also tried to cheer Arthur up by taking him to the local pub. Arthur would go there, sit there, have his regular pint of bitter and come back. David tried in many different ways to get the whole family to cheer up, but he felt like he was failing. He told Granny once that he was getting busier at the office and that his department was under a lot of pressure—because on the one hand the war was costing too many young men and on the other hand there were uprisings under the British rule in the whole of south Asia.

Then one day the bombings on London started again. The whole house shook as if someone had dropped a bomb right on top of it. Power in the whole neighborhood was knocked out. Katherine got up and lit candles in the living room and in the study. They all sat in the study all night. Arthur fell asleep right in his chair and Katherine fell asleep right by his feet. The next morning they woke up when they heard knocking on the door.

"Arthur, are you in there? Katherine, are you alright?" David was yelling from outside while knocking on the door.

"Katherine," he shouted again. As he started to go around the house toward the back, Katherine opened the door.

"Oh, Katherine, thank god, you are alright. I was so afraid. I came as soon as I could. All the roads are closed and there is rubbish on the roads everywhere. They really got us this time. I was listening to the radio in the morning, they were saying that hundreds are feared dead." David went on and on. Then he hugged Katherine and again said, "I am so glad you are alright."

Arthur and Granny were standing behind them. When David opened his eyes he saw both of them staring at them hugging. David immediately let go of Katherine and straightened up. He gave a mild salute to Arthur and said, "Sir, I......I....."

"Don't hesitate lieutenant, come in. I am so glad to see you," said Arthur and then he turned to Katherine said, "Will you make us some breakfast dear?"

Katherine was also kind of embarrassed. She said of course and hurried inside.

David and Arthur went into the study and started talking about the reports on attacks. Then David became serious.

"Sir, I....I..."

"Go on lad, what is it?" Arthur tapped on his arm.

"Sir, they have asked me to transfer to India. It seems like Viceroy of India needs someone to be there all the time with him. I may have to leave next week."

Katherine was just about to enter the room with a tray in her hand. But she stopped at the doorstep listening to this conversation.

"I don't know whether to take this assignment, but I am afraid I may not have a choice."

"No, no, David. It is a great opportunity for you. You will love India," Arthur paused for a minute and then gathered his courage to say a few more words.

"Well, I have been thinking. I was going to call for you and ask you to do something for me."

"Anything Sir, you don't need to hesitate." David held Arthur's hand in his hands.

"Well, ever since we lost Ram Singh, it has been very hard on the whole family—especially Katherine. She needs to get out of this. She deserves better. And I am afraid I cannot give her anything better in this house. So, I was... I......" he hesitated again.

David just tapped his hands.

"I wanted to ask you….if….if you love Katherine…to marry her…and take her away from here," he tried to complete his sentence as best as he could.

Katherine heard that and she stumbled. The cups and the dishes in the tray she was holding made a noise and both David and Arthur looked up. Katherine walked in as if she had heard nothing. She kept the tray on the table and asked them if they wanted her to make tea for them. Then she started to leave.

"Katherine, wait," said David with a clear voice. Katherine's heartbeat started going up. She slowly turned around, but she didn't see David. Then she noticed David on his knees kneeling in front of her.

"Katherine….will you….." and before he finished his sentence Katherine started crying and said, "Yes, David, I will. I will."

Arthur looked up. This was totally unbelievable for him. Things were happening so fast.

Katherine helped David up and kissed him. Now she was not embarrassed to kiss him in front of her father. Arthur's happiness was flowing from his eyes. And Granny was watching all of this from the other side of the room too.

Arthur walked up to David and shook his hands, "Congratulations my dear friend."

"Now, you can go to India with my Little Princess. I am glad. I could not give her that dream, I am glad I met you. Now it's your job to make all her dreams come true," he laughed rather loudly.

"No, no, Sir. You can't get off that easily. The least you could do is to send us by First Class and make our journey by ship more comfortable," David laughed.

They all started laughing. Laughter was heard in that house after a long time.

Then things happened so fast. Katherine and David got married that Sunday. Katherine wore a beautiful white dress. But then she added a peacock feather as broach. As she got ready by her dressing table. She paused for a minute and looked the turban on her dressing table.

'I wished you were here to see this day Ram Singh,' she murmured with tears in her eyes.

Arthur came to her room shouting, "Come on dear, we are getting late you know."

He took one look at her and paused himself. The peacock feather caught his eye.

"Is that from a male peacock or a female peacock dear?" he asked with his tongue in his cheek.

"Dad, of course it is from a male peacock. I know that much now!" Katherine exclaimed.

"The male peacock is the beautiful one," they both chimed together and started laughing. Then they both paused for a bit remembering Ram Singh. Arthur hugged her and said, "Your brother would have been very happy today. He would have insisted on at least some Indian customs at the wedding."

It was a very small gathering in the church right around the corner from their house—which fortunately was still standing. A small group of people had gathered. Some of David's colleagues, some of Katherine's students and their parents had come to attend. Arthur had managed to get the word out at the pub and at New Delhi restaurant. So, a couple of his friends from the pub and surprisingly some of the Indians from the restaurant also showed up.

David and Katherine set sail in just a few days. Arthur and Granny came to the docks to see them off. It was very hard for Arthur to let them go. But he knew that was the right thing to do for Katherine.

Arthur couldn't say a word on the dock. He handed a letter to Katherine and made her promise that she will read it after arriving in India. The only one talking there was David. He kept on telling them about the ship—Margaret II—how he got the First Class reservations on that ship with his assignment as the Special Security Agent to provide security guard to the Viceroy of India and also about the recent riots in India which had created the need for such a post, and so on. He asked Granny and Arthur if they wanted to see their cabin on board, but they both declined. All three of them were just listening and looking at each other. Finally, Arthur put his hand around David and said, "There are more things to life than First Class cabins David. Take good care of my Katherine. I am glad that one way or another, her dream of going to India is getting fulfilled. I just wished……"

"What? Go on. You just wished what?" David was a bit annoyed.

"Oh, no, nothing. I just wished Ram Singh could have been there with you."

"Don't worry, Father. Ram Singh will always be with me," Katherine said it with a heavy voice and watery eyes. Then she showed him a necklace that Ram Singh had given her when David proposed to her.

"Oh, that belonged to his grandmother—he told me. The day he left from his house, his grandmother woke up early in the morning and as he was leaving she gave her that necklace," Arthur remembered clearly.

David was getting visibly annoyed. No one was paying attention to his recently attained glory. He started yelling at the porters to be careful with their luggage and to bring it to the First Class cabin no. I.

"Oh, by the way David, don't forget to take Katherine to Bombay. When I left India, they had just finished building the Gateway of India on the shores of Bombay. It is very impressive I heard. I saw some photographs of it in the newspaper when King George had visited India. You should see Taj Mahal and Qutub Minar in the north, stay on a house boat in Dahl Lake in Kashmir, visit Mysore

Palace and sit on the 40 Kilo solid gold throne and also don't forget to go to the temples in the south—there you will find out what culture is all about." Arthur couldn't stop.

"But, Sir, I am on a mission there. I am not sure how much time I will get to be a tourist in India." David said it rigidly. It was as if he was telling Arthur, 'I am fulfilling your request to take Katherine to India, now leave me alone.' Arthur got that message and kept quiet. Katherine went over to Granny and hugged her goodbye.

"All my life everyone I loved left me. First, Arthur's father, then Arthur..."

"But Granny, Dad came back and so will I. Don't worry. I will be back before you know it. Just promise me you will take good care of yourself. And get someone to help you around the house. I know Dad will hesitate to spend the money, but….."

"Why do all of you think I am stingy? I will spend any amount of money when it is necessary, but when it is not necessary I will not spend a single pound," Arthur replied rather grudgingly.

"Ok, ok Dad. We agree. You will not hesitate to spend the money to get some help—maybe you can ask one of your chums from New Delhi Restaurant," Katherine had a winner's smile on her face and she winked at Granny.

"Well, why employ one of the foreigners. Sir you could ask Susan in our office—there are lots of families that need work these days. All those wives with their husbands gone to war or the children are trying to make their ends meet."

"Those lads in New Delhi Restaurant are also trying to make their ends meet. Besides they don't even have families here. Many of their family members got killed back home in India."

There was a group of Indian immigrants at a distance who had to come to the docks to see one of their friends off. There was a young sikh boy that kept on looking at Katherine. She looked at him and smiled and bowed her head down to say, 'Ram Ram' (good bye in Hindi). For some reason she thought about Ram Singh—the boy looked exactly like Ram Singh the first time Katherine met him entering into their house. Katherine smiled with fond memories.

Right then, the ship horn blew once. David turned around and said to Katherine, "Come on darling, its time to go."

Her smile vanished. She hugged Arthur. He kissed on the cheeks and then on her forehead and said, "Don't worry about us now dear. You have to start your own life with David. And obviously you are off to a great start."

He took out an envelope from his coat pocket and gave it to her. It was duly sealed and seemed kind of heavy.

"Don't read it until you reach India dear. Enjoy your journey. There is a lot do on the ship—this is kind of a honeymoon for you."

Katherine put the envelope in her purse and carried the curiosity on her face.

CHAPTER 6

Writing Makes Man Perfect

That evening they went down to the First Class Dinner Hall all dressed up. There were a lot of people there: A lot of rich people, a lot of diplomats and their wives. David immediately found a few people he knew and started talking to them. Katherine found herself totally out of place. She was there physically, but her mind was still at home with Arthur and Granny.

'Granny must have made her pot roast for dinner and Dad must be drinking in the library looking at the photographs or putting on his old records,' she started thinking to her self.

"Katherine, Darling, are you alright?" David asked.

"Oh, yes. I am not very hungry. Would you mind if I go for a little walk on the deck?"

"Are you sure? Why don' you at least have some bread? Would you like to drink something?" David was trying very hard to keep her there.

"No, thank you David. I will see you in the room in a little while."

"No, wait, I will come with you."

"Oh, no. Don't be silly David. Why don't you finish you dinner and then come find me."

Katherine went back to the room, changed into something more comfortable and warm and then walked up to the deck.

She wrote a small note to David and kept it on the desk so he would see it as soon as he entered.

'Dear David,

I am just going on the deck to take a stroll. Come find me.

Love,

K.'

She kissed the note right beside her signature and left a lipstick mark. Then she left the room and walked up to the deck. It was a nice evening. She walked a little on the deck, looked around and then found a quiet corner and sat down, took out the letter Arthur had given her and started to read.

'My Little Princess,

Oh I am going to miss you so much. It's not going to be the same without you here. I love you so much.

But, I must apologize to you my love. I must apologize to you on two accounts. One, for not being there in your childhood years to take you to the park, to teach you how to ride a bicycle and to do your math homework with you. I am so sorry that I could not be there for you when you needed me the most. I hope you will forgive this old hopeless fellow. You see darling, I was so much in love with your mother that when I lost her, I didn't know what to do or where to go. So, I did the simplest thing a man can do. I ran away.

I sometimes wished I had had an affair with someone—just to reduce the intensity of my feelings for your mother. And you know my dear, what hurts the most is that I know that she loved me with the same intensity—but never said a word.'

Katherine couldn't stop crying. An old lady walking by saw her crying and said, "What's the matter my child. Are you alright?"

"I...I am alright ma'am. Thank you."

Katherine left that place and went and sat down somewhere else.

'I ran away all the way to India. I didn't know where I was going. I just wanted to get away from those memories. And very soon a whole new world opened for me.

The second reason of my apology is that I couldn't be there with you in India. I wanted to take you there myself. I wanted to show you all the wonderful places around India. I wanted to take you to the Taj Mahal—the greatest building on earth, the Red Fort in Delhi, the Mysore Palace and best of all—Lake Palace in Jaipur—I know the King of Rajsthan—Maharaja Uday Singh—personally. I would have been a proud father to introduce you to him. He speaks better Queen's English than any of the British officers there.'

Katherine chuckled a little and looked around. 'Only my Dad knows how to make me cry and laugh in minutes,' she thought to herself.

'When I arrived in India, the British Raj was at its peak. The anti-British sentiment wasn't as strong—except for a few factions in some areas. It's really surprising what hunger does to one's pride. Many Indians would come to me asking for work and I knew that deep down they are dying while they are bowing in front of a foreigner, but hunger does wonders my dear. I hope I never go hungry. I have seen the spite in their eyes while eating the bread and soup I gave them before they worked for me or did anything to earn it.

Well, do one thing my child. Whenever you pity any one of them, let them earn their keep. Just because we British have a few more guns than they do, it doesn't give us the right to kill their pride.

Oh, another thing. You are going there at the beginning of spring, but April is when Indian summer starts. It is going to be very hot there. So, take care of your health. Drink plenty of water. That's the bad news; the good news is that you will get excellent mangoes next month. Once you have these mangoes, my dear, you will know why they are called king of fruit.

And, take care of David. He loves you very much. I have sensed that he may not have the same views about India and Indians, but that doesn't make him a bad person. I am sure he will change his opinion once he sees what's going on there and when he meets some wonderful people.

Keep writing to me and I will do the same.

Yours lovingly,

Arthur.'

Katherine folded the letter and got up and went toward the balcony. She stood there for a long time watching the ship move through calm waters. The moonlight was bouncing off the gentle waves. It was a tranquil scene. Katherine wiped her eyes and took a deep breath. That fresh air smelled very nice.

All of sudden, someone hugged her from behind.

"Ah, so you are out here. I was looking all over for you."

"Oh, Arthur, you were sleeping like a baby. I didn't want to wake you up. I couldn't sleep."

"How silly of me! How could I sleep on such a wonderful night with such a beautiful wife with me? And….. wait a minute….how could I sleep on my Wedding Night? Come on darling, let's go to the room. Let's have some Champagne. Its getting cold out here, warm me up!" David smiled at her. Katherine blushed.

He held her glowing face in his hands, kissed her.

He then hugged her and said, "I love you so much Kay."

"I love you too David. I never want to lose you. Promise me, you will never lose me."

"I promise, Kay, I promise."

He hugged her again for a long time.

"Ahhhh, do you want to spend our first night together here on the deck or…."

"Oops, sorry darling. Let's go."

There was no one on the deck. They held hands together and went to their room.

The next morning, Katherine woke up looking out the window. The sun was coming up. She looked at David. He was fast asleep. He had a slight smile on his face. Katherine kept looking at him for a while. She caressed him gently. Her hands must have been cold as he shivered a bit. She pulled the blanket over him and patted him back to sleep.

She then got up and went into the bathroom. She started a nice hot bath in the tub. While she was taking the bath, she herself didn't realize when she went to sleep.

She kept on getting flashes in front of her eyes. It was Arthur, Granny, Ram Singh, the bombarding and Ram Singh's death. Those images were disturbing her.

All of sudden, she woke up with some kind of touch—it was David sitting beside her.

"Room for two?" he asked with a huge smile on his face.

"Yes, of course darling," Katherine sat up straight.

David got in to the bathtub and they kept on talking for several hours. They talked about their own aspirations, what they want to do in life, how many children they wanted to have.

"But no matter what darling, our first one has to be a boy," he said. "I want to be able to play with him while I am still young."

"Oh, that's not fair. I want a daughter first. I will be so lonely at home, when you go to work. I want someone I can talk to."

"Ok, then, let's do this. We will have first daughter, then son, then daughter again and then another son."

"Four children?" Katherine just looked at him with awe.

"Yes of course. I am of the firm belief that every one of my children should have a brother and a sister," David announced.

"Oh, come on you are just looking for an excuse to get close to me," Katherine was blushing again.

"Do 'I', The Chief Army Officer, on Special Assignment to The Viceroy of India, need an excuse to get close to my own wife?"

He laughed and reached across the tub to hug her. She tried to escape going under water.

It was almost I O'clock in the afternoon by the time she woke up. She was hungry. She called the attendant and ordered lunch. She got up and cleaned up a little bit, made her hair and changed into something light. While she was waiting for lunch, David was still sleeping. She sat on the bed right beside David and started to write a letter.

'Dear Dad,

I don't know how to start this letter. I miss you Dad. I miss Granny too. I miss Ram Singh. This war has really changed everyone's life.

I read your letter. Yes, I admit, I cried. I cried, because you felt it necessary to apologize to me. I know you Dad. I know you didn't run away—I know you enough to realize that you wouldn't have done it unless you had to do it.

When you left for India, I was too little to know what was happening. When I grew up, I started asking Granny about you and mother. She used to tell me that both of us were in India and they couldn't take me with them because no one below ten was allowed on the ship. Before I could discover the truth, I heard that you were coming back. It was at that time when Granny told me that mother had passed away. I cried a lot that day Dad. Granny gave me her photograph framed in a nice golden frame. I used to keep it with me all the time—just like some of my friends used to carry their dolls. I would take it to bed with me and pretend as if mother was singing me a lullaby. I always felt that someone was sitting on my bed, patting my forehead. I could feel someone's fingers running through my hair. Then I would wake up in the middle of the night and realize that she wasn't there. But, when you came home, I forgot all about it. Those few years were the best years of my life. I was so happy with you, Granny and Ram that I used to pray every night to god to keep our family of four together forever.

You have given me a lot in my life Dad. You gave me your passion for life, your genuine heart, your thirst for learning and exploring. Anything worth doing is worth doing well—I learned that from you Dad. So, don't ever say again that you couldn't do anything for me.'

David woke up a little.

"Good morning love," he said, in a groggy voice.

"Morning? You mean good afternoon? But, it's ok dear. I have ordered some lunch for us. I will wake you up when it gets here."

She kissed him on the cheeks and patted him back to sleep. He held her left hand and wouldn't let go. The ship was sailing the calm waters. Katherine looked out the window—the vast ocean was glistening with sun shine.

'How lucky I am', she thought to herself. 'Here I am floating in the air—with a handsome loving husband beside me and a whole wide world I am about to explore.'

She started writing again.

'I am beginning to enjoy my married life. David and I are in love with each other. I hope that never subsides. And you know Dad, he wants to have four children. Four? Is he just saying this to show me that he loves me or does he really mean it? I don't know. But whatever it is, I love the feeling. I can only imagine how you must have felt when you were in love with mother, but for me, there is so much excitement of being married, spending time with David, and going to India. But I miss Granny, I miss Ram Singh and most of all, I miss you.

You must promise me Dad. Promise me that you write to me. All the time. Convey my sincere regards to Granny and yes, go easy on your Scotch—don't drink every night. I know you are shaking you head right now and filling up your glass with more Scotch. Just keep that bottle down. And ask Granny to stop knitting. How many sweaters are you going to need in one single winter anyway?'

Katherine put the pen down and lost herself in thoughts. She started thinking about her house, Arthur and Granny. She was lost in thoughts for a long time.

Arthur put the letter down and looked at Granny—sitting on her favorite chair, knitting a sweater. She didn't have much to keep herself busy. If she didn't knit another sweater, what else was she going to do? Was she really knitting sweaters or was she collecting her thoughts together to give them a familiar shape? Arthur took one of the scarves she had knit and wrapped it around his neck. He felt the warmth of wool as it touched his cold neck. He looked up at Granny and kept on staring at her for a while. He then continued to read. "Ok, ok, I got it. I don't know who is grandma anymore!" Arthur murmured to himself.

'If it is safe outside, take her for a walk. I know she must be cooped up inside the house. When Ram Singh was around, she used to go with him to the market around the corner. She didn't need her cane then. Now she needs it. So, if you go out with her, don't forget to take her cane with you. And also remember to stay with her. Otherwise you will walk fast and she will be left behind.'

'Well then, I have got to wake him up and have him take a bath. It seems like a nice day outside. We will go for a walk. It is beginning to get warmer. The daytime is sunny and warm—I am enjoying that. The nighttime is a bit cool and breezy. We will reach a port on the Western Indian coast tomorrow. I can't wait to see what India is like. All of my imagination about this mystical country and all those hopes that I have kept inside me for so many years! I am so anxious about getting there and seeing it with my own eyes that I am not paying attention to many things. Yesterday I was getting ready for dinner and David caught me humming a Hindi song. I think he was kind of mad at me, but he didn't show it. Some times I think he doesn't like Indians or India. But then I think, if he doesn't like it, why is he going there?

The other day there was an Indian server in the dining room. David was really upset at him. Why? Because this poor chap spilled some water on the table while pouring it for David. There was this fat lady that tried to sneak through a small space and ended up bumping into the server. But the server was quick enough to hold the jug of water high and he tried to make sure he didn't spill the water on anybody. But, David yelled at him anyway. He called him an ignorant peasant. I felt so bad for that young man. But I couldn't say anything.'

Katherine realized she had gone over several pages and now it was time to get up and get ready for afternoon tea. She quickly wrapped up the letter, signed it, folded it and put it in an envelope and addressed it to Lieutenant Arthur Whisman. She wanted to give the letter to the postman before David woke up.

She quickly went to the upper deck at the main desk and gave the letter to the clerk. He promptly sealed it and stamped it.

"Thank you Ma'am. We will make sure it reaches Lt. Whisman as soon as possible," he smiled courteously.

When Katherine came back to the cabin, David was already up. He was in the bathroom shaving. Humming to himself and then once in a while using the razor as a drumstick. Katherine started laughing. David realized that Katherine was standing right behind him and watching him.

"Oh, no, you don't. You don't get to watch the show without paying for it." David came running after Katherine with his shaving brush in one hand. He caught hold of Katherine and smudged the shaving cream all over her face.

"Oh, darling, look what you have done. Now I have to wash my face again," she pretended to hit him and then tapped him on his cheeks.

"Now, darling, please get ready quickly. I am starving for some cheese sandwiches and biscuits with my tea," she pushed him aside and pointed him to the bathroom.

David and Katherine were enjoying their tea, cheese sandwiches and biscuits and talking and giggling at the table.

"Hello, Lt. Sutherland," the ship's vice captain greeted him with respect. "Ma'am," he bowed a little more.

"Sir, I understand there was an incident with one of our servers at your table yesterday. I just wanted to let you know that I have taken care of it. He now works in our boiler room."

"Well, thank you very much Captain," David was delighted to hear it.

"Is that really necessary?" Katherine interrupted David's moment. "I mean, it wasn't his fault. That lady......"

"Ahhh, huh," the vice captain coughed and pointed slightly toward the right. That lady was sitting two tables down, laughing and talking to her elite friends.

"Well, that lady tried to go through a narrow passage behind him and knocked him with her big bottom....." Katherine whispered, but with a lot of stress.

"Katherine, let's not meddle in the ship's management. Let them do whatever they feel is appropriate. Thank, you sir. Thank you for taking the time to let us know about it." David tried to finish the subject.

Now the whole room was looking at them. It was getting very embarrassing for David. But Katherine couldn't care less. She wanted the right thing to be done. David pulled her hand and sat her down. She reluctantly sat down. But she didn't even touch the biscuits and tea. David kept on talking about something, but she had tuned him out.

After tea, David asked her if she wanted to take a stroll on the deck. But she declined. She said," You go ahead dear. I want to go look at the paintings in the art gallery. I hear there are lots pf paintings by Picasso on display."

"Ooh, paintings!" David sneered at the idea and said, "Ok, then, I will go find my friends and challenge them to game of tennis. I will work up a sweat and then go take a bath. I will see you in the room at 1800 hours...errr....I mean around 6 pm, ok Love?"

They both kissed. As they were kissing, some ladies were walking by. They giggled at the couple.

"Well, she is my wife you know," David yelled at the ladies.

"David!" Katherine shouted at him.

Instead of going to the art gallery, Katherine went straight up to the Captain's office to discuss that poor Indian boy's case. The confidence and urge to do the right thing was showing on her face very clearly. The captain tried to argue with her for a little while and then gave up. It was clear that Katherine wasn't going to back down.

He called that Indian boy up to his office. When that boy came to the office, he was so frightened that he couldn't speak much.

"What is your name?" Katherine asked in a very gentle voice.

"Ummm"

"Tumhara naam kyaa hai?" Katherine asked his name in Hindi. Everyone in the room was totally surprised. The boy was also surprised.

"Hamaaraa naam Ram hai. Hum Durgapur ke rehne waale hai, (My name is Ram. I am from Durgapur)," the boy answered as if he wanted to get it off his chest in a hurry.

The captain and his staff was staring at Katherine and the boy. Finally, Katherine said, "Captain, would you mind if I talk to Ram out on the deck?"

"Well, of course, Ma'am, by all means," the captain opened the door—as if he was saying, 'take this problem out of my room and do whatever you want to do'.

Katherine and Ram went on the deck. She sat down on a wooden chair and he sat right at her feet. Ram was about 15 years old. He didn't look anything like Ram Singh, but still somehow Katherine felt like his older sister. They talked for a while.

She found out that Durgapur is a nice village and very popular one because of a man-eater tiger story a few years ago. Ram told her all about the tiger and how he was killed by the Maharaja of Tarapur District, with the help some British officers and a few Indian servants. Ram's father was one of them and Ram had heard the complete story about the hunt from his father.

Ram's cousin used to be a very good carpenter. He got a job on the ship. When there were some riots and some of the local teenagers were shot by British soldiers, Ram's mother decided to send him with his cousin for any kind of a job on the ship. Ram didn't want move away from his village and his friends, but he was forced to move by his parents. His cousin convinced him that he will see different countries and enjoy good food on the ship. But, just after a couple of days, Ram started getting bored on the ship. There was nothing to do—except work, eat and sleep. There was no fun.

Then one day, when the ship had stopped at some port in Africa, Ram and his cousin went into town. His cousin drank some kind of liquor and they all ate a lot of different kind of African food—some of almost like Indian curry. That evening when they came back, his cousin fell sick. He had high temperature and he was throwing up a lot. All the servants wanted to keep it quiet about his illness. But, somehow the Captain found out and Ram's cousin was asked to leave the ship. Ram had no idea what happened to his cousin after they sailed away, but since that day, he had not spoken to anyone on the ship. He used to do his work and sit quietly in his room. So, today, when someone showed him some affection, he could not stop talking and crying.

During a silent pause in between, Katherine had signaled the waiter and softly ordered some food, 'Baira, ek toast, ek cake aur ek cup doodh leke aao, jaldi (Waiter, get me some toast, a piece of cake and some milk, quickly)' she ordered.

As the food arrived, she offered it to Ram. At first, Ram hesitated. Then he devoured it, as if he had not eaten for days. He was wiping his tears once in a while, but still eating quickly. It was clear to Katherine that the food these people receive is different from the food for passengers. But, she decided not to say anything about it.

Later in the evening as she was getting ready for the last dinner on board, all of a sudden David stormed in the cabin and started yelling at Katherine, "Katherine, what were you thinking? Why are you doing this?"

Katherine was completely baffled. "What are you talking about David?"

"Why did you have to take that...that....peasant boy and talk to him and feed him? Why did you have to humiliate me like this? The whole ship is talking about it." He was really angry. He was pacing up and down the hallway. But Katherine was still puzzled as to why he was so angry.

"I had told you to stay out of the ship's business. Let them handle their own employees and treat them the way they want. Who are we to say anything?"

Now, Katherine was also getting angry. David was not leaving any room for her to express herself. Obviously she was not free to do anything she pleased—no matter how justified that was. Katherine was wondering whether to start yelling back or to be subdued about it and then reason with him when he cools down.

"David, look, I did something that any other human being would have done. I just talked to the boy and gave him something to eat. It's alright. I am not going to deal with it any more. Come on Darling, let's not fight over such a petty little thing," Katherine pleaded.

"You think this is petty little thing? My wife goes and entertains some servant boy and you think it's a little thing? Alright, Katherine, remember, we are going to India on an official mission, I have duty to perform and so do you......"

David kept on talking how it was important for her to stay away from peasants and all Katherine could think of was that poor little boy with no one on the ship to care about him. But, she decided to keep that emotion to herself. She kept of nodding and saying, 'Yes Dear' every once in a while.

Finally, she took David's hand in hers and said, "Come on Darling, now, let's get ready and go to dinner. This is our last dinner on the ship. Let's enjoy it."

David had calmed down by now. He looked his beautiful wife, gave her a long kiss with his eyes closed and then said, "Ok, Mrs. Sutherland, let's get ready for dinner." They both smiled and started getting ready.

Dinner was very nice. The chefs had outdone themselves that evening, with so many interesting preparations decorated nicely. But, Katherine was finding all the food to be very bland. She was looking around to see if anyone else thought it was bland too. There was an older gentleman sitting at the next table. He leaned over the Katherine and whispered, "The feast is great, but its needs spice, doesn't it?"

Katherine was totally startled. She looked at him as if this man could read her mind.

"Ma'am," he bowed. "Here, take this and put it on your fish, it will taste a lot better," he again whispered.

Katherine took the small paper and opened it to see what was in it. There was some kind of dark brown and red spice.

"Oh, Garam Masala!" she exclaimed.

"So, looks like you know your spices, Ma'am!" the gentleman was also startled.

She sprinkled some on her fish without letting anyone see that. Gave the paper back to that gentleman and said, "Thank you very much. I do need some spice in my food."

He just signaled, 'You are welcome' with his eyes and turned back to his table and got engrossed in the conversation again.

Katherine finished the fish and pretended as if she was back in the conversation.

After a while, she told David she wanted to go to the ladies room. As she stood up, everyone at the table stood up. She kissed David on his cheeks and said, 'I will be right back, Darling.'

When she stepped out of the dining hall, she sighed almost loudly as if she was breathing fresh air after a long while. As she started going toward the ladies room, she noticed there was someone standing in the corner.

"Who's there?" Katherine stepped back a little.

"Mai hun Mem-Sahib, Ram (It's me, Ram, Madam)," Ram came out of the dark.

"Ram," Katherine yelled out in a whispering voice.

"Tum yahan kya kar rahe ho (What are you doing here?)," Katherine looked around to see is anyone was around.

"Mai aapako Thank You bolane ke leeye kabase idhar khada hai Mem-Sahib, (I have been waiting here for quite while just to say Thank You to you, Madam)," Ram said in his innocent and sincere voice.

"Aap kabhi bhi Durgapur aao Mem-Sahib. Hum bhi aap ko hamari Ma ke haath kaa khana khilayenge. (Please come to Durgapur any time Madam. You will enjoy my mother's cooking).

Aap Delhi se Bambai jaane wali rail gaadi me aaoge, to hamara Durgapur bilkul beech me hai Mem-sahib. Durgapur ke baad aata hai ek bada tesen— Bhusaval. (If you take a train from Delhi to go to Bombay, Durgapur is right in the middle. Aftger Durgapur is a big station called Bhusaval).

Aap Durgapur aao aur hamari ma, baba, aur chhoti behen Seeta se milo (You come to Durgapur and meet with my mother, father and my little sister Seeta)."

He then put his hands together and with tears in his eyes said, "Thank you Mem-Sahib. Hum aapka pyaar kabhi nahi bhulenge, Mem-Sahib. Aap ko keesee bhi cheez ke zaroorat pade, hum ko boliye Mem-Sahib. Thank you Mem-Sahib (Thank you Madam, I will never forget your affection, Madam. If you need anything, please let me know. Thank you Madam.)"

Katherine took his hands in hers and said, "Come on Ram, now don't make me cry here. You are welcome. Mai Durgapur zaroor aungi aur tumse milungi. (I will definitely come to Durgapur and look for you.)."

"Now, get going from here before anyone sees you. Chalo jaldi se neeklo idhar se."

Katherine stood there as he rushed away.

"Uh hmmmm," someone coughed in back. Katerhine was startled.

"The ladies room is this way, Ma'am," said that same older gentleman sitting at the next table.

"Thank you," said Katherine and walked away quickly.

CHAPTER 7

India—The Land of a Million Mysteries

As the ship drew closer to the port of Bombay, everyone was gathered around the balconies watching the port. They were all dressed up and ready to get off the ship. Some of them were talking about their luggage; some were talking about how they are going to get to their destination.

Katherine and David were standing in the balcony of their room holding hands. Every so often Katherine was squeezing David's hand showing her anxiety.

Back home in London, Granny was sick in her bed. Arthur was sitting right beside her reading a book.

She woke up coughing. Arthur gave her some water.

"Arthur, where is my Katherine? I want to see her Arthur."

Arthur thought to himself, 'She must have reached India by now. She has her own life now Mum. Please don't wish for something that is impossible for me to give you.'

"Arthur!" Granny yelled.

"Uh, Mum, she must have reached the West Coast of India by now Mum. I will send her a letter and ask her come visit us as soon as she can," Arthur consoled her the best he could.

He took his watch out from his pocket and said, "It's almost noon Mum. Time for your pills."

"No, Arthur, I don't want any more pills. All I want is to see my Katherine. I miss her Arthur. I miss her very much."

"So do I, Mum, so do I," Arthur said dejectedly. 'But life must go on, Mum,' he murmured to himself.

He got up and fetched Granny's pills and gave them to her with a glass of water.

"I am going to make some lunch, Mum. What would you like to eat?"

"I don't want to eat anything. I have no taste in my mouth. These pills are making me sick."

"I will make you some soup, how is that?"

In Bombay, David and Katherine had arrived at the Officer's Club. They were sitting down for supper. The whole environment was exactly as she had imagined. They were sitting out on a verandah. There was a warm light breeze. The décor of the entire dining area had a very official look with white curtains, white tablecloths, and even the waiters in their white clothes and white hand gloves. There were two Sikh sentries—with white Sherwani (a long high-neck shirt) and red turban with golden lace around it. Katherine was looking around with a light smile on her face—as if she was in heaven.

The waiter came to their table, greeted them and gave them very nicely decorated menu cards.

Looking at the menu card, Katherine started ordering food.

"I will have some Mulgatani Soup, Chicken Curry and some Butter Naan. Oh, and don't forget to bring me some pickles—I love those spicy pickles."

David was looking at her with a mixture of awe, anger and embarrassment. Even the waiter was surprised.

"Take it easy Darling, we are here to stay. You don't have to have all Indian food at once."

"Oh, come on David. I have been waiting for this day all my life. Let me enjoy it."

David saw the determination in her eyes and backed off.

"Alright. But, what would you like to drink?"

"I will have some sweet lassi," Katherine ordered and started looking around indicating that she didn't want any discussion about it. The waiter noticed her Hindi accent when she said lassi and knew right away that she knows some Hindi.

"Ok then. She will have lassi," David ordered in a very British accent. "And I will have Scotch on the rocks, please."

"What about your food, Sir?"

"Oh, yes, I will have some Chicken Soup and a Spagetti with Chicken Marinara."

"Oh, by the way, do you some of those papadams?" Katherine asked.

"Yes, of course, Ma'am. Would you like one?"

"Mmm, we will have a couple of those, please."

As the waiter walked away, before David could say anything, Katherine took his hand in hers and said, "Thank you very much dear. I am really grateful to you for giving me the experience of my life. My father has been telling me about India for so many years and now I can see it with my own eyes. Thank you so much. I love you Darling."

David didn't know what to say. He just looked at her.

As their drinks were served, they started talking about their plans for the next few days.

"I have to report on duty tomorrow morning. Then we will decide where we go next. Most likely we will go to Delhi from here."

"Oh, yes. We can take the train to Delhi. There we can go see Red Fort, Kutub Minar, and Darling, I have to go to Agrah to see the Taj Mahal."

"Darling, darling, slow down. I am here on an official duty—not for vacation. Besides, we are here to stay for many years. Don't worry; we will visit all these places. We don't have to go there right away."

David was right. Katherine also agreed and decided to shut up for a while about her excitement of being in India.

They had their supper, while talking about other things; remembering Granny and Arthur.

The next day they got up early in the morning. David got ready in his Army clothes. He was looking very handsome. As Katherine sat down for breakfast, she looked at him with a lot of love, pride and admiration in her eyes.

"What? What are you looking at? You are looking at me as if you never seen me in these clothes before!" David was almost blushing.

"So, what are you going to do all day?" asked David as he sat down to have some tea. Katherine started to reach out for the tea-pot and the waiter quickly moved forward.

"Allow me please, Ma'am," he said promptly.

"Well, I might go into town and see the town."

"Be careful, darling. You don't know anyone here. Besides, there may be some riots or processions here and there in town. Don't go that side. Why don't you stay here close to the camp—you can even walk to the sea-side. I will tell the officers to arrange for a car for you along with English-speaking driver. How's that?"

"Thanks lot dear. I would love to do that."

Katherine sat in the car on the back seat, and asked the driver to take her to the town. It was quite warm that day. Katherine wasn't used to such humidity and the heat. Although she was wearing light colored clothes, she was beginning to sweat a lot. As the car started to speed up a bit, the wind cooled her off.

She walked around town—looking at shops; observing the locals and looking at various things on the side walk sale. Every once in a while some little kids would follow her and try to sell her something. But, she shooed them away speaking in Hindi telling them she didn't want to buy anything.

She was enjoying the stroll around town so much that she didn't even remember to have lunch. At one place she saw a small hut. There was a man at squeezing sugar cane juice from a hand-driven churn. Several people had gathered around drinking sugar cane juice. Katherine was really curious. No one had told her about this. As she went toward that shop, everyone stopped talking and drinking. They all started staring at her.

"Yeh kya hai?" (What is this?) she asked the man at the churn. He was surprised to hear her Hindi.

"Yeh, ganne ka ras hai mem-sahib (This is sugarcane juice madam)," he answered.

"Hamey ek gilaas dedo (Give me one glass)", Katherine said.

Very hesitantly the man gave her a glass of sugarcane juice. She first tasted a little bit and then she gulped the whole glass down. As she finished, she stuck her tongue out and wiped her lips—she didn't want to waste any of that taste. Then, finally, she made a sound with her tongue in her mouth—giving the final seal of approval to the man. The whole crowd was looking at her—some women giggling and some men gaping at her in awe. She gave the man one whole Rupee and walked away without waiting for her change.

Finally, toward the end of the day, she ended up at the sea-side area. She saw the Gateway of India—a large monument that the British have built. It was built to commemorate the visit of the first ever British Monarch, King George V and Queen Mary in 1911. It was formally opened to public in 1924. It is 26m high structure, complete with four turrets and intricate latticework carved into the yellow basalt stone. There was a large open area with a lot of people walking around, a lot of street-hawkers selling various things like peanuts, balloons, etc. There were some families with small children and the children trying to persuade their father to buy them a balloon. Katherine was taking millions of snapshots to store in her memory.

It was nice and breezy there. She stood there looking at the Indian Ocean—as if she was looking to see if beyond the sea.

"Madam, we should go now Madam. It's almost Five O'Clock—time to get ready for supper," said the driver walking politely behind her.

At dinner, Katherine couldn't stop talking about her day and all the things she saw. David was just nodding his head and saying 'Hmm', 'Uh, huh,' and so on. He kept on asking the waiter for more Scotch with almost every story she had.

Finally, he had to stop her. He held her hand and said, "K, love, stop. You are going at 100 miles an hour and I have something important to tell you."

Now Katherine was embarrassed. She stopped and started playing with the food on her plate.

"Oh, Katherine, I am so glad you got to experience India—the way you wanted to, the way your father wanted you to. But, we are here to live for a long time in India and I am sure you will experience a lot more. For now, I need to focus on my duties and my duty is to leave for Delhi tomorrow."

"What, Delhi? Tomorrow? Oh, David, I haven't even seen anything around Bombay. How can we leave so soon?"

"Well, my love, we don't have to leave. I, on the other hand, must leave. They are expecting me in Delhi in 2 days. There is a meeting with many of the

State governors in Delhi next week and I need to attend that. We will have plenty of time afterwards. I promise you this Christmas I will take you to Kashmir and you will have a White Christmas. Okay love?"

"Oh, David, Christmas is so far away! I just started enjoying here. Can I stay here a few more days and then join you in Delhi?"

David thought for a minute. On the one hand, he wanted her to join him—perhaps because he didn't want her to befriend any locals or worse yet help any poor peasant out of pity. On the other hand, he thought, it is perhaps alright for her to be left alone for a while. She will be safe at the military base and he can focus on his tasks.

"Of course, darling, why not? But you have to promise me you will behave yourself!" he laughed.

Now Katherine was happy. She looked at him with her eyes full of love. She bit her lower lip and smiled.

"Come on darling, we need to go and pack up your bags—if you have to leave tomorrow," she hurried him up.

They hurried back to their room. As Katherine was helping him pack his bags, they were playing around with each other. Just as almost all the bags were packed and ready, things got a little hot and heavy and they found themselves rushing to bed kissing madly—as if they had been away from each other for a long time or they were going to away from each other for a long time to come.

The next day, David left. Katherine went to the train station to see if off. The train station—Bombay Central Train Station—was bustling with people and lots of activities. Seemed like there were a lot of people going on the train. Many of them looked like they were going on some kind of a pilgrimage—they had lots of orange flags in their hands. At one point Katherine stopped to look at them. David thought she was going to stop and talk to someone, so he hurried her up, "Come on Kay, let's go. I am getting late."

The porter put David's luggage in the First Class compartment. David went in and looked around. There were several white people. He nodded hello to them and walked out to see Katherine. Katherine was standing out side and looking around with her usual thirsty eyes. As he came out, she hugged him and gave him a passionate kiss. They stood there for a while and talked. He gave her names of a few people in case she needed any help.

The train whistle went off and everyone hurried to get on the train. David went up the steps of the train and turned around to hold her hand. As the train started rolling, Katherine started walking holding his hand. As the train picked up speed, she started running, but then had to leave his hand. For some reason she thought she shouldn't leave his hand at all. Just as their hands drifted apart the train whistle went off again and Katherine stopped running. She stood there for a while and saw him waving back at her. She stood there for a long time. The whole train rolled off from the station. She saw the back of the train with a big X marked on the back of the train.

She was completely lost in some thoughts, until the station master stood behind her gently asking her, "Is everything alright Madam? Do you need any help?"

She quickly gained her composure and said she was fine.

CHAPTER 8

Duty Calls

David was introduced by Lord Linlithgow, Viceroy of India to the room full of governors from almost a dozen states—many of them were English—except for a couple of them—from Kashmir and Hyderbad States. David had a seat right by the Viceroy. David stood up and bowed to everyone.

Behind the governors seated at the table were several Indian sentries standing up straight—waiting to take the command from their masters. Right behind the Viceroy was a large painting of Queen Elizabeth and the Union Jack. David was proud of the whole set up. He was looking at the paining, the British flag, the Viceroy and the room full of dignitaries and beaming with pride.

"Gentlemen," Lord Linlithgow started his speech with a very statesman-like voice.

"I am going to contact Lord Gowrie, Governor General and ask him for several things and concessions for all of your states. First and foremost, I feel very strongly that we need more aircrafts. Now, I know that England is fighting a long and hard war in Europe; however, we cannot ignore the growing demands of India and all the neighboring regions. I will also ask him to consider supplying us with more war supply—because of the local insurgence of violence and war-like tactics of the local militant groups. Of course, I will keep any details of such insurgence out of this correspondence—which may lead to some misunderstanding of how we are managing this entire region. In addition, I will also ask His Majesty to nominate an officer of high rank to be a member of an Eastern Group Supply Board in India who would be fully familiar with the requirements and also with the resources of his Dominion and in a position to take decisions on behalf of the Dominion. The object of the Board would be to co-ordinate efforts so that needs of each area should be met according to the changing strategic position, and also that the fullest use should be made of the available resources."

He looked around the room. Everyone was listening intently. He paused for a little bit, sipped a little water and continued.

"One of the things that I have to ask of all you is that we would need to provide some incentive to His Majesty's government in order to get such a request approved quickly I suggest that each of the your states agrees to pay at least 50% more in taxes over the next two years."

As soon as he said that, there was a big commotion in the room. Everyone started talking to each other. The two Indian Governors stood up very aggressively. David became alert immediately. He stood up with one hand on his gun hanging from the belt. Lord Linlithgow signaled David to stay calm.

"Gentlemen, may I please have your attention? Please calm down. I know it is very difficult for you to fathom the reason behind such a request. You see, there are many other territories that are helping His Majesty in this time of war. They are providing soldiers, a lot of raw material and many other things. The least we can do is to pay the price of our own protection. Consider this insurance for your own well-being."

"But, Sir," spoke up Governor of Hyderabad. "These past few years have been extremely difficult for us to pay the taxes we owe. Now if you are talking about increasing it, there will be big danger of some more local unrest in our area. After all, there is only one crop a farmer gets every year. What else can he do?" he lowered his tone toward the end—almost as if he was begging Lord Linlithgow to reconsider.

"I understand, Your Majesty, Khan-sahib. We will try to help you figure out some way of squeezing out more from your constituents. And, besides, I was not asking you to remit the increase in taxes. I was merely telling you before the decree comes to you in writing," his voice became very strict toward the end.

David had not worked Lord Linlithgow for too long. But, he had come to know in just a few days that when he says something he really means it and he will get it done. Resistance is futile—when Lord Linlithgow has made up his mind. It was clear that the whole room knew that. But, some of them were shaking their heads—as if they were anticipating some kind of a storm on the horizon.

David was proud of his new master. He liked the determination and the way he had handled the questions from this audience.

Katherine was sitting in the train's canteen compartment and writing a letter to her father. Sipping a cup of tea and nibbling on a couple of samosas with some chutney, she was deep in her thoughts writing to Arthur about his experience in Bombay.

'. . . . . .and when I tasted that ice cold sugarcane juice on that hot sunny afternoon, I thought I had died and gone to heaven. I couldn't get enough of that sweet taste. I kept on licking the glass. And, you know what Dad, the locals were looking at me as if they had just seen a ghost—a white ghost.' She paused for a little.

The train was slowing down as if it was coming to a stop. She looked out the window and didn't see any station or even a town for miles and miles. She stopped the ticket master who was hurriedly passing by her.

"Yeh kya ho raha hai? Hum yaha kyu rook rahe hai?" (What's going on? Why are we stopping here?) She asked him.

"Madam-ji, kuchch nahi, bas signal ke liye khade hai. Bas abhbhi neekal jayenge." (Nothing Madam, we are just waiting for the signal. We will leave very soon.) He answered promptly. He wasn't even surprised that she spoke to him in Hindi. It was obvious he must be meeting many English people on the train speaking Hindi.

As the train stopped in the middle of nowhere, Katherine went to the door and leaned out to smell the fresh air. There were lots of fields in front of her. The wind was sweeping across the fields and painting a new picture every minute. Far away on the horizon, she could see some mango trees and some people around them.

She was completely lost in her thoughts when she was awakened by the train whistle as the train started moving slowly. Katherine stayed at the door for a while. As the train picked up speed, it picked up the rhythm from the wheels going over the rail joints.

Dhagdaa….dhagdaa…..dhagdaa…dhagdaa…dhagadaa..dhagadaa……
kooo…oooooo…

The whistle from the engine also added to the rhythm of the train.

Katherine looked toward the front of the train. As the train was turning left, she could see the engine spewing smoke. It was a beautiful sight captured in her mind. On the background of dark green trees, there were plush yellow shiny fields with wind blowing them and the train combing through it.

'A mechanical—but practical conveyance brought by the British in the middle of this vast natural beauty!' Katherine thought to herself.

Dhagdaa….dhagdaa…..dhagdaa…dhagdaa…dhagadaa..dhagadaa……
kooo…oooooo…

dhagdaaa dhagadaaa…..

The train kept on catching speed. When the wind became unbearable, Katherine came inside and sat down at her table and started writing again.

'Dad, you won't believe the beautiful sight I just saw……' she continued writing the letter.

As the train pulled into the station at Delhi, Katherine was standing at the door looking for David. It had been over a week she had not seen or kissed him. She was getting impatient. As she saw some officers on the platform, she quickly looked at them to see if David was among them. But, they were talking among themselves—some smoking cigarettes and some tapping the ash off the cigarettes. Finally, the train stopped and Katherine started wondering what happened to David—whether he got the telegram of her arrival or not.

Suddenly, an older looking army officer approached Katherine and asked, "Eh, excuse me ma'am, but, are you Mrs. Katherine Sutherland?"

Katherine was baffled for a minute and then she said, "Well, yes, I am." And she still kept on looking around for David.

He took off his hat and introduced himself, "I am Lieutenant Graham Smith. It is a pleasure meeting you."

"Oh, yes, it is a pleasure meeting you too," Katherine answered mechanically while looking around for David.

"Are you looking for General Sutherland, Ma'am?"

"Yes, of course, I just hope he got my telegram," Katherine answered quickly and then wondered how come he knew about my husband.

"Pardon me, Ma'am. Perhaps I should explain better. I work for him and he did get your telegram. But he was busy with his work and sent me to receive you at the station. I can take you home and by the time we reach there, he should return as well," he tried to explain as quickly as he could in one breath.

"Umm, alright then," she was visibly disappointed that David did not come to the station to receive her.

Graham called the porter and asked him to bring a large cart. Katherine had a lot of luggage. They went to the car parking lot. Graham had an official Government vehicle for them. Graham told the driver of the other car to make sure all the luggage was fit into the car and if it had to go on top of the car he should tie it with a rope. Then they themselves got into another car and took off toward the residence of high level military personnel in Army Colony.

Katherine once again was looking at Delhi streets with her thirsty eyes. The air was kind of brisk and a lot drier than Bombay.

As they arrived at the villa assigned to David, a couple of servants ran toward the car. Katherine got out of the car and immediately started looking around. It was late afternoon. And the golden sun was beginning to sketch very interesting patterns in the sky. Katherine looked up in the sky. Many schools of birds were flying back to their nests. In the background she also heard a mixture of military band at a parade, a Muslim chanting of 'Allah Ho Akbar' going on from the mosque and bells ringing at the Hindu temple.

'What a unique combination of sounds and traits,' she thought to herself.

As they were climbing the stairs, the other car with all her luggage drove in. Graham told the driver and the servants to carefully unload the car and take the bags to her room. They all promptly ran to help the driver.

Katherine went up to her room and took her scarf and hat off, threw it on the bed and immediately went to the balcony. She looked out at the city—those crowded streets, the small hut-like houses trying to form a line, but not being able to keep it in line. A slight haze with golden sun shining on a few glass windows was making it look like a rich lady's necklace shining in the twilight with an occasional bling.

A servant girl came in the room very hesitantly and asked in a bleak voice, "Mem-sahib, bath?"

"Ha, ha, humaare nahaanekaa paani lagaado, (Yes, yes, I will take a bath.

Prepare hot water for me)," Katherine told her and looked away—as it she didn't even want to look at the girl's face with a complete awe about Katherine speaking in Hindi.

"Ji, Mem-sahib, (Yes Madam)" the girl said and almost ran away.

Just as Katherine was done with her bath and was getting ready for dinner, she heard someone yell, 'Arrey Sahab aa gaye,'. She came out of the bedroom into the inside balcony overlooking the drawing hall. David was just walking in. He handed his hat, his jacket and a small leather brief case to the servant and as he looked up, Katherine was looking at him with nothing but pride and love in her eyes.

He quickly ran up the stairs, ran to her, held her in his hands and gave her passionate kiss. All of sudden they both realized that some of the servants were staring at them. Embarrassed, they moved a step away from each other—while still gazing at each other's faces.

"Come on love, let's get ready quickly, we have to go to the Governor's mansion for dinner," David went in the room unbuttoning his coat.

"Oh, no, David. I am so exhausted. I want to rest at home. Can we please just stay at home?"

They kept on trying to reason with each other. Finally, they both gave up and agreed that David would go to dinner and Katherine would stay home.

As David got dressed up in his black suit, white starched shirt and black bow tie, Katherine was relaxing on the bed lovingly looking at him.

"Stop staring at me. Haven't you ever seen me before?" David came and sat beside her on the bed. They talked for a little while and then David realized he was getting late.

"Ok, I need to get moving. I will be back in zippy. Take good rest my darling," he kissed her and took off.

She just sat there on the bed thinking. She wanted David to cancel his plans and sit with her—at least for that first evening together. Then she thought there will be many more evenings like this one. She got up and sat at the table to write a letter to Arthur.

She kept on writing for quite a while.

"Mem-saab, would you like to have your dinner now?" an old gentleman came at the door of the bedroom and asked. They all used to call him Mama-ji (Uncle). He had been working at the Army officer's residence for over 20 years.

Katherine woke up from her deep thoughts.

"Yes, Mama-ji, what time is it?"

"It's almost 9 O'Clock Mem-saab."

Katherine went down stairs. The dining room was very big with a large dining table in the middle. It was obviously designed to hold large dinner parties. A setting for one was arranged on one end of the table. She sat down and looked at the whole room, the large table, the empty chairs and she called out, "Mama-ji!"

"Yes, Mem-saab," Mama-ji came out hurriedly as if there was something wrong.

"Have you had your dinner yet?"

"No, Mem-saab, but we will all have dinner after you are done."

"Nonsense. Let's all have dinner together."

Mama-ji was startled. He did not expect that at all.

There was a small table in the kitchen. They arranged a setting for her at the table and they all sat down in front of the table with their plates. Her setting included a nice dinner plate, napkin and silver cutlery, while they all had steel plates. When she saw that, she pushed away the cutlery and started eating with her hands.

After a while they all got used to the new Mem-saab and started talking in Hindi, introducing themselves and talking a little bit about their families. Most of them were from nearby villages around Gudgaon—which was about 30 miles from Delhi. Some of them had their wives at home with small children, but they had to be in the city working. Katherine thought to herself, 'Here I am thinking that David should have stayed back to have dinner with me and here are these people who have not see their wives for many weeks'.

They kept on talking, eating and joking around a little. After a while Katherine realized she had eaten quite a lot and she was full.

"Mem-saab, aapko kheer to khaanihee padegi (Madam, you must try the kheer—desert)," pleaded Mama-ji.

When she realized that refusing it was not an option, she tasted a little bit. It was made of almonds and dates enriched with milk and flavored with saffron. Once she tasted some, she couldn't put it down. She finished the whole bowl, without a single word and then looked up—everyone was looking at her as if she was starving and had tasted food for the first time in many days. Katherine was embarrassed. But, then started laughing it off, "What? Stop looking at me like that. It was very good."

From that day onward, Katherine was very friendly with all of them, but only when David wasn't around. She knew that David would be upset if she was too friendly with the servants. Whenever, David wasn't around for dinner, she would have dinner with all of them the same way in the kitchen.

Then one morning, Katherine woke up not feeling well at all. She rushed to bathroom to throw up. David was very concerned. He woke up and ran to her help. Later than morning he called the doctor home. The doctor came by and examined Katherine.

He called David in the room—who was pacing up and down the hallway.

"Congratulations, Captain," the doctor said.

Katherine was lying on the bed—a bit exhausted, a bit blushed.

David ran to her and held her hand. Just as he was about to kiss her, she pointed to the doctor. Then David realized that the doctor was still in the room.

"Well, I will take your leave sir, I will send some pills for her. Let her take complete rest for a few days." Mama-ji took the doctor's bag and walked out with him.

"Thank you doctor. Thank you very much," David completed his formalities in a hurry and turned his attention to Katherine.

They sat there talking for a long time. He knew that Katherine really wanted a son. He also wanted to have a son—his thinking was that while he is young, he should be able to play with his son. But, knowing that she wanted a son, he said, "I want a daughter and I am going to name her Margaret."

"But, I want a son and I am going to name him Michael."

"Ok, then, it is decided, Margaret for a girl and Michael for a boy," David put his seal pf approvals—as if he wanted to get that out of the way.

Suddenly, Mama-ji came by the door and knocked gently, "Sahab, Lieutenant Graham is here from your office."

"Ok, Mama-ji, tell him I will be right there." He then turned his attention back to Katherine. He didn't say anything for a few minutes. So, she had to break the silence.

"It's alright, dear. Go ahead. Go to your office. I know you are a busy man. And it's not like you had planned to take a day off or anything."

"Are you sure? I can stay here with you." David was actually relieved that she herself said it.

"Go on, I will be right here when you get back."

David rushed out and ran downstairs. He was speaking so loudly running down the stairs that even she could hear it.

"Hello, my friend Graham. How are you? What a wonderful morning, isn't it?"

Katherine sat up in bed to adjust the pillows and got the writing pad and pen to start writing to Arthur.

'Dear Dad or should I address it more like Dear Grandpa:

Yes, Dad, you are going to be a Grandpa and Granny is going to Great-Granny! Can you believe it?

I came to Delhi a few days ago. Just as I was getting used to this dry hot weather, there is another change in my life. Seems like there are a lot of changes on my life lately. You, Granny and David are living very steady life.'

Arthur was reading the letter to Granny. Granny was lying in bed—sick. She had tears in her eyes.

"Oh, bless her heart, my child Katherine. Arthur, I miss her so much. I want to see her again. I want to hold her in my arms, Arthur. Tell me, Arthur, I will see her, won't I?"

"Yes, of course, Mum. You will see her—just not now. In a few months, she will be back and we will all be together." Arthur—the tough Army lieutenant almost had tears in his eyes. He was clearly not used to that. He got up very awkwardly and went up to the cupboard pretending to look for something.

"Arthur, come here. Read her letter to me." Granny started to get up and suddenly started coughing trying to get up.

Arthur ran to her bed and said, "Mother, don't exert yourself. I am right here." He helped her sit up and gave her a glass of water.

They could hear some sirens going off and ambulance passing through the neighborhood immediately followed by a fire truck with its bell ringing. They both looked at each other and shook their heads in dismay.

Arthur continued reading Katherine's letter further. They sat there reading the letter and talking about Katherine and David until it started getting dark.

CHAPTER 9

Circle of Life

Katherine's due date was drawing closer and at the same time, due to the Viceroy's decree of increased taxes there were all kinds of protests all over the country. David was torn between his duty as an officer and as a husband. Katherine's doctor had told them that her condition had become a little more difficult and that she probably would have long and hard labor—unless they decided to perform an operation. Katherine was scared. She wanted David to be with her all the time.

Around the same time, the Viceroy decided to visit the State of Madras, a Southern Indian province. David tried to talk him out of it and tried to warn him that there are a lot of unhappy and enraged people along the way. He insisted that the Viceroy stays put in Delhi for his own safety. But, David knew what was going to happen.

As David was packing up to leave, Katherine was sitting on the bed—looking very big and very exhausted too! She was not saying much. David was also quietly packing his things.

"Oh, come on darling, I will be back before you know it. It is just a question of another week or so."

Katherine just grumbled and mumbled something. David ignored her for a while. As he finished packing his bag, he turned to her. He sat beside her and pulled her face his way. She tried to look away, but David kept on holding her face.

"You know, Love, my sentry was saying that it is considered bad luck in Hindu custom if a loved one doesn't smile while bidding goodbye to you on your way to a journey," David tried to get a smile out of her.

After a few seconds, Katherine smiled and then hugged him.

"Ummm, I hate you…I hate you…."

"Okay, then, I hate you too!" said David and hugged her really tight.

"Promise me, you will send a telegram every day."

"I promise—I will personally send a telegram to you every morning," David put his hand on his chest.

"Promise me you will be back in a week."

"I promise, I will be back in a week."

Then David turned to Katherine's big belly and shouted, "Now you promise me you will wait till I am back."

They both laughed and hugged each other again.

They sat there for a while, until Mama-ji came to the door and knocked, "Saab, its time for your train Saab," he reminded David.

David turned around and asked Mama-ji to carry his bag.

Katherine stood in the balcony bidding David goodbye with half a smile and drying tears on her cheek.

"Darling, tell Margaret to wait till I am back," David shouted from the car.

Katherine started laughing and then went inside.

The next couple of days went rather uneventful. Katherine would wake up and walk up and down the hallway; read newspaper full of news about riots everywhere and then try to keep her mind busy with some other kind of reading or just sitting in the kitchen talking to the servants.

Every morning at 10 O'Clock she used to get a telegram from David.

'Arrived in Durgapur. Stop. Nice town. Stop. Wish you were here. Full Stop.' Signed David.

Then one day, there was another telegram. Mama-ji brought the telegram and kept it on her bed. Kathrine was busy doing something in the garden. Mama-ji thought it was David's regular telegram. So, he didn't pay much attention to it.

That afternoon after lunch Katherine cam back to her room. It was getting a bit hot that day. She put on the ceiling fan and sat on the bed. She saw the telegram right beside her. She then relaxed on the bed and opened the telegram.

'Princess.Stop.'

It was from Arthur. All of a sudden Katherine sat up. Her heart had started racing.

She started reading further.

'Princess. Stop. Sorry to say Mum is no more. Stop. She went peacefully. Stop. She loved you. Stop. I love you. Take care. Stop.'

Katherine dropped the telegram from her hand. The whole room started spinning and then she started really fast. She was going out of breath. She wanted to shout, cry out loud, but she couldn't. Finally, after a minute or so, her voice came out, "NOOOOOOOOOO".

The whole house heard her shout. Everyone dropped whatever they had in their hands and ran upstairs.

Mama-ji ran as fast as he could. Everyone had gathered around Katherine as she was curled up on her bed crying in pain holding her stomach.

"Aye, Chhotu, jaa doctor ko bulaa, jaldi, jaldi" (Hey, Chhotu, go call the doctor, hurry, hurry), yelled Mama-ji.

David was running down the hallway at the hospital. He saw the doctor in the hallway and asked, "Doc, where is my Katherine?" The doctor pointed him to a room.

He ran into the room. Katherine was sitting up in bed. There was a cradle right beside her. She was rocking the cradle looking at the baby. As soon as she saw David, she started crying, "David, Granny......"

He hugged her and said, "I know, I know darling. I am soooo sorry." He hugged her tight and looked at her again. "How are you?"

"I am fine," Katherine was still crying. He hugged her again—this time he saw the baby in the cradle. He looked at Katherine and asked, "Margaret?"

Katherine just nodded and smiled. He smile was like a rainbow after a stormy rain peeking from dark black clouds.

David got up and went around the bed. He picked up Little Margaret.

"So, you couldn't wait for your Daddy to come back, huh? I told you to wait. Even at this age you are not listening to your Daddy, huh?"

Then David pretended to be a little baby, "Daddy, Daddy, it wasn't me. Mommy told me to come out!"

"Uh, huh. So, your Mommy put you up to this, huh?"

They both started laughing.

CHAPTER 10

Destination Durgapur

It was the spring of 1942. The weather was beginning to get warmer in Delhi and so was the political situation. Everyday there was news of some riots, some fires, police brutality and hundreds of freedom fighters getting arrested and jailed.

David was very busy. He used to leave home very early in the morning and wouldn't come back until late at night. He had instructed Katherine not to step out of the house with Margaret. Katherine was getting cooped up inside the house.

One day, Margaret started crying right from early morning. She wouldn't stop crying for several hours. Finally, Katherine asked Mama-ji to prepare the car to take Margaret to the doctor. Mama-ji tried to reason with her that he would go and get the doctor home. But, Katherine insisted that she has to take Margaret right away to the doctor.

It was early afternoon—getting really hot on the streets. After lunch, generally, a lot of people would go home and take a siesta—an afternoon nap. It is called 'vaama-kukshi' in Sanskrit. Katherine had found out about this a little while ago. It was very interesting. The doctor was explaining to her that 'vaama' means left side and 'kukshi' means to sleep on the side. So, if after a meal you sleep on your left side it is better for digestion. It was noted in the ancient writings of 'vedaas' in India.

Katherine sat in the back of the car with windows rolled down. Even though it was hot, even though the car wasn't going that fast, the breeze was refreshing her. She stuck her face right in the window and breathed the air in deep. She felt refreshed. She kept looking out the window until Margaret caught her attention again with a weak cry.

David rushed in the house. He was sweating and he also had some blood on his forehead.

"Mama-ji," he shouted out. There was no answer.

"Mama-ji," he shouted again. Still there was no answer.

"Chhotu," he shouted out. Chhotu came out of the kitchen—kind of scared.

"Ji Saab?" (Yes Sir?) he said in a timid voice.

"Sab log kidhar haai?" ("Where are all of them?") David asked in his irritated voice. It wasn't clear if he was irritated at the riots, the heat, the fact that no one was home or the fact that he had to speak in Hindi with a peasant. He took his jacket off and threw it on Chhotu's face.

"Saab, who sab Bebi ko leke doctor ke yahaa gaye hai," ("They have all gone to the doctor with the baby") Chhotu answered as if he was saying, 'why are you yelling at me? What have I done?'

"WHAT? They all went out? KATHERINE." He yelled looking up at their bedroom—as if Katherine was there.

It was getting late in the afternoon. The clock in the living room struck 5 O'Clock and David started getting even more upset. He poured a drink for himself and gulped it down. Then poured another one. Just as he was sipping that one, a car drove in the main gate. He ran to the door. Katherine was getting off the car. She was holding Margaret in hand. Margaret was sleeping.

"WHERE THE HELL….." David started shouting from the door. Katherine shushed him.

"Shshsh…she is sleeping. Let me put her in her crib and then we will talk."

When Katherine came down, David was on to his third drink. He was getting a bit excited now.

"If I have told you once, I've told you a thousand times. It is not safe for you to go anywhere. Where the hell have you been?"

"Calm down David. We went to see the doctor."

"To see the doctor? Why didn't you send Mama-ji with the car—the doctor could have come here."

"No, the doctor was very busy. In a stampede over on the south side, some small children got hurt. There were a lot of people at the hospital. The doctor was attending to all these children."

"Precisely. That's the reason I didn't want you going outside."

"But, David, I had no other choice. Margaret was crying all morning. I am glad I went to see the doctor. Now she is feeling much better."

Now David was beginning to calm down. It was obvious that something else was bothering him. He gulped down the drink and went for another one. Katherine went behind him and hugged him from the back. He shrugged her off.

"Come on David, what's wrong?"

"These bloody Indians. Now, the Indian National Congress has passed a declaration of 'Quit India' movement in Bombay. Who the hell do they think they are?"

"Well, David, we are foreigners in this country. After all, this is their country. Isn't it?" Katherine said it rather softly—she knew David would burst out in anger. And sure enough, he did.

"What the hell do you mean by that? Running this whole country for the past 200 years, is that some kind of a bloody joke? What do these peasants know about running a country? You can ask anyone—who brought all the industrial development to this country? Who brought railways and post office and...and..... education and universities and...who trained thousands of soldiers?"

"Huh, as if these things wouldn't have come to this country if it were not for the British!", now Katherine was also not going to let it go.

"Who robbed the country of all the treasures that have been preserved for hundreds of years? Who made slaves out of these peasants and who forced them to make opium so the British can bring it to China and drown the Chinese in this filthy habit? Who brought corruption in this country's government? You go ask anyone!" she said it as if she was making a counter argument in court.

"Come on, you don't really believe these things, do you? You must be talking to these bloody peasants. MY WIFE can't be talking like this."

Mama-ji, Chhotu, the driver and the cleaning lady, all of them were listening to all this from the kitchen door. All of sudden, they heard some unrest on the streets. They heard a lot of people gathering around and shouting, 'Inqilaab Zindaabaad' (Long Live Freedom).

"Think about it David. Just because the sun sets every evening it can't be due to the Indians and just because it rises every morning, it can't be because of us!"

"Shut up!" David slammed his glass on the bar.

Right at the same time, a rock came through the window and fell by the sofa. Katherine got scared. She ran toward David. He took her in his arms and ducked behind the sofa. His jacket and gun belt was on the other side of the sofa. He first looked at the rock and kicked it to make sure it wasn't a grenade or something. Then he ran toward his gun belt, grabbed the pistol and came back to Katherine who was squatting down.

"MAMA-JI, put off all the lights," David yelled out.

The crowds chanting 'Inqilaab Zindaabaad' was still going on and the noise was drawing closer to their house.

Little Margaret heard something and woke up. She started crying. Katherine realized that Margaret was alone upstairs. She got up and started running toward the stairs. David yelled out in a whispering voice, "Katherine!" But she didn't even look back. She kept on running and taking two steps at a time and ran up the stairs. She ran inside the room and held Margaret very close. Margaret was still panting.

Some time went by. It seemed like the noise outside was dying down. The procession went passed their house. They could still hear the crowds shouting,

'Inqilaab Zindaabaad'. After some time, Chhotu came running inside the house. He called Mama-ji and told him that the crowd was gone. He had made sure that the procession had taken the next left turn and gone away from the house and that there were no more people in front of the house. So, Mama-ji put the lights on and called out for David and Katherine.

David went straight to the bar and poured another drink for himself. Katherine came downstairs with Margaret in her arms. Margaret was completely awake now, but she still looked exhausted—perhaps it was the medicine that Katherine got for her earlier that day. Nevertheless, Margaret looked a lot more comfortable.

David was standing by the bar shaking his head. He turned around in spite and saw Katherine coming down the stairs with Margaret. He walked up to them and hugged both of them. He kissed Margaret and took her in arms.

"What are we going to do darling?" Katherine asked. She was obviously worried. "I mean, how long will this go on? Are we going to hide like this every time there are people protesting in front of our house?"

David didn't pay attention to her. She started getting angry.

"David! Are you listening to me?"

"Come on darling, its not that bad. These things will go on for a while and then it will come to an end. It has to. Besides, I will arrange for a few more gurkhas to guard the house."

These are a group of brave recruits from Nepal—who had been fighting for the British since Robert Clive's decisive victory at Battle of Plassey in 1757. From this war the British had come in contact with a unique and vigorous fleet of soldiers from city-state of Gorkha. The young men used to come down south from Nepal for jobs in security services for rich people. They would take on any kind of hardships, such as staying up all night to guard a house. A typical sign of a gurkha is a black round hat and a big dagger hanging from their belts.

"A few more of the guards is not going to make me feel safe, David. I don't want to be a prisoner in my own home. Nobody wants to be a prisoner in their own home." She emphasized the word nobody. David understood the meaning of that immediately. What she meant was that the Indians were imprisoned in their own homes and they are not going to rest until they are free—so this unrest is not going to stop.

Mama-ji and Chhotu were listening to this conversation from the kitchen door.

'Ab jaake eenko pataa chalaa apane hi ghar me agar kisiko kaidi banaayaa jaataa hai to kaisa lagataa hai (Now they have started realizing how it feels to be a prisoner in your own home)' Mama-ji murmured.

"Alright then, let me see what I can do. Perhaps we can move out of the city to be away from all these processions," said David—still busy playing with Margaret.

The next morning, Katherine woke up late. David had gotten up and gone to work before she woke up. Margaret was also sleeping soundly in her cradle. Katherine woke up and stood in front of the window. She opened the window to let some fresh air in. It was mid-morning, but she could feel the air warming up. She stood there for a while yawning and looking outside. Every once in while she looked at Margaret—looking so blissful sleeping in her cradle and cuddling up to her favorite blanket.

After a while, Katherine decided to get ready and went into the bathroom. As she was getting ready, all of a sudden she heard the loud noise of a glass breaking. She ran out in her gown and saw that Margaret had woken up and she was crying. The window was broken and there was a big rock in the middle of the room.

"Margaret...." She shouted and ran to her. Mama-ji and Chhotu were in the kitchen preparing lunch or something like that. They heard the noise and dropped whatever was in their hands and ran up the stairs.

Mama-ji knocked on the door strongly and yelled out, "Mem-saab, are you alright?" He didn't hear anything from the room—only Margaret crying. He yelled out again, "Mem-saab, aap theek to hai? (Madam, are you alright?)"

Then in a minute or so, Katherine yelled out, "Yes, yes, Mama-ji, I am alright." And she walked up to the door holding Margaret tight to her chest. She opened the door and Mama-ji and Chhotu ran inside to see what had happened. They found a big piece of rock in the middle of the room and all shattered glass spread around.

"Don't worry Mem-saab, it may be just these naughty children from that house on the corner."

Mama-ji had actually found a piece of paper wrapped around the rock—which read 'Inqilaab Zindaabaad—Bhaarat Chhodo' (Long Live Freedom—Quit India). But he quickly put it in his pocket. Katherine noticed that he had put something in his pocket very quickly. But she didn't want to confront him right there.

When things calmed down, Katherine came down to the kitchen to have a cup of tea. As Mama-ji prepared a cup of tea for her, she looked at him and asked, "Mama-ji, aap ko kyaa meela ooper kamare me? (What did you find in the room Mama-ji)".

Mama-ji tried to avoid eye contact with her and tried to deny there was anything. But when she pushed him, he took that piece of paper out his pocket and gave it to her. Katherine read it and kept it right in front of her. She didn't say anything for a while. Then she got up as if she had decided something. She started walking out of the kitchen and while walking said to Chhotu, "Chhotu come help me bring some of the suitcases down from the attic and come help me pack our things."

When David came back in the evening, he seemed to be in a hurry again. He went straight upstairs, took a quick wash, changed from his uniform into a suit and came down.

"Darling, I have to go to the Governor's Mansion for dinner. We have a meeting with the Chief of Police from Madras State."

"David, I need to talk to you," Katherine said it in a cold voice. David knew she was serious.

"David, I need to get out of here. It is not safe here for Margaret and me."

They talked for a little while. David tried to convince her that it would get safer soon and that he would feel better if they were with him.

"But, you are not here all the time anyway. And I don't want to live in fear all the time. Just this morning someone threw a big rock through our bedroom window. I don't want to live in fear, David."

Finally, after some more discussion, David promised her that he will look into sending them somewhere safer.

Then, a few days later, David told her that they could move to Durgapur— it was one of the stations on the railway line that went from Delhi to Madras via Bhopal junction. Bhopal—a larger town, almost like a city—was a couple of hours away. When Katherine heard about Durgapur, she was very happy. She remembered Ram from the ship.

Then, one late afternoon they arrived in Durgapur. David stayed with her for a few more days, until she was settled enough and then he took off to Delhi. Katherine was lonely for a couple of days. She asked around about Ram, but no one could tell her his whereabouts.

One evening when she was coming back to the haweli after shopping in town, she was passing by the large banyan tree. A few children were playing there. There was a group of 10 to 12 year old girls. They were playing a funny game and while playing they were whispering something and giggling away. Katherine stopped there for a minute and started watching. She was mesmerized—maybe thinking about her own childhood.

All of a sudden a little girl said, "Excuse me, you are standing in my way." Katherine's reflex action was to quickly say sorry and move backward. But then she realized that this girl was speaking very good English.

"Tumko itni achchi Angreji kaise aati hai?"(How come you speak such good English?) Katherine asked and now it was the girl's turn to be startled.

"Aapko itni achchi Hindi kaise aati hai?" (How come you speak such good Hindi?) the girl responded immediately.

Katherine was impressed with her bold and witty remark. They talked for a while, exchanging names and other information. Then Katherine started leaving, but came back and asked Seeta, "Seeta, how would you like to work at the house for me? It's not much heavy work, just some things here and there. But you will keep me a good company."

"Oh, madam, I will have to ask my parents. If they allow me, I will."

CHAPTER 11

Calm before the storm?

Katherine was very happy. Most of all it was the feeling of safety and then it was about experiencing real India. She used to walk to the village, mingle with the locals, joke around with the ladies and Seeta was always there taking care of Margaret, like her own little sister. There were many local festivals that Katherine would take part in. She was feeling very comfortable and at home. She had kept up with writing letters to Arthur. Every once in a while she would also receive letters from him. But his letters had started getting shorter and shorter, while Katherine's letters were getting longer and longer. She wanted to describe all the things she was doing and how she was enjoying taking part in festivals like holi (a festival of colors—celebrating the beginning of the harvesting), Diwali (the festival of lights—celebrating Lord Rama's return from Sri Lanka after defeating the evil king Ravanaa) and so on.

Every so often she would get telegram from David that he would be visiting them soon. So, she would wait for him, but sometimes he wouldn't even show up. Instead, she would get another telegram, 'Sorry. Stop. Cannot come. Stop. Will come next month. Full stop.'

The nearest big town was Bhopal—which was about 2 hours by train. But, Katherine never felt like going to the town. When she needed anything from the town, she would ask Seeta to go find someone that is going there, give them a list of things and some money.

Fortunately, there was a doctor in Durgapur—a very nice young man who was educated in Bombay University, but had to move to the village to take care of his ailing mother. He wasn't very happy about it, but he had no choice. Also, very few people would go him for their medical needs. They would go to the local doctor—called vaid—who would normally practice ancient Indian medicine and not allopathic medicine. So, when Katherine would go to Dr. Satya, he would be very happy that he didn't have to convince someone about allopathic medicine.

Once Katherine was busy writing a letter to Arthur in the morning and when Margaret woke up and started crying, Katherine called Seeta. But Seeta wasn't in the house. Normally Seeta used to come to the haweli in the morning to help Katherine and then go to school from mid-morning to mid-afternoon.

Then she used to go home, help her mother and then again come back to the haweli later in the evening to help with dinner. But that morning, Seeta had not come to work. Katherine was surprised, but then thought, something must have come up. So, she got up and picked up Margaret herself.

That afternoon she went to the village looking for Seeta. She saw Seeta's friends playing under the banyan tree. She asked them about Seeta. They all hesitated to answer her. Katherine's suspicion and concern was growing. She ran into the village asking about Seeta to different people—Dr.Satya—who was sitting in front of his dispensary, the postman, the grocery shop owner (known as Baniyaa-ji) and whoever else she met along the way.

Finally, she found Seeta's house. She went and knocked on the door rather strongly. An older gentleman—wearing a dhoti, kurtaa and Gandhi-like glasses—opened the door. He had a very worried look on his face. When he saw that it was Katherine, he quickly came out and closed the door behind him.

"Mem-saab, aapko kyaa chaaheeye? (What do you want Madam?)" he asked as if he really didn't want her there.

"Seeta kahaa hai? (Where is Seeta?)" Katherine demanded.

"Mem-saab, who ab aapke ghar aa nahi sakatee. (She cannot come to your house from now on)" the man said.

"But why?" Katherine knew that something big was happening here and she was afraid that Seeta's father must be getting her married or something like that. It was very customary in those days that a girl would get married in her teen ages. But, Katherine knew that was wrong.

The man didn't answer her and just turned around saying, "Namaste Memsaab. (Greetings Madam). Aapne hamaare liye jo kuchch bhi kiyaa hai, ooske liye dhanywaad. (Thank you for everything)."

Now, Katherine was getting upset. She grabbed the man's shirt from behind and yelled, "What do you mean? I want to see Seeta. Where is she?"

The man was angry, but he didn't say anything. He just forced his hand to get it away from Katherine's hands.

"Who, ab aapko nahi meel sakati (She cannot meet you now)," he said, walked in and locked the door from inside.

Katherine stood there yelling out, "Seeta, Seeta, please come out. I want to see you." But there was no answer. So, Katherine went around the house and started searching for a window or something to find Seeta. Finally she found a small window that opened ever so slightly and someone from inside whispered, "Mem-saab, I am here."

Katherine went near the window. Seeta started to cry. Katherine said to her, "Seeta, please don't cry. Tell me what is going on. I will help you."

"No, ma'am, you cannot help us. My father wants to get me married to the sahookaar."

Katherine just blew up. "WHAT?" She was trying to hold her rage, but she couldn't. She started stepping up and down. "They cannot do that to you. I will not let that happen."

Seeta kept on crying. She didn't know what to say. After a couple of minutes, Katherine regained her composure and asked her, "Seeta, listen to me. I will help you. I know I can. Just ask your father to open to open the door for me. Let me talk to him."

Suddenly someone came in that room and saw Seeta at the window talking to Katherine. It was Seeta's mother. She yelled at Seeta, "SEETA! Kheedaki band karo. (Shut the window)."

Katherine put her hand through the bars of the window and stopped her from shutting it.

"Suniye, (Listen). Aap muze bataaiye keetane rupaye chiheeye oos sahoo-kaar-ko (Please tell me how much money do you need to give to the sahookaar)." Katherine asked as if it was a simple transaction, pay the money, close the account and you can go home!

"Mem-saab, aap hamei hamaare haal pe chhod do (Madam, please leave us alone). Aaap-ne itane deen Seeta ko naukari deke bade ehsaan keeye hai humpar (By giving a job to Seeta, you have done a lot for us already). Lekin, ab Seeta aapke ghar nahi jaa sakati (But, Seeta cannot go to your house)."

"Par kyu nahi? Mai oos sahookaar ko paise de doongi. (But, why not? I will pay that sahookaar off.)"

As Katherine was saying this, she just realized that this was sahookaar's dirty trick. He knew that Seeta was getting very friendly with the Angreji Mem-saab (English Madam). And the freedom fight was catching on like wild fire all across the country. So, he thought, now is the time to leverage the situation. So, he came to Seeta's father and showed him the papers that Seeta's grandfather had signed for the lease of their house. The illiterate father of Seeta did not even read what that was. He sat down as if he had lost all strength in his knees.

"Eetanaa karajaa mai kaise chukaa paoonga Dharamdaas-ji? Hum gareeb log hai. (How can I repay this much money? We are poor people).

"Gareeb, ae? Arrey eetanaa badaa khajaanaa ghar me chhupaa ke rakkha hai, aur bolataa hai, hum gareeb hai ! (Poor? You have been hiding such a big treasure in your house and you call yourself poor?)" the sahookaar looked at Seeta—who was listening to the conversation from behind the main door.

"Aur, Gori mem-ke ghar kaa khaanaa khaake, woh khajaanaa aur bhi rang laayaa hai! Ha! Ha! Ha!" (And eating at the English Madam's house the treasure has even more luster!) he laughed devilishly. His assistants also started laughing with him.

Seeta's father was scared. She looked behind him at her mother in such a pity, that she closed the door and dragged Seeta inside.

"Yaa to hamaaraa karajaa chukka do—nahi to yeh khajaanaa hamaare hwale kar do (Pay by your loan or give me that treasure)!" he said it matter-of-factly and walked away.

"Dharamdaas-ji, Dharamadaas-ji," Seeta's father went after him. But the sahookaar didn't stop.

Katherine knew that she had to something about this or 12-year old Seeta would be married to the 45-year old sahookaar right in front of her.

Katherine went around to the main door.

"Seeta, open the door. Open the door right now," she yelled. "You give me one day, I will be back here with that lousy piece of paper and I will make sure that no one from that sahookaar as much as looks at you from now on." Katherine was determined.

She went home in a hurry. Wrote something on David's official letterhead, took some money from the closet, carried Margaret and went back to Seeta's house. She left Margaret there and went straight to the sahookaar's house. When she knocked on the door, the guard opened the door and started yelling, "Sahaab-ji, Gori-memsaab, Sahaab-ji, Gori-memsaab."

Sahookaar came down hurriedly mumbling, "Arrey yeh susari to bahot jaldi pahooch gayee yahaa, lagataa hai badaa lagav hai Seeta-se. Ab aaye ga mazaa. (Oh, this woman came so quickly. Seems like she really loves Seeta. This is going to fun)" he came down rubbing his hands, as if he was already counting his money.

As he came down, Katherine went rushing toward him.

"You—Dharamdaas," she almost bumped into him.

"Tumko maloom hai mai yahaa kyu aayee hun? (Do you know why I am here?)"

Dharamdaas was taken aback a little. The animal in him had started to bow down a little.

"Ha, ha, hamaari puraani hawaali kaa kuchch kaam hogaa (Yes, yes, may be you are about that old mansion of mine)," he tried to play dumb.

"Nahi. Tumko achchi taraha se maloom hai ke mai yahaa Seeta ke baareme baat karane ke liye aayee hun (You know very well that I have come here to talk about Seeta)," she shouted again.

"Seeta? Kaun Seeta? (Seeta? Seeta who?)" again he tried playing dumb.

Now, Katherine was getting really upset. She almost grabbed his collar and said, "Jyaadaa hoshiyaari mat deekhao. (Don't be too smart.) Tumhe maloom hai mere pati military ke sabse bade officer hai (You know my husband is the chief of military)".

Now, Dharamdaas was getting worried. He started wiping sweat off his forehead.

Katherine dangled the envelope in her hand in front of his eyes and said,

"Maine unake leeye ek sandesh leekha hai (I have written a memo to him). Woh Seeta-ke karazekaa kagaz muze dedo waranaa mai yeh sandesh daroga-ji ko de doongi aur Dharamadaas tum jail me jaaoge chakki peesane (Hand over those loan papers otherwise I will give this to the police and you will go to jail)," she said it as if she had a bomb in her hand.

Now, Dharamdaas was really scared. These sahookaars were evil people, but many of them were very timid. They would extort the people, but when it came to any kind of police action, they would get really worried. The locals never had the guts to call the police. But Dharamdaas knew that this English woman not only had the guts, but also that the police would definitely listen to her more than him.

He immediately yelled at his servant—who was standing there watching all the fun.

"Aye, dekhate kyaa ho? Jaao woh Seeta-bitiya ke gharwaalonke karaje-ka kagaz laao (Hey, what are you looking at? Go get that loan paper for Little Seeta's parents)," he ordered his servant as if he himself was about to hand it over.

When Katherine went over to Seeta's house with that loan paper in her hand, everyone was waiting for her right outside the front door. When Seeta saw her coming running toward the house, she knew that Katherine had got the paper. Seeta ran toward her and hugged her.

Her father took the paper from Katherine and started to cry and started to bend down to pay respects to her. She lifted him up and just put her hands together, "Nahi, nahi, Kaka, aap to muzse bade hai. (No, no, Uncle, you are elder to me)".

In the background Seeta's mother was wiping her eyes with her saree. Seeta was still hugging Katherine and looking at her parents as if saying, 'See what my Mem-saab can do for me? Pretty amazing, isn't she? That's MY Mem-saab.'

Once again days were going by fine. Seeta and Margaret were growing up like sisters. Katherine was enjoying the life. Every once in a while she would read in the newspapers about David and how he was heading the British police and army in various situations of turmoil. Of course, Katherine knew that any newspaper that was openly available would not print anything against the British Raj.

She found out that there was a Hindi newspaper—Inqilaab (i.e. Freedom)—that was printed in Bhopal by some underground freedom fighters. She asked Seeta to find if there was any way for her to get that newspaper. Seeta didn't know what she was talking about. But she said she had seen her brother visit the family during the holidays and he was showing some newspaper to her father—but being very secretive about it.

She saw that one day her father was reading that newspaper and then kept it under his pillow as he heard someone knocking on the door. Just as he went to answer the door, Seeta sneaked in his room, took the newspaper and hid it under her jacket. Then she ran toward the haweli—she just yelled out at her mother and told her that she was going to the Mem-saab's place and she will be back before dark. Her mother yelled back with something she wanted from the grocer, but Seeta ignored and ran away.

When Katherine got the newspaper, she started reading it hurriedly. The headline caught her attention and she was completely stunned.

'General Sutherland Ke Haatho Sau Sattayaagraheeyon Ki Hattyaa' (General Sutherland Killed 100 Freedom Fighers)

She immediately rolled up the newspaper and told Seeta to go play with Margaret. Then she sat down in the verandah and continued reading.

'General Sutherland was turning out to be the most strict and ruthless head of the British police and army. The British Government had decorated him with many medals for saving various British dignitaries' lives. But he was the worst enemy of the Indian freedom fighters.'

Katherine knew that she had to take all this information with caution. Not all the information or data was accurate—but just like the old Hindi adage, 'If there is smoke, there must be a fire somewhere'! So, she knew that David was doing his duty very well from British government's perspective, but he was not very well liked by general public. Deep down in her heart she also knew that if she had confronted him with all of this, he would brush it off and then say, 'Come one Katherine. I came here to do a job. If I start to go soft on anyone committing a crime, I cannot perform my duties. And, before you ask the question, let me tell you, deciding what is a crime and what is not, is not my job.'

'Oh, David…!' Katherine was caught in a dilemma. Her heart was telling her that what David was doing was wrong, but her mind was telling her that she should support her husband.

As she was flipping through the newspaper, she saw a photograph of David. She put her hand on his face and murmured, 'Oh, I love you so much David. I miss you so much. I miss you smell.'

She had put her hand on the picture. Just as she started moving her hand, all of a sudden she saw something that just shocked her. In the photograph, David was standing close to a woman in white dress, holding her hand and leaning toward her so much as if he was trying to kiss her. The woman—Lady Sarah Knightly from Edinburgh—was looking at him as if they were married.

Now, Katherine was completely lost. She just sat there looking dumb-struck.

CHAPTER 12

Beginning of one thing, end of the other

"Congratulations, General," said Lady Knightley looking at David with a light blush on her face.

There was some kind of a celebration going on. It was a big hall, hundreds of British army officers, dignitaries and Lord Gowrie, Governor General himself was there. He was greeting the guests. Many of them were mingling, having a drink, munching on some snacks and a group of them was even doing the traditional British Circle Waltz dance in the middle of the hall.

"Thank you very much, Ma'am," David kneeled down and kissed her hand.

"Oh, come on David, you don't have to this formal with me," she whispered.

"In that case, you don't have to call me General either, Ma'am!" They both laughed.

The celebration was for the birthday of Queen Elizabeth. On that same occasion, Lord Gowrie had decided to honor several army personnel with medals for heroic efforts in the Indian Territory.

Just as the big grandfather's clock in the hallway started striking 6 O'clock, David went up to the slightly elevated stage and asked the musicians to stop the music and clapped to get attention from people still talking.

"Ladies and Gentlemen, may I have your attention please?"

The crowd still wouldn't settle down, there were still some people talking away.

"Ladies and Gentlemen, may I have your attention please?" he said it bit loudly and bit more authoritatively this time.

"Ladies and Gentlemen, I am not used to this. Usually, when I want attention, I don't ask, I order attention!" Everyone started laughing.

"Oh, well, now that I have your attention, I don't have to give you an order!"

Once again there was laughter in the room.

Lord Gowrie whispered to an older-looking army officer standing right beside him, 'See? I think, not only is he the best army officer we have, but he is also an excellent orator!' The gentleman looked at him—as if he was insulted by that comment.

'Err, but, he has a lot to learn from you, Sir!' he corrected himself.

"So, let me introduce His Highness Lord Gowrie, the Governor General," David concluded his short speech and asked Lord Gowrie to come on to the stage.

"Thank you David. You are a fine soldier. Don't even think of a career in opera, okay?" The whole audience started laughing.

"Ladies and Gentlemen, thank you very much for coming to this special occasion. Today we are celebrating 30th anniversary of coronation of Her Majesty the Queen of Great Britain. Long Live the Queen."

"Long live the queen," everyone chimed in.

"I am sure you realize that on this occasion we are celebrating not only Her Highness' birthday, but the very foundation of the British Government in India. Our foundation is solid as it ever was and under the British government, even the Indians a flourishing. We have successfully brought railways and post office to this country and connected north to south and east to west. Without our firm commitment to building this society, this country would have been divided into pieces by many greedy Maharajas with small kingdoms and the whole region would have been utter chaos. Under our direction this country has become one of the biggest exporters of spices, silk, gold and many other precious materials to Europe and beyond. Under our guidance they are teaching their children modern science and mathematics—which they never dreamed of learning. Many of the Indians have gone to England for studying further in law and sciences. Of course, some of those are coming back with the teachings from our own universities and using that knowledge against us. They have come back after years of comforts and higher education and now walking around in loin cloths carrying a stick and waving it in front of our own eyes. But, we know how to deal with them—after all—they forget that WE are the ones that taught them the science of politics." The whole crowd started laughing and thumping.

"When I came to this country, I was shocked by the society that is so openly divided by religion, caste system and languages. With our missionaries—thank you father," he raised the glass to a group of Christian missionaries attending the reception.

Then he continued, "With our missionaries helping the poor untouchables and giving them equal opportunities in attending schools and doing jobs side by side with the other caste members."

"Under our regimentation many Indian soldiers are becoming great fighters and helping the allied nations in the world war and also helping us maintain the control in Middle Eastern countries like Iraq. The Gorkha unit and the Sikh unit are the most notable warriors who are helping the British Government right here at home and abroad. There are many British officers who will be decorated today—but out of all of them, the most notable and my most favorite is General David Sutherland. What is has done in just the past three years is remarkable."

David stood up straight and smiled at people around him, bowing to Lord Gowrie. He then looked at Miss Knightley—who was looking at him with a lot of admiration and affection. He smiled at her and looked away—knowing full well that she was still staring at him.

"David, my friend, please come on up here," Lord Gowrie asked David to come and stand right beside him. The whole crowd started clapping as David was taking a light bow. He looked at Miss Knightley again and this time there was a definite visible connection between the two.

"So, this, ladies and gentlemen, is David Sutherland—the shining star of the British Government."

Now David was beginning to blush a little.

In that whole crowd, there were a few of David's lieutenants. They were whispering kind of sneering remarks toward David.

'Just look at him. How can he take all the credit when we know for a fact that all he does is order!'

Lieutenant Graham Smith was also standing among them. He didn't like the fact that they were all commenting on their commanding officer.

'Oh, yeah? So, Lieutenant Barnett last week when you were pinned under your G.P., who came to rescue you? Who was there to get you out of there? Should he have stayed in his office giving orders while you were just about to get killed by that angry mob?'

All of them kept quiet after that. They knew that David was giving orders, but he was not afraid to confront any kind of violent situation.

Just as Lord Gowrie was asking one of the helpers to bring David's medal to him, David spoke up, "With all due respect, Sir. Any officer is nothing without his brave and loyal lieutenants. I would like to request that we first decorate these courageous young lads."

"Of course, of course," Lord Gowrie answered, as if he was going to do just that.

David then called each of them and asked Lord Gowrie to pin their medals on their proud chests.

Then the whole ceremony was over. They all started drinking and enjoying the appetizers again.

While this whole ceremony was going on, some of the servers—who happened to be Indians—some of them Sikhs—were staring at the whole show with hate oozing out of their eyes. One of the younger servers was carrying a tray full of some appetizers, as he was approaching David and Miss Knightley, he tripped on something and spilled a little bit of chutney on David.

"You ignorant fool!" Miss Knightley shouted out. "Can't you even walk properly?"

She immediately took her handkerchief and started wiping the chutney off David's jacket. David just kept looking at her.

Some of the senior servers came to rescue of the young fellow and took him away. The lieutenants also came running toward David.

"People, people, come on! It's just a little accident. I am fine. Go back to your places, enjoy the evening."

Miss Knightley was still cleaning his jacket.

"David, this stain is not going to go away. Come with me." She grabbed him by his hand and took him to the hallway and looked around for the wash room. She spotted one at the end of the hallway. She took him inside without caring about whether it was men's or women's wash room. Just as she went in, she locked the door behind them and planted a long kiss on David's lips. David was totally surprised. But, then he also realized that the attraction was mutual and he held her face in his hands and reciprocated. It was steamy in that wash room—partly because it was a closed room without any fan in there.

When they walked out of that washroom, both of them looked a little flushed. They had to make sure there were no visible signs of their steamy encounter on their face or on their clothes.

They went back into the main hall and re-joined the group—just as they were walking into the big dining hall for dinner. All throughout dinner, they kept on looking at each other—as if they were a couple.

From that day onward, Miss Knightley—Sarah—and David were spending a lot of time together. She was seen going in and out of David's house in the mornings and evenings. Mama-ji and Chhotu would look at her and then just look at each other. She didn't care what they said—neither did David.

There was a different kind of mood in their house. Sarah was acing as if she was David's wife and David was acting as if he was never married to Katherine.

David's heroic acts in protecting the governor and the British Raj continued on. Every once in a while he would come up with new ideas to clamp down on the people fighting for their freedom. He kept of winning Lord Gowrie's confidence even more and kept on getting increasing freedom to enforce what he felt was the right thing to do.

CHAPTER 13

End Of One Thing And Beginning Of The Other

The unrest in the communities all around India was growing tremendously. Almost every day there was some news of some incident somewhere. Gandhi, Nehru, Lala Lajpatrai, and many of their followers had started various movements—Non-violence movement, Non-Cooperation Movement, and most of 'Quit India' campaign was catching on like wild fire everywhere in India.

Many small villages—like Durgapur—though away from this whole hustle-bustle, still would get lots of news about what was going on everywhere in the country.

Seeta's brother and his friends would visit once in a while—they would come late at night at home. Her mother would cook a meal for everyone; they would eat in the dark—with lamenting lights. Talk among themselves about various plans of 'baghaavat' (i.e. revolution) and when her father would finally tell them to stop it and to get back to their families, they would disperse.

One morning, Seeta came running to the haweli, shouting right from the entrance, "Mem-saab, Mem-saab….."

"Yes, Seeta, what is it? Is every thing alright?" Katherine came out of the bedroom worried.

"Yes, Mem-saab, everything is fine. I have some news for you," Seeta was panting. She couldn't even complete her sentence.

"Ok, slow down, my dear. Slow down and tell me what is happening."

After a few minutes, when Seeta had calmed herself, she started saying, "There is big news. Tomorrow a big procession is coming by the train. The badaa governor-saab is coming by train and he is going to stop here for half day."

"The badaa governor-saab? Oh, you mean The Governor General! Oh, you mean, Lord Gowrie is coming through here? So, that means, David must be with him too. Is that right?"

"Yes, Mem-saab, that is what I wanted to tell you. I heard my brother and my father talking about this news."

"But, wait, how come David has not sent me any telegram? Usually, he sends me one before coming?"

Just as she was saying that, she saw mail-baabu (postman) coming their way. He was hurrying up on his old bicycle. He got off and ran toward the gate and without even looking up he yelled out, "Mem-saab, telegram!"

Katherine was right there. She took the telegram and read it fast. It was very short.

'Coming to Durgapur. Stop. 9 am. Stop. Dying to see you both. Stop. Love, David. Stop.'

Katherine's face lit up with happiness. She said, 'Thank you very much, mail-baabu, you are the best!' Mail-baabu blushed for no reason and then realized that he had blushed for no reason, so he turned his bicycle while saying, 'No mention, Mem-saab, no mention.' And he rode off on his clunky old bicycle.

Katherine grabbed Seeta and said, "Seeta, let's go, let's go get some groceries, we will prepare a feast tomorrow."

The next morning, Katherine got up early. She was in a very good mood—for obvious reasons. She got ready quickly and then woke Margaret up and got her ready. All along she was humming some song. She didn't even know what she was humming, but it was some kind of a happy song—that's all that mattered.

Around 8:30 in the morning, she started walking toward the train station. While walking she thought to herself that she was going a bit early, but when she reached near the station, she knew she had thought wrong. The whole station area was like the center of the local weekend market. There were a lot of people starting to gather there—the whole area was decorated to welcome Lord Gowrie. Police had started gathering their troops. Some of the officials of the town—like Mr. Patil—head of the local panchayat (village government council) were running around instructing people what to do etc.

Seeta also got up early. There were a lot of people in their house—she had never seen them before. Her brother was acting as if he was the leader of them all and he was rallying up the troops together. She quickly got ready and had her glass of milk and ran out.

"Maa, mai station jaa rahee hoo. Mai waheese Mem-saab ke ghar jaooingi aur raat ko vaapas aa-oongi. (Mother, I am going to the station. I will go straight to Mem-saab's house from there and then I will be back only at night from there.)

"Beti, apnaa khayaal rakhanaa. Kahee-bhee beehc raaste theheranaa nahi. Koeebhee khataraa ho sakataa hai. (Be careful Seeta. You never know what kind of danger there might be.), her mother shouted back—as if she knew that Seeta was going leave that morning, but then get into some kind of trouble.

By the time Seeta arrived at the station with a couple of her friends, the crowds had started gathering. It was almost like a melaa—a fair at the fairground. Seeta and her friends tried to get into the station, but the guard stopped them and asked for a special pass that was required that day to go on to the platform and join the procession to greet the Governor General. Obviously, they didn't have that, so they had to step back.

The crowd was increasing. Katherine was also trying to get into the station, but even she was having difficulty getting in. Then all of a sudden, the station bell started ringing. That was the indication that the train had arrived at the previous station and that Station Master had telegrammed the Station Master at Durgapur. The whole crowd started going wild.

As the train approached the station, it had slowed down quite a bit. Seeta and her friends, who could not get into the station, had secured a place a little higher on the fence of the station, so they could see what was happening on the platform—at least partially.

Katherine barely made it to the entrance of the station and the station master spotted her.

"Mem-saab, come here. I will take you near my office," he said in broken English. He cleared people around her and took her near his office. Just as they reached there, the train pulled into the station. The station was full of people. There was a lot of noise and chaos. A local village band—which usually plays at weddings—was also there, playing some tunes that sounded like some songs, but one couldn't recognize which song—even if one tried hard.

As the train pulled in, the driver gave a couple of whistles and let out a lot of steam. Many people from the train were gathered at the windows and doors of the train. One of the first class bogies was occupied by all officials. Katherine spotted David looking out from the window. His deputies were standing at doors on both sides with guns. Lord Gowrie was also spotted in one of the windows, waving at the crowd.

As the train stopped and the dust settled, David and Lord Gowrie came out at the door and there was a big noise—many shouting were mixed together —

'Gowrie Moordaabaad' (Down with Gowrie)

'Gowrie-saab zindaabaad' (Victory to Gowrie-saab)

Then the station master got up on a raised platform with a horn in his hand and he shouted at the top of his lungs, "Bhaaeeyo aur Beheno" (Borhters and Sisters)

"Zaraa shaant ho jaaeeye" (Please be quiet).

Still some shouting was going on. It took him a few rounds to calm everyone down.

"We welcome Gowrie-saab to Durgapur. Hum Gowrie-saab kaa Durgapur me swaagat karate hai," he repeated himself in Hindi. And he offered Lord Gowrie a garland of flowers. Lord Gowrie didn't let him put it around his neck, but took it in his hand and thanked the station master.

Once again there were some boo's and some ooh's and aah's—followed by shushing by some people.

David was busily looking around—Katherine thought he was looking for Margaret and her. But then she thought, may be he is just making sure security all around is well arranged. But, then when David and Katherine saw each other through that thick crowd, they smiled and gave each other a flying kiss. Katherine was relieved—in a way.

The station master signaled Mookhiyaa-ji (the village leader) to come forward.

Mookhiyaa-ji came forward rather hesitantly.

"Hum puren gaaon ki taraf se Gowrie-saab kaa swaagat karate hai. Welcome Gowrie-saab," he completed the ritual of repeating his Hindi sentence in English—in his typical Indian village English.

"Yeh bahot achchi baat hai ke aaj Gowrie-saab yahaa aaye. Good you came," once again that repetition in broken English.

Katherine and David were smiling and looking at each other—laughing the attempt of the local people to speak in English. Katherine was smiling but thinking to herself, 'At least they are all making an effort to speak our language.' Whereas, David's smile was more of a snooty smile.

"To mai ab Gowrie-saab se binati karataa hun ke wo kuchch kahe. I would like to request Gowrie-saab to say something," Mookhiyaa-ji was so proud of himself that he had completed his small speech without making any mistakes.

He asked Lord Gowrie to take the center stage.

While all of this was going on, there were a few people still coming toward the station. There were a few young people walking briskly toward the station. They went on one side of the station. There were a few hoarse carriages parked there. The horses were untied from the carriages with some hay in front of them. A couple of the young fellows reached down the stack of hay and took out two guns and a few hand grenades and started running toward the station. They split and went on both sides of the main entrance and tired to find a convenient place to stand from where they could see the center stage and also have something to rest the guns on.

One of the gunmen was standing right beside Seeta and her friends. But they didn't pay attention, because they were too busy looking inside the station and watching the whole show.

Just as Lord Gowrie had taken a center stage and he was about to start talking, the young fellows took their position. One of them made tweeting sound—a signal to each other. As soon as David heard that sound, he became alert. But, then for a minute or so, nothing happened, so he relaxed thinking that it was really a bird chirping.

"Ladies and Gentlemen," Lord Gowrie started talking. The whole crowd went silent.

"I have come to Durgapur to see how the government can help you build a local school and perhaps a hospital," no one knew if this was pre-determined or if he was making it up as he was going along. But, when the station master translated it into Hindi, "Saab keh rahe hai ki sarkaar Durgapur me school aur aspataal banaani wali hai," the whole crowd started shouting 'hurrey' and started clapping.

"But, before that happens, every one of the villagers has to sign an agreement that they will not participate in any action against the government," he said it in one single breath and looked station master for translation.

"Lekin sabhi gaon waalonko ek aisa wachan denaa hogaa ki gaon kaa koi bhi sarkaar ke kheelaaf kabhibhi kuchch nahi karegaa," station master slowed down as he was translating it—as this whole thing was a surprise to him and he didn't know how the villagers would react.

As soon as the crowd heard that, there was silence in the crowd. Only the old electric fans on the ceilings making meek rusted sound could be heard.

All of a sudden, from out side the station some people started shouting, "Inquilaab Zinadaabaad," and a couple of shot were fired toward the center stage. One of the guards fell down. Obviously, the gunman from right hand side had missed Lord Gowrie. The gunman on the left side of the stage tried hurriedly to get solid footing to shoot and in doing so he stepped on Seeta's hand—which was just leaning on the railing in an uncomfortable position. But she immediately shouted and took her hand away from his foot. In doing so, he has made the gunman lose his balance and his gun went off with many shots fired at the same time, a few guards fell down.

David ran toward Lord Gowrie and pulled him down and told him to stay down. All of this happened in a fraction of a second, and before the crowd could realize what was happening, the guards had opened fire toward the two sides of the main entrance—a couple of people got hurt. The whole station was in chaos, every one started running to get out of the station.

David took the frightened Lord Gowrie carefully back in to the train and told him to stay down. He ran out again and from the door of the train he started firing shots toward the gunmen on both sides.

Seeta was also frightened. She took her friend's hand and said, "Kamli, chalo bhaago," (Come on Kamli, let's run). But, Kamli wouldn't move. She had her head down and she wans't moving.

"KAMLI!" Seeta shouted out. She didn't know what to do.

Katherine was ducking down with Margaret in her arms and she tried to escape from the station, but there was no way to get out. The whole crowd was rushing over to the gate. A couple of times Katherine popped her head up and tried to look for David. When she saw him standing up in the door of the train with two guards guarding him, she was relieved. Finally, somehow she managed to escape through the crowd and got out of the gate. She looked on the side and caught a glimpse of Seeta crying and screaming, "Nahi, nahi. (No. No.).

She rushed over the Seeta and tried to grab her by her hand and said, "Seeta, chalo mere saath. (Seeta, come with me)." But Seeta won't budge. She kept crying and pulling back toward her friend Kamli. "Mem-saab, Kamli !" she was crying her heart out.

In the mean while, there were police whistles going off. The members of that young gang were running in many different directions.

As this whole storm was finally settling down, David took the horn in his hand and yelled out, "EVERYBODY, LISTEN. Every one go home right now. But, don't even think of going anywhere. Because we are coming to get whoever did this. Go home and stay home. Don't get out until we tell you do so." He then gave the horn to one of his deputies and said, "Tell them in Hindi."

The deputy took the horn and explained it in Hindi. Many elderly people along with the women and children shook their heads and started going home.

Katherine grabbed Seeta's hand and took her to the haweli with her. Little Margaret was pretty shaken up. But she wasn't crying. She first cried as it started happening. But, then she kept quiet as she saw her mother struggle to get out and grab Seeta to get out of there. Katherine with Margaret in her arms and crying screaming Seeta ran to the haweli with all their energy and just sat down as soon they reached there—as if they had just enough energy to get them home.

They all sat on the veranda for a while. Margaret and Seeta were exhausted. They dozed off right there on the veranda, while Katherine just sat there thinking—thinking about what's going to happen next. She knew that something big was going to happen, just didn't know what.

Later that afternoon one of the teenage boys came running to the haweli and started yelling, "Seeta, Seeta, gazab ho gaya. (Seeta, it's a disaster). Pulis sab ke gahr me ghus rahi aur maar peet karake puchch rahi hai ke tumhara bhai kidhar hai. (Police are forcing their way in to every house and asking for your brother.)"

"Lekin Bhayya ne kyaa kiya hai? (But, what has my brother done?)" Seeta asked very innocently.

"Aye, kyu bakwaas kar rahaa hai rey? (Hey, why are talking rubbish?)" Katherine came out and wanted to shush the young boy away. "Chalo neeklo eedhar se (Go on, get out of here)," she said and kicked the boy out of haweli.

"Seeta, listen to me. I will talk to David. You trust me, don't you?"

"Lekin, Mem-saab, pulis bhayya ko kyu dhoondh rahi hai? (But, Mem-saab, why is the police looking for my brother)" Seeta asked again.

Katherine was holding Seeta down. She knew that Seeta wanted to go into town and see what is going on. She kept on explaining to Seeta that everything will be alright, just let David come home and she would explain everything to her and make sure her family is alright. But, Seeta didn't listen to her at all. She freed herself from Katherine and ran toward town.

As Seeta was entering town, she started seeing the devastation this whole incident had started creating. On both sides of the cobble stoned street leading into town, many doors were visibly busted open and some of them were on fire. She could clearly hear some women and children crying, some of the men were sitting out side the house with their heads in their hands showing that they had given up. As she went closer, she could her soldiers' footsteps and a harsh hoarse voice calling out the parade orders, "Left, Right, Left, Right, Left Right." A commanding officer was sitting on a horse and leading the troop. He would stop at every corner and the corporal then order the company to halt. Then the officer was asking half of them to go on one side of the street and the other half on the other side. They would go knock loudly on the door, if no one opened the door, they would break down the door and go inside. Then you could hear women screaming and men coming out saying, "Humko kuhch pataa nahi ji, sach me hum ko kuchch pataa nahi (We don't know anything sir, we really don't.)" Then the soldiers would set something on fire and come out. Many of the people whose houses were already raided were running around with buckets trying to bring some water and put out those fires. But, no matter how much they ran or how much water they threw at the fire, this fire was not going to be put out.

Seeta sneaked around the back alley and went to her house. The troops had not reached here house yet. But, as soon as Seeta knocked on the door, there was ghastly silence in the house. Seeta knew that they were all in the house, but they were not opening the door.

Finally, she whispered out loud, "Mai hun Seeta, darwaza kholo, (It's me, Seeta. Please open the door)."

Someone opened the door ever so slightly and pulled her in to the house quickly and shut the door behind her. As soon Seeta got in to the front porch of the house, she saw that there were several people waiting around there. Some of the young men looked familiar. There was a group of them gathered in a circle in one corner. As they saw the door open, they all looked back. Seeta's brother was among them. He looked at her and then looked at them. Some of them signaled him to take her inside. He came hurriedly toward Seeta, held her by her arm and said, "Kahaa thi tum ab tak, aye? (Hey, where were you until now?)"

Seeta tried to answer him, "Mai.....mai to.... (I....I...)"

"Kuchch mat bolo, chalo ander chalo (Don't say a word. Just get in, get in)," he literally dragged her inside.

"Lekin, Bhaiyaa, suno to. Mai Mem-saab........(But, Brother, listen to me.

Mem-saab….)," she tried to reason with him—still trying to loosen his grip on her arm.

"Kuchch mat bolo us Gori Mem ke baareme (Don't talk about that White Woman)," her brother was now getting angry.

"Lekin, Bhaiyya, mai Mem-saab ko bol doongi. Wo General-saab ko ma-naayengi aur wo tum sabko chchod denge (But, Brother, I will talk to Mem-saab. She will convince General-saab and he will let all of you go)," Seeta said it all in breath so fast that her brother had no chance of interrupting her this time.

"Paagal, ladki. Tumhe kuchch maloom nahi hai (You silly girl, you don't know anything)," he made a snide remark.

"Muze maloom hai, Bhaiyya. Koi bure log hai, unhone General-saab aur Gowrie-saab ke upar goli chalaayee aura b Genaral-saab samazate hai ke tum aur tumhaare dost bhi usame shaameel hai (I know Brother. Some bad guys fired guns at General-saab and Gowrie-saab. And now General-saab thinks that you and your friends are involved that too)," again she said it in one breath without a pause.

Her brother sat down with his head in his hands and just looked up at her—as if he was admiring her courage and appreciating her innocence at the same time. But then, all of a sudden he thought of something. Perhaps she could help them. Just like she had gotten help from Mem-saab to get rid of the sahoo-kaar, she could help them escape this time too.

He told her to stay in the room and said he would be right back.

He went outside and talked to his friends. Some of them shook their heads in disbelief, but some of them were beginning to see some hope in this idea. Somehow they had to get out this house and go in to the forest where many of their other friends were waiting for them.

He came back in to the room whispering loudly right from the door, "Seeta, Seeta," but there was no answer. He looked around in that small room and once again looked outside the door, but she was nowhere to be seen. Then he noticed the window open slightly. He looked outside the window and saw Seeta running up the road.

"Seeta, meri behen, yeh kyaa kar rahee hai tu? (Seeta, my little sister, what the hell are you doing?) he murmured to himself, but then closed the window immediately. As he closed the window, he heard some noise over on the other side of the street and saw some smoke in the sky.

Seeta was running up the cobble stone street and getting tired. But she didn't stop. She had her head down as she was running. All of a sudden she heard Katherine's voice.

"Seeta, Seeta, oh my child, you are alright," Katherine came running and hugged her tight.

Seeta struggled to get out of that strong hug as if she was saying, 'this is not the time to hug me, Mem-saab. Help me.'

"Mem-saab, Bhaiyya......General-saab...," she tried to speak but couldn't. So, she took a few deep breaths.

"Slow down, slow down," Katherine said while wiping the sweat off her forehead.

"Mem-saab, General-saab ko kuchch galat fehemi huwee hai. Wo samazate hai ke mere Bhaiyaa aur unake dosto ne General-saab par goli chalaayee. (Mem-saan, General-saab has a misunderstanding. He thinks that my brother and his friends fired shots at the General and Lord Gowrie)."

Katherine was listening intently.

"Aur wo mere Bhaiyya ko pakadane aa rahe hai (And he is coming to arrest my brother)," she said it in way that Katherine understood that she was asking for help.

"Alright, alright. You go home. I will go find David and find out what is really going on. OK?"

But Seeta just stood there.

"Come on, go home. You will be safe there. Let me see what I can do. I will help you if I can. Come go, Seeta, go," Katherine almost begged her to go home.

Finally Seeta agreed. She turned around and started walking slowly. Katherine stood there watching her walk down. Seeta stopped after a few steps and looked back. Katherine was gone—Seeta could hear Katherine footsteps almost running toward the center of the town.

Katherine was walking down the road and thinking that how she would convince David to let go of everyone in Durgapur. Now that only a few constables were killed, none of the British entourage was hurt, why should he care that much? But, deep down, she knew that David wouldn't listen to her. She was feeling like she was caught between rock and a hard place. Just as she came to the main intersection of roads, engrossed in her own thoughts, she was looking down and walking. She almost bumped into a group of police parading down the road in one line. They had their guns on their shoulders as they were marching in rhythm of the leader, 'Ek...do....ek....do....ek.....do..... (One.....Two..... One......Two.......)'

Katherine reached the police station in the center of the town. But David was not there. She asked around, but everyone kept quiet. They all said that he had gone with a group of soldiers to look for the people who fired shots at him.

Katherine just stood there for a minute, not knowing what to do or where to go next. Then she decided to go toward Seeta's house, so she started walking really fast—almost running down the street.

As she came to one of the crossroads, she saw Seeta's friend running toward her carrying Margaret. Katherine had found one of Seeta's friends and asked her to stay at the haweli to look after Margaret. When Katherine left, Margaret was sleeping and she thought she could be back with Seeta before Margaret woke up. But, she wanted to make sue Margaret was safe, so she had asked Seeta's friend to stay there.

"Mem-saab, Mem-saab, Baby ooth ke rone lagee, Mem-saab (Mem-saab, the child woke up and started crying)," she explained running down the road—carrying the still crying Margaret.

Katherine went up to her and took Margaret from her. When Margaret saw her mother, she started crying even harder, as if complaining about leaving her with a stranger.

"I am sorry, Baby, I am sorry. But I had to go and find Seeta. Don't cry baby." Katherine hugged her and tried to calm her down.

After a few minutes she realized that she still had to go and make sure Seeta was safe. She took Margaret with her and started walking fast toward Seeta's house.

Seeta started walking down the road. Every few seconds she was looking back, making sure that Mem-saab is not coming back. As she walked down, she was thinking what else she could do to help her brother. As she almost reached her house—which was on the corner—she turned left to go to the front door. On that straight road, she heard some soldiers marching a few hundred meters away. All of a sudden, Seeta realized that they might be coming to her house to arrest her brother and his friends. So, she started running toward them. She went past her house and kept on running. The marching line of soldiers was quite far away. By the time she reached them, she was tired. So, she bent down to catch her breath. When she looked up the soldiers were right in front of her and she saw David leading them down the road.

"Left....Right.....Left......Right......" his determination to catch those rebels was evident in David's commanding voice.

She saw that David right in front of her. So, without thinking she started talking, "General-saab, General-saab"

"COMPANY, HALT." David halted the parade.

"General-saab, I am Seeta. I work with Mem-saab. I have seen your photo, General-saab."

David thought that the girl was going to tell him something important.

"Do you know where Vikram Singh and his friends are hiding?" he demanded an answer.

"General-saab, you misunderstand. My brother did not fire," she went straight to the explanation.

"Your brother? Where do you live?" again that demanding voice.

"Over there," she pointed toward her house.

"But, General-saab, you misunderstand."

"There is nothing to misunderstand. Now, get out of my way."

"But, General-saab, Mem-saab, said, you will understand."

David ignored her completely.

"COMPANY, ATTENTION! March Forward!" He ordered and started again with, "Left…..Right…..Left……Right……"

Seeta started running with them to catch up.

"General-saab, please listen. I know Mem-saab, I know Margaret, I have seen your photographs, General-saab," Seeta was trying to connect with David while running beside him. But he was completely ignoring her and kept on marching forward.

When they came near a few houses around the bend, David ordered the soldiers to go inside and find the rebels. The soldiers dispersed and started knocking on the doors and when no one opened, they knocked the doors down with the back of their guns and barged inside. There were a lot of noises of soldiers shouting and the women in the house crying for help, some old men begging them to leave them alone—but the soldiers kept on smashing down the stuff like buckets and kicking on the hay stacks looking to see if there is anyone hiding under the hay stacks.

David was standing outside on the road. As the soldiers were finishing a house, they were coming out and reporting to David that there is no one but the women, old men and babies in the houses. David was getting increasingly frustrated—he would yell at some of them once in a while, "WHAT ARE YOU LOOKING AT? Go—go to that house and look for these bastards!"

Seeta was still there trying to convince David—who had successfully ignored her—until she said, "That is my house General-saab. Please don't go in there."

David turned around and saw a few soldiers knocking in Seeta's door. He started running toward the house. He pulled his pistol out from his waist belt and started to run toward the house. He knew something was going to happen, so as one of the soldiers was about to knock the door down, David shouted, "NO! Get away from that door."

And just then a gun was shot from inside—it knocked the door of the house down and killed the soldier standing straight in front of it—as he was slightly distracted by the shout from David.

David started running toward the house, but then jumped down and moved on the side of the door hiding behind the wall.

Katherine was right around the corner. She heard David's shout and then a gun shot and she ran fast around the corner. As she turned left she saw a whole bunch of soldiers with their rifles pointing at Seeta's house, a soldiers lying on the ground in front of the broken door. She looked around. Hearing the loud gun shot Margaret had started crying. When Katherine looked on the left of her, she saw David squatting down and thought to herself, 'Oh, Thank God!'

David heard the little girl's cry and looked up. To his surprise Katherine was there with Margaret.

"KATHERINE! What are you doing here? Didn't I tell you to stay at home? And you brought Margaret HERE with you? What's wrong with you?"

Seeta saw Katherine coming around the corner and ran to her. Just as she was talking to David, Seeta went and hugged Katherine. Seeta looked David and said, "General-saab, Mem-saab," as if she was saying, 'See, didn't I tell you, I know Mem-saab?'

Katherine sat down and hugged both the girls.

David yelled again, "KATHERINE, take them and go back to the house."

The gun shots were still going on. The difference between the rifle shots and the shots from a home-made pistol was very audible. The shooters from inside the house had an advantage of hiding behind the wall and the door. But the rifle shooters—the soldiers of British army—had the disadvantage of being completely exposed out on the streets. This disadvantage was evident in casualties.

After a while, there was a brief period of silence. It was gravely ominous silence.

This whole saga was going on all afternoon. It was coming close to evening and the orange red sun was shining down on the streets. David realized that the rebels might be short of ammunition. So he decided to speak up and challenge them to come outside.

"Vikram Singh, tum bachake nahee ja sakate (Vikram Singh you won't survive this)," he said it in his broken Hindi.

In all of this turmoil, Seeta—who was hiding behind the wall of their front neighbor's house—chuckled at David's Hindi.

"Agar mai mere ghar se bachake nahee ja sakataa, to tum bhi MERE ghar se bachake nahee jaa sakate General! (If I cannot escape alive from my own home, you will surely not escape alive from MY home)" a manly voice challenged David from inside.

Then suddenly the door was kicked open and someone from inside came out with pistols in his both hands and shouted, "Inqilaab zindaabaad!"

David had taken a shelter right next to the door. He stooped down and aimed at the man from a very short distance. He shot the man several times before the man could see David, he fell down. As he fell down, he fired several shots in the air and then fell down to his death.

There were screams from inside the house and an elderly lady's voice, "NA-HEE! (NO!)"

Someone sneaked up behind the door and slammed the door shut as quickly as possible. Seeta, Katherine and Margaret had turned around and started running to take a shelter away from the gun shots. There gun shots all around them. Katherine was leaning down to avoid getting shot. She asked Margaret to run beside her. She held Margaret's hand and started running again. The gun shots were still going on. As they were running, Margaret tripped and fell down. Katherine thought she just tripped and fell down. She didn't even imagine that Margaret would get shot. She just picked her up in her arms and quickly ran behind the brick fence of the house in front of Seeta's house.

As the noise died down and the dust was settling down, the golden sun was shining on the road. The man—Vikram Singh—was lying dead in front of the door of Seeta's house. David was sitting on the road with his back to the wall of Seeta's house. Seeta was on one side of the brick fence and Katherine and Margaret were on the other side. Katherine quickly went around the brick fence and sat down. She held Margaret in her arms.

That ghastly silence was so ominous that Katherine shivered a little bit. She noticed that Margaret didn't shiver at all. And for the past few minutes she also didn't hear Margaret crying. Suddenly, she was scared. She looked at Margaret who was calmly sleeping in her arms and wondered hoe come this child is sleeping in such noise and all the running around. She saw that Margaret's hair was coming on her face, so she took her hand from under Margaret and tried to wipe the hair away from her face. She noticed a blob of blood on face as she wiped her face with her palm. Katherine got really scared. But then immediately noticed that the blood was on her palm itself. 'But I am not hurt!' she thought to herself.

And then she realized that Margaret had been hit.

"NO!" she yelled at the top of her lungs. She yelled so loudly that the birds from nearby trees flew away chirping with an ominous sound.

"MARGARET!" she yelled again.

Everyone stopped doing whatever they were doing and looked back.

Katherine lifted Margaret in her arms and went running to David crying, "David, our little Margaret!"

David was also stunned with the site of lifeless body of his daughter in front of him. He didn't know what to say.

Seeta heard the cry and ran toward Katherine and kneeled down to hug Margaret. She was crying her eyes out. "Mem-saab, Baby ko kyaa huwaa Mem-saab (Mem-saab, what happened to the baby)?" They both started crying.

David sat there for a few minutes and then gathered himself. He got up, stood straight up over the three of them and pointed the gun at Seeta's head and yelled, "You bastards, you killed my only daughter. Now I will kill yours if you don't come out."

There was no answer from inside the house. There was only some murmuring. Katherine looked up at David in total disbelief. She could not believe, David was pointing the gun at Seeta's head.

"David, what do you think you are doing?" she yelled out. But, David didn't pay any attention to her.

"DAVID!" she shouted again.

"SHUT UP, Katherine. You don't know what these people are capable of doing," he turned his head back and without even looking at Margaret he told Katherine to shut up. Then he turned around to the house and yelled out in spiteful voice, "Are you listening in there? I am serious. I will kill this girl."

The door opened slightly and someone saw what was going on out on the street. Again there was some murmuring inside in Hindi. Then a minute later the door opened wide and everyone came out with their hands up in the air.

David ordered his soldiers to arrest each and every one of them.

Seeta looked up and saw that they were getting arrested. She started crying.

"Nahee, nahee. Mem-saab, Mem-saab, aap kuchch bolo Mem-saab (Mem-saab, please say something)," she was sobbing.

Katherine was sitting down, looking at the ground. She didn't know what to do. Then she spotted a pistol right in front of her. She paused for a minute and then gently kept Margaret on the ground, wiped her own tears off and picked that pistol. She quickly got up and ran behind David. She hid the pistol in her hand behind her dress and then as she reached close to David, she raised the pistol up to his head and yelled, "DAVID. Ask your men to drop their weapons and leave those people alone."

David looked back and saw Katherine standing there with a pistol in her hand. He could not believe it.

"Katherine! What the hell do you think you are doing?" he asked in total disbelief.

"DO IT!" she yelled.

The men had stopped arresting the locals. They were frozen in their boots, not knowing what to do next. David was still not issuing any order.

David wasn't sure Katherine would do anything with the pistol in her hand. He didn't even know if she could operate the pistol. He never taught her how to shoot. But, Katherine had a winner's confidence on her face. She pointed the gun at his foot and fired a shot.

David almost jumped up. He looked at Katherine—again in disbelief—this time it wasn't like, 'I don't think you can operate that pistol,' it was more like, 'I can't believe you shot at me!' kind of a look.

So, he hurriedly asked his men to drop the guns and release the arrested men. The released men were very happy; they hurriedly got back into the house and locked the door from inside.

Katherine then, lifted the life-less body of Margaret, took Seeta by her side and started walking away from the scene. David didn't know what to say.

"Katherine, I…..I…am so sorry!" he said it meekly.

Katherine stopped and gave him a real disgusted look, and said, "Sure you are David. I am sure you are sorry. But what are you sorry for? Are you sorry that you couldn't arrest all those rebels or are you sorry because fully ironed jacket got all crumpled up? Because you sure are not sorry about Margaret—you didn't ask even once if she is ok or what happened to her? What are you really sorry for David?"

Then she kept on walking with Seeta right by her side and Margaret in her arms.

CHAPTER 14

Ashes To Ashes

The next morning was kind of cold, foggy and gloomy. The sun was just peeking out and showing a haze. But the dark orange color of sun was still very evident. Although it was very early in the morning, almost the whole town had gathered near the river bank. Many of them were wearing clean white clothes.

They were all very quiet. Except once in a while you could hear someone whispering and someone crying. There were two things going on there at the riverbank. On one side, there was a Hindu priest sitting down in front of a pile of logs. He was chanting something in Sanskrit and every once in a while he was dipping a leaf in small pot of water and sprinkling it all over.

Then a whole group of people arrived in plain white clothes carrying a dead body of a young man in a wooden stretcher on their shoulders. There were incense sticks, flowers, some red powder and some yellow powder spread all around the body. They set the wooden stretcher with the body on a pile of wood.

The Hindu priest started chanting some mantras again. And on the other side, digging of the grave for a small baby was completed. The lifeless body of innocent Baby Margaret was lowered into the grave and at the same time on the other side the fire was lit under the logs of wood underneath a lifeless body of a patriot young boy.

Katherine was crying her eyes out and so were Seeta and her entire family. David had come to the funeral that morning. But, he was standing far away. Katherine, Seeta, Seeta's parents—all had noticed him. But all of them ignored him. He also did not make any attempt of going up to them. He just stood there with his head down.

There was no Christian priest in the town, so Katherine had to do whatever she remembered of the funeral process herself. She had brought roses and asked the local carpenter to make a small coffin.

The sun had risen completely now. It was completely round and radiant orange now. So much so that anyone looking straight at sun would have to squint. David was standing on the side. He also started getting sun in his eyes. So, he took his military hat and wore it and pulled the flap a little bit over his forehead to block the orange red sun. He was standing there in full uniform, looking very official and straight faced—as if he was saying, 'I did what my duty called for'.

Just as Katherine finished reading some verses from the Bible and asked someone to lower the coffin into the grave, on the other side the Hindu priest had finished his verses and he asked Seeta's father to carry a clay pot of water on his shoulders and walk around the pile of wood. As Katherine took a fistful of sand in her hand and sprinkled it on the coffin saying very softly, 'Ashes to ashes, earth to earth….', Seeta's father took a macheti in his hand and lit fire to the wood.

Seeta was standing right between the two. Katherine was wearing full black clothes and Seeta's mother was wearing a pure white sari. Seeta was wearing white chudidaar and she had taken a black chunni. Her mother did not like that, but in her grief she was in no mood to talk Seeta out of it.

Seeta stood on the side of her brother's burning pyre. The light wind was blowing black sooth all over. Small pieces of sooth flew all over and some of it went toward where David was standing. As he got some black sooth on his uniform, he murmured a curse and swept it off his uniform. When it caught hold of the middle of the wood pile, Seeta's mother burst out crying and sat down helplessly.

Katherine stood there looking at Margaret's grave being filled in with soil. Seeta comforted her mother for a few minutes and then walked over to Katherine. Seeta went over and took Katherine's hand in her hand. Katherine hugged her with just one hand and kissed her hand.

It was very tense, but silent half hour on such a beautiful morning.

Then Seeta went back to her parent, told them something and before she could hear their refusal, she walked back to Katherine and in a very light voice she said, "Let's go Ma'am."

A few days later, Katherine and Seeta walked up to a small Red Cross plane at Delhi Airport and boarded it to take off to England. Katherine had talked to some officials in Delhi to persuade them to let them take the plane. They told her that it was dangerous to take a plane during war time. Even though it was a Red Cross plane, there were no guarantees that it wouldn't be caught in crossfire.

"Sir, when my little baby was lost to crossfire, I don't care if I lose my life the same way. I just have to go back to my father."

"Your father Ma'am, was senior to me in Royal Army. He taught me a lot of things, Ma'am. Please come tomorrow morning. I will arrange everything."

"Thank you very much officer."

"Oh, and Ma'am, please give my most sincere regards to your father."

'What a legacy!' Katherine thought to herself. 'That annoying old man with all his bad habits of drinking and talking loudly, has made so many friends in the world!'

Seeta was excited to fly in plane. But they didn't say anything to each other. Every once in a while there were just looking at each other and smiling meekly.

When they reached London it was raining slightly and getting very dark. It was dusk time, but still there were no lights anywhere. The blackouts were still in force. Katherine took a taxi and went home with Seeta.

When Arthur opened the door, he saw Katherine and Seeta standing outside. He kept on looking at them for a few moments and then spread his arms and hugged Katherine, "Princess, my Little Princess. Oh, I missed you sooo much."

Katherine hugged Arthur tight and started crying, "Me too, Dad, me too."

CHAPTER 15

The Donation

It was a cold and rainy morning in London. Traffic was very heavy. Mr.Thakur was making his way through crowd out of the tube and up the stairs on the street. He was trying to walk as fast he could. He was wearing a suit, a trench-coat, a scarf around his neck, a hat and carrying an umbrella in one hand and a small leather briefcase in the other. As came into the office with his wet umbrella and wet shoes, the water dripping from both, he tried to shed the water, but finally gave up and went in. He opened the lock with his keys and went inside. He kept the umbrella in the corner and murmured something.

'Kahaan se maine yeh Lodon aane ki soch lee (Why did I ever think of coming to London?)' he said to himself.

'Achcha khaasaa Delhi me thaa (I was fine in Delhi),' he went into the small make-do kitchen to make himself some hot tea.

Mr.Thakur was the newly appointed representative in London working for India Literacy Project. The India Literacy Project, (ILP), founded in 1990 in the USA by a group of young Non-Resident Indians inspired by Dr. Parameshwar Rao, a nuclear scientist trained in the U.S. He returned to India in 1967 to dedicate his life to improving the lives of the rural poor in India.

Mr. Thakur and Ms. Jenny Jackson were the only two people in ILP's small office in London. Ms. Jackson did everything from accounting to office management and Mr. Thakur was in charge of campaigns for fund raising and trying to recruit teachers from the U.K. and neighboring countries to send to India on assignments to rural Indian villages for education of the millions of children—who cannot afford any kind of school and their parents force them get a job—even in this day and age of modern society.

When Mr.Thakur came to the office, Ms. Jackson wasn't there. He did his regular chores of paperwork, answering emails and returning some phone calls and so on.

Then around 11 am, he left the office to go the bank and then to have a quick lunch.

When he got back around 1:30 that afternoon, the office door was open. Ms. Jackson was sitting at her desk.

"Oh, hello Ms. Jackson, how are you today?" he asked very courteously.

"I am fine, Mr. Thakur—though I would rather still be in bed—but I am fine. And you?" even in this gloomy cold and rainy weather Ms. Jackson was as bubbly as ever.

"I am alright," he sat down at his desk. And started looking at the mail that had arrived while he was away.

There was a strange envelop in the mail—it was addressed to Mr. Thakur at ILP. He was surprised and curious.

"Ms. Jackson, what is this?" he asked.

"Oh, that came in through the courier service this morning. Were you expecting something from someone?" Ms. Jackson answered promptly.

"No. I was not expecting anything."

"Well, it doesn't matter. Open it," she said it as if she was about to append it with 'you moron'.

"Oh, yes," said the dumbfounded Mr. Thakur.

He opened the envelope and took out the contents. It was a neatly folded piece of paper and there was a bank check inside. He saw the amount on that check and his jaw dropped to the table. He literally froze there.

"Mr. Thakur, are you alright? What is it?" Ms. Jackson came over to his desk immediately.

She picked the letter and started reading it. It was a very short note.

'Dear Mr. Thakur,

I found out your name from a mutual friend. Please accept the enclosed bank check made out in the name of India Literacy Program.

I wish to donate this amount to your organization with only one condition. The entire amount should be used to build a school in the town of Durgapur—which used to be a small village near Bhopal Junction in central India. It should be called Margaret Sutherland School.

I trust you will follow my mother's wishes.

If you need any more money to build and operate a fine school in Durgapur, please do not hesitate to contact my secretary, Mr. Mick O'brian.

Sincerely,

Miss Seeta Katherine Sutherland'

Ms. Jackson picked up the bank check and looked at the amount.

"ONE MILLION POUNDS!" she shouted so loudly that Mr. Thakur unfroze with a jolt.

93510